House Rules

By the same author:

THE PASSIVE VOICE
HIS MISTRESS'S VOICE
A MATTER OF POSSESSION
AGONY AUNT

House Rules

G.C. SCOTT

CARROLL & GRAF PUBLISHERS, INC.
NEW YORK

Carroll & Graf Publishers, Inc.
19 West 21st Street
New York, NY 10010-6805

ISBN: 0-7394-0960-3

Manufactured in the United States of America

House Rules

One

'You do not want to go with any of these women,' said a voice behind him. Richard turned to confront a short young woman with dark hair and dark-blue eyes. She was in her mid-twenties, he guessed, and she was extraordinarily beautiful.

'And do you know what I do want?' Richard asked her.

'Maybe,' she said as she took his hand and led him back towards the *Reeperbahn*. 'All those ladies under glass,' she said, gesturing toward the glass-fronted rooms in which prostitutes displayed themselves to the passing crowds, 'all those women are greedy professionals, in it for as much as they can get. You cannot blame them. We all want as much as we can get for our work. But their usually perfunctory service is less easy to forgive or tolerate. They owe their customers a good time, at least.'

'And what do you offer your customers?' Richard asked as they turned out of *Herbertstrasse* on to the *Reeperbahn*. She led him towards the *U-Bahn* station. Even as he followed her, he wondered who she was. This was the very first time he had ever been picked up by a woman.

She frowned slightly at him. 'I don't have customers. I have clients, or, better, friends. And I offer them the chance to discover what they want to do.'

'And are your tastes so catholic that you can satisfy every one of them?'

'No. Of course not. But once I know that I cannot help them, I can usually send them to someone who can. But don't ask so many questions. You will take all the surprise and mystery out of it.'

The crowds on the *Reeperbahn* made progress slow, but Richard was in no hurry to reach the destination towards which his new companion was leading him. Part of the fun of Hamburg's red-light district was the show on the streets. A blonde Valkyrie in a rubber suit was offering some unthinkable service to the passers-by, and Richard edged closer to hear her. It seemed, from what he could make of her rapid-fire German, that she was offering to take anyone back to her room and beat them with whips while they kissed her feet and begged for more. It wasn't exactly his idea of fun, but someone in the crowd struck a bargain with her, and the two went away together.

'She'll spend maybe ten minutes actually whipping him, not very hard. The rest of the time she will sit around in her rubber suit letting him look at her. Not much like what he is expecting, but that's the way things usually go.'

Shops selling every kind of sex toy, and pornography that would be banned instantly in his native England, lined the pavements. The crowds of pimps, prostitutes and tourists filled both the pavements and the street. The crowd parted to reveal a dark-haired woman of perhaps thirty. She was attractively dressed in a white knit dress that ended just above her knees and clung to her body. Her hands were tied behind her back, and a sign hanging around her neck told passers-by to take her back to her rooms in *Herbertstrasse* and do whatever they wished with her.

Richard thought it might be difficult for her to insist on being paid for her services if the punter simply neglected to untie her hands. Or, even more sinister, what if someone in the crowd were to take her back to her rooms and torture her, or even kill her? But then, he reflected, she doubtless had a minder in attendance to ensure that neither of these possibilities were realised.

As if reading his mind, Richard's new companion nodded towards the bound woman. 'She promises to do anything she is told, but all she provides is a screw under the eyes of her pimp who, as often as not, threatens to send a video tape of the action to the police. That usually gets more money from the poor man. On tape, what they are doing looks very much like rape. And in any case, no one likes to have that kind of information about his sex fantasies getting out. Just another con,' she finished contemptuously.

'How do you know so many of the people here?' Richard asked her.

'I have lived here for three years,' she answered simply.

Richard stopped suddenly, and the girl turned to look at him in surprise. 'Who are you?' he asked. 'And where are we going?'

'Do not ask too many questions. There should be some mystery in first encounters. And,' she added, 'things will be easier this way if you find you do not like what I offer you. You can forget me more easily if you do not know my name.'

'But suppose I do like what you offer? How will I find you again?'

The girl smiled up at him and said, 'If that is the case, we will exchange names and addresses and arrange for the future. Now come along.'

The crowds thinned out as they walked away from the centre of the red-light district. When they reached the *U-Bahn* terminal by *Die Landungsbrüken*, they were practically alone. The girl led the way to the platform. The train was not very full, and they rode in comparative privacy. Richard kept his questions to himself, and the girl said nothing more about their destination or herself. He was able to look more closely at her now, and he confirmed his first impression: she was undeniably beautiful. Her dark hair was cropped short and seemed to fit her head like a helmet, a style he always associated with Audrey Hepburn, and which gave her the same air of *gaminerie*. Her eyes were dark blue, almost black. She wore her clothes with style. Her dress revealed a good deal of her thighs as she sat beside him. Her legs were rather on the full side, which he preferred to the fashionably slender legs in vogue among models. She wore glossy white tights and high-heeled shoes. The effect was stunning, now that he could see her clearly. Richard was suitably stunned.

They got off at *Die Jungfernstieg* and walked a short distance along the lake side. 'This is the *Binnenalster*,' she explained to Richard. 'That is, the inner Alster lake. I live along the street here. If this were a fairy story, I would be a young maiden leading you to a castle, but I'm afraid you'll have to put up with an apartment only.'

They turned into *Gertruden Strasse* and entered the building on the corner. It was some five floors high, and her apartment was on the fourth floor. The windows along one side overlooked the lake, and she left the room dark so that they could stand at the window and see the lights of the water-taxis moving slowly across the dark water.

'I have only one rule,' the girl said in the darkness. 'You may do anything with me so long as I can do anything with you. In that way we will discover one another's likes and dislikes, and the reciprocity of the transaction should keep us from doing anything really harmful to one another. Unless you're a psychopath, that is.'

Richard smiled and replied, 'I don't think I am. No one has ever told me I was crazy.'

'Then that's all right,' she said. She drew the curtains and turned on the lights. 'Welcome to my home,' she said as Richard looked around.

The room in which they stood was carpeted in dark blue. The furniture looked comfortable rather than luxurious: a couch and armchairs, coffee table, TV and video recorder. Fashion photographs hung on the walls. They were from many periods, from the twenties on up to the present. Richard walked over to examine them more closely.

Seeing his interest, the girl said, 'I am – or I would like to be – a fashion designer. But I haven't enough money to set myself up in business yet. Once I begin I would like to design my own exclusive lines. Come into my work room and look at some of my designs.' She led Richard into one of the bedrooms and turned on the light. There was a large drafting table along one wall, a sewing machine and worktable along another. There were drawings and bolts of cloth, a dressmaker's dummy, all the paraphernalia associated with a designer's studio, but on a much smaller scale.

'Have you studied design?' he asked.

She nodded. 'For five years, in school and at college. I have always been interested in the subject. And I think I have found a niche I can fill.' She picked up a sketch from the drafting table and beckoned Richard to come and look at it.

The sketch showed a male figure wearing leather shorts which fitted like his own skin. He was locked into them by means of a leather waist belt which passed through several sturdy belt loops and locked with a padlock. There was a zipper up the back which locked to the belt with a second padlock. The front was designed to both contain and emphasise his genitalia. The garment had long legs that fitted tightly, obviously to prevent access to his cock.

'How does he go to the toilet?' Richard asked.

'He doesn't, unless his keeper lets him,' the girl replied.

'His keeper? Who might that be?'

'Oh, anyone at all,' she replied airily.

'You?' he asked.

'Maybe. It would depend on the man. But these would be for sale to anyone who desired to control their partner. There is a female version as well.' The girl picked up another sketch and handed it to Richard to study. This one was obviously designed for a female figure. The waist was much smaller, the hips larger in proportion, and the legs were cut high, leaving little more than a thong running up the crack of the bottom while covering the entire vulval area. The same arrangement of locking belt and zipper was provided.

'Wouldn't these be rather warm to wear for a long time?' It was the only thing he could think of to say that might conceal his rising excitement.

'I suppose I could arrange a few small holes to let the air in,' the girl replied. 'While keeping everything else out,' she added.

Richard felt a wave of excitement as he looked at the drawings. He imagined how it would feel to be locked into the leather shorts, unable to touch his own cock, and how the girl would look if she were locked into the female version of the chastity belt. There was no other name for the things she was showing him. He had never thought seriously about that sort of thing before, but the idea interested him now. However, it was only an idea, a fantasy. The garments existed only as drawings.

'Have you made up any of your designs?' he asked.

'A few. I haven't the money or the time now to do it full time. When I have saved twenty thousand marks, I'll make a real beginning. I think it would be fun to make and sell that sort of thing. And I know it is profitable, just by looking at the prices others sell their ready-made things for. I plan to offer clients a personal fitting service if they wish. I will design their choices directly on their bodies. But of course I will need some place a bit bigger than this. I will need a room where I can accommodate more machinery, as well as somewhere more intimate where I can take my measurements and do fittings.'

'Have you thought of getting someone to back you with cash while you get started?' Richard asked.

'I have approached several people here in Hamburg, but so far I haven't been able to afford to travel farther afield. But I'm nearly at the point where I can begin. Only another few thousand marks. And of course I need a commission from a client.' Changing the subject abruptly, she said, 'Let's talk about what you'd like to do this evening.' She led Richard back through the sitting room and into the second bedroom.

The time for negotiations had arrived. Ruefully, he thought that it always came to this. Being picked up by a beautiful woman almost always came down to the matter of how much. Only in fantasies does a woman choose a complete stranger and take him home for a night of passion out of sheer love for the sport. He didn't grudge the money. It was the mechanics of haggling and the embarrassment of handing it over that he disliked.

The girl, however, said nothing about payment. Perhaps, he thought, she was the type who waited until afterward. Or maybe the type who left the amount to the discretion of the man. That might prove even more awkward, but he would have to deal with that. He wasn't going to walk out at this juncture.

Standing before him, she looked down with a smile. 'Undo me,' she said, turning so that he could get at the long zipper up the back of her clingy dress. It purred downward, and she shrugged out of the garment to stand before him in bra, panties and the sheer, glossy tights he had noticed earlier. She seemed to expect some comment, for she stood still while he looked at her.

Richard couldn't think of anything that didn't sound banal, so he merely looked at her. He thought she was beautiful, but even that didn't do justice to her. She removed the rest of her clothes. Watching a woman undress before his eyes usually made him silent. She let him look his fill before undressing him.

'Lie down on the bed,' she directed him. The girl went to the bureau and returned with a pair of handcuffs. 'Put your hands through the bars of the headboard,' she told him.

In a daze, Richard obeyed. She locked the cuffs on his wrists, leaving him helpless on the bed. He felt his heartbeat quicken as she stood looking down at him. His cock was becoming erect even though she had not yet touched it. The bizarre and novel situation was enough to arouse him.

The girl smiled as she sat on the bed beside him. When she touched his cock, he flinched involuntarily. She smiled again at his reaction, holding him in her hand. 'Good so far?' she asked, and he nodded, fascinated both by the situation and his ready acceptance of her domination.

'Relax and let me do the work,' she told him. She climbed on to the bed and sat astride him, facing his feet. With one hand she grasped his cock while she cupped his balls with the other.

There was nothing he could do to influence her actions, and his helplessness was brought home to him when she squeezed him sharply. He gasped in surprise. However, this reminder of his vulnerability was exciting rather than frightening. This was one of his wildest fantasies come true. He had heard rumours of clubs in London where men and women met to practise bondage and flagellation, but had dismissed them as too fantastic even while he wished he could find one himself. But no one in East Anglia was likely to know about such places. He had come to Hamburg half hoping to find someone to introduce him to domination and bondage, and had been more than half minded to choose one of the women who advertised themselves as dominatrices along the *Reeperbahn* and in the *Sankt Pauli* area. He could hardly believe his incredible luck in being picked up by a woman who looked like being the girl of his darker dreams.

Meanwhile the girl was stroking his cock slowly and expertly, and Richard felt himself growing more and more excited. She seemed bent on making him come. 'What about yourself?' he asked her. 'If you keep on like this I'll come and won't be able to do anything for you.'

'And does that bother you?' she asked in her turn.

He thought for a moment before replying, 'Yes.'

'You are most unusual then. Most men are selfish enough to remain silent and let me go on.' She paused and looked back at him over her shoulder. 'Yes, I see you are concerned,' she continued. She shifted herself so that her crotch was above his face as she bent to take his cock in her mouth.

Richard raised his head until he could lick her labia. He smelt the aroma of her musk mixed with a faint perfume, as from talcum or bath salts.

'Umm,' she said. 'That's good. Do you feel better too?' The words were blurred because she didn't stop sucking his cock. Without waiting for a reply, she shifted so that his tongue could reach her clitoris. She settled herself atop him and continued to arouse him.

Richard worked his tongue inside her and felt the tiny hard grape of her clitoris. With lips, tongue and gently nipping teeth he toyed with her, being rewarded by an occasional groan as she became excited in her turn. The task of arousing her took his mind away from what she was doing to him, so that the danger of an immediate solo eruption receded. He really preferred a long, slow sexual encounter to one that ended too soon.

He was so intent on what they were doing to one

another that her first orgasm caught him by surprise. Abruptly she bore down on his face and moaned softly. At the same time she nipped his cock. He tensed as he felt her teeth, but then she released him as her mouth opened in a longer, deeper moan of pleasure. He felt her shudder as the spasm passed through her body. When it passed, she resumed working on his cock. Richard wanted to hold her against him, but the handcuffs prevented any more active participation on his part. He had not foreseen that aspect of bondage when he was fantasising about it, but he found that his helplessness was turning him on in ways he had never thought possible. He was finding it hard to hold back his own orgasm as he lay beneath this extraordinary young woman who had picked him up on the street.

She moaned again as a second orgasm took her. Richard buried his face deeper in her crotch as she bucked atop him. When the peak had passed, she lay quiet for a few moments, then she shifted until they were face to face so that he could enter her. As she guided him home, she sighed with satisfaction. She lay flat against him so that her breasts were pressed against his chest. Then she began to fuck him, rising and falling on his cock and rubbing her breasts with their engorged nipples against his chest. Her next orgasm shook them both, her body shuddering as a series of peaks washed through her. She was moaning continuously, the sound rising and falling as she gasped for breath. Her mouth was wide open and her eyes closed tightly as she concentrated on her pleasure.

Richard felt as if his cock were enclosed in a burning liquid tunnel which sucked greedily at him as she moved wildly in her orgasm. He was trying hard to prolong this episode. It was one of the wildest sexual encounters he had ever experienced, and he wanted it to last. At the same time he knew that he was being pushed steadily closer to the brink. When he could delay himself no longer, he too groaned with the release of tension. The girl bucked wildly as she joined him. He thought she would fling herself off into the air, so wild were her movements. Then abruptly she slumped against him, her breath sawing in her throat.

Richard was alarmed. She seemed to be having a fit of some sort. He thought, belatedly, of those stories about having a heart attack during sex, and he wondered if that had happened to her. She lay limply against him, and he was helpless to do anything. He tugged at the handcuffs, but there was no escape. He could do nothing but look at her. And as he did he noticed that she was still breathing, albeit stertorously, and her heartbeat was strong. He could see the tiny pulse beneath her ear. All the vital signs were there, and gradually he realised that she had fainted. That was something none of his other partners had ever done. Quite an accomplishment, he thought with a quiet pride.

He lay more quietly as the initial alarm faded and his breath slowed towards normal. Indeed, there was nothing else he could do until she regained consciousness and unlocked the handcuffs. Or didn't. He felt a thrill of excitement as he contemplated being held for hours. It would hardly be against his will.

They lay for what seemed like hours, until eventually she stirred and opened her eyes. For a moment she looked wildly at him, then recognition came to her and she smiled. She bent down and planted a kiss on his mouth before rolling off him. Richard felt a sense of regret as he slid out of her, but she was still smiling. She stood up warily, as if she didn't trust her legs to bear her weight. Then she moved off to the bathroom. Richard could hear water splashing, and then the sound of the toilet flushing. Eventually she came back, looking refreshed but still tousled. She was still smiling as she bent to unlock his handcuffs. She laid them on the bedside table before laying herself on the bed next to him.

Free now, Richard turned over and gathered her against him. She rested her head against his shoulder and kissed him again. They lay together, and gradually she drifted off to sleep. Her head rolled on to the pillow. Richard looked for a long time at the girl lying beside him. Her hair, dark against the pillow, shone softly in the glow from the bedside lamp. He stroked it idly, drowsily, before falling asleep himself with an odd sense of better things to come.

When he woke in the morning, the other half of the bed was empty, but there was a heartening smell of fresh coffee and breakfast being cooked. He got up and followed the noises to their source. The girl was standing at the stove wearing an apron.

'Cooking in the nude may be provocative, but there is a real danger of getting hot spatters on one's tits. Or other vital parts,' she added, with a glance at Richard's cock. 'But come and sit down while I finish our breakfast,' she continued.

Richard sat at the scrubbed pine table and admired the girl as she moved familiarly about the kitchen. She poured coffee for them both and presently set two omelettes on the table. Toast, butter and marmalade completed the setting. As she sat down opposite Richard, he voiced the thought that had been on his mind since they had met. 'Do you think it proper we should have breakfast without knowing one another's names?'

'Is it any less proper than what we did last night without knowing one another's names?' she retorted with a smile. 'But perhaps you're right. Breakfast is a different matter, in the cold light of the morning. I am Helena Witt.'

'Richard Stanfield. Are you related to Katarina, of figure-skating fame?'

'I don't think so. I am not from Chemnitz, or Karl

Marx Stadt, as it used to be known. I come from Neumunster, near Kiel. Where do you live?'

'In England. Near Bacton, on the North Norfolk coast.' He went on to explain that he lived in a large old house in the country, a house inherited from his aunt, who had had ambitions for a large family but less success in acquiring one. 'I was her favourite nephew,' he told her. 'I used to spend my school holidays with her and my uncle, rattling around in the old place and in the woods nearby. On special days we would make an expedition to the seaside: places like Mundseley and Cromer. They – my aunt and uncle – loved the North Norfolk coast and detested Great Yarmouth, which they thought unspeakably vulgar, with all those amusements and gawking visitors.' He found himself eager to tell her more about himself. She was easy to talk to, and he felt impelled to share his confidences and experiences with her. But he stopped himself from running on about himself with an effort and asked her about her past.

'Later,' she told him. 'I would like to keep some secrets. It makes me more mysterious and desirable, I think. Don't you agree?'

'You may be right,' Richard agreed. 'I know you're mysterious and desirable enough for me as you are.'

'Thank you,' Helena said, with another smile. 'And thank you for saying nothing about my surprising you last night. It was bad manners, to say the least.'

'Not at all. I was flattered I could help you come as you did. No other woman has ever fainted in my arms, so to speak.'

'I was surprised myself,' she said. 'That has never happened to me before.' She looked at him solemnly.

'Well, in that case, maybe we should keep one another company. Maybe something like it will happen again.' Once again Richard was surprised to hear himself speaking so openly about his feelings with a stranger.

The English reputation for reserve was not normally undeserved in his case.

Helena smiled abruptly, her solemnity disappearing. 'I am so glad you feel that way. I feel the same. I think we will go on to discover some wonderful things together.'

They were silent after their mutual revelations, embarrassed perhaps by their own frankness. But there was an underlying current of excitement as they ate their meal.

At the end of it, Helena asked him if he had anywhere important to go that day. Richard said no, he was having an indefinite holiday from England. She seemed pleased by his answer. He was happy, because her question implied that she wanted to spend more time with him. Helena stood up.

'Do you mind doing the washing-up, Richard? I need to get ready to go out for a bit.'

Richard nodded and watched as she took off her apron and hung it up. Nudity became her, he decided. As he washed up the breakfast things, he could hear her moving about in the apartment. The small domestic noises were reassuring. As he was finishing up, Helena came back. She was dressed and carrying a large canvas hold-all in addition to her handbag. She said she would be back in a few hours and he should make himself at home while she was out. Did he have any special requests for dinner?

'Anything, so long as you're around to cook it. I'm not much good at *haute cuisine*.'

She nodded, and withdrew. Richard heard her high heels tapping across the floor, then the sound of the door opening and closing as she left the apartment. He dried his hands on the apron Helena had worn and poured himself a second cup of coffee. He liked being alone in her apartment. Her leaving him there implied a certain degree of trust in him.

He took the coffee through into the bedroom, where he noticed she hadn't made up the bed. He smoothed the sheets and drew the quilt up over the pillows. Then he picked up the clothes she had worn the last evening, hanging up her dress and taking the underwear through into the bathroom as he went to take a shower. There was a wicker basket more than half full of her underwear and tights. Richard added the things he carried to the collection and stepped into the shower. He had left his toilet things at the guest house and so had to use Helena's things. That added another degree of intimacy to the novel situation.

He dried himself on her towel and put it into the basket of things to be washed before going in search of his clothes. He remembered Helena undressing him in the bedroom but couldn't find his clothes there. Puzzled, he looked into her wardrobe, in case she had hung them up. That seemed unlikely, since she had left her own things lying around. There was no sign of his clothes anywhere in the bedroom, so he wandered out into the living room. They weren't there either. Could they possibly be in the other bedroom, the one she had turned into a work room? They weren't, although Richard spent a good deal of time there both looking for his clothes and studying the drawings Helena had made of her fetish fashions. As on the previous evening, he felt a stirring of excitement as he looked at the drawings of the male and female chastity belts she had designed. He thought again how exciting it might be to be locked into one of them.

After he had looked all around, he reached the only possible conclusion: Helena had taken his clothes with her, stranding him there. He recalled the canvas hold-all she had carried, which had seemed so incongruous with the way she was dressed. He had no idea why she had done this, and he felt a flare of resentment. They had seemed on the brink of a relationship, of exchanging confidences, maybe even of becoming partners. And now this. But in spite of Helena's playing this trick on him, he could see the funny side. He could think of a lot of men who wouldn't mind being stranded without clothes in the apartment of a beautiful young woman who had showed a sexual interest in them. And now it had happened to him. Richard wasn't afraid of being stranded permanently. This was Helena's home, and she would be back eventually. It was merely a matter of being patient until then. Then he could take any measures he thought appropriate. He toyed with the image of turning Helena over his knee and spanking her until she sued for mercy.

But suppose Helena returned without his clothes? There was nothing he could do in that case. Spanking her, or doing anything else along those lines, would not produce the clothing he would need when it came time to leave the apartment. He shrugged the thought away. There was nothing he could do except wait and see.

Richard wandered around the apartment once again, looking into wardrobes and drawers and reading Helena's bookshelves. He turned on the television, but there was nothing on except the bland daytime fare. It was no better in German than the programmes he had seen in English. For want of something to do, he brought Helena's basket of washing to the kitchen and sorted through it. As he put her underwear into the washing machine, he could smell the faint odour of her that clung to it.

While the washer was going through its cycle, he settled down with one of Len Deighton's Berlin spy thrillers. He got up to put the damp washing into the dryer and returned to the book. When he looked up again it was nearly one o'clock. His stomach said it was lunch time, so he explored Helena's refrigerator. There was *schinkenwurst* and cheese, from which he made sandwiches.

Helena had still not returned by two o'clock, when Richard went back to the kitchen with the dishes. He washed them in the sink and left them on the drainer to dry. He took Helena's clothing from the dryer, folded it, and put it away in the drawers in the bedroom. Then, having nothing else to do, he set about tidying up the apartment. Helena didn't appear to be especially untidy, but there were things to put away and others to replace in their proper places. The workroom alone he did not touch. He thought she would probably have arranged things in there to suit her work habits, and would not appreciate his efforts to rearrange them.

As he was putting the vacuum cleaner away, he heard the key turn in the door. A moment later Helena entered, calling over her shoulder to an unseen companion to come in. She noticed Richard with the vacuum cleaner. So, a moment later, did her companion, a statuesque blonde in a dark, severely cut pinstripe suit of the type worn by lawyers and bankers. Helena smiled mischievously at him. Her companion looked at him with undisguised astonishment, turning in a moment to outright appraisal.

Richard was embarrassed, of course, but Helena seemed not to be. To his further embarrassment, he felt his cock stiffening as he looked at the two beautiful and stylishly dressed women who stood looking at his nudity.

'Margaret, meet homo erectus. Richard, this is my aunt, Margaret Wagner. I've invited her round to look over my drawings and discuss my business venture. If she likes what she sees, she may be persuaded to lend me enough capital to start making a few things to display in the shops.' Helena smiled brightly at him and then, somewhat more tentatively, at Margaret.

It was apparent from the way Margaret was looking at him that she already liked at least part of what she was seeing. Richard was flattered at her interest, but taken aback at his abrupt inclusion in Helena's social circle. He tried not to let his surprise show. He didn't want to do anything to upset her plans if he could help it, but he was not at all sure he was ready to handle this complication to his fledgling relationship with Helena.

'I see you've trained him well,' Margaret said, with a gesture that included both Richard's nudity and the vacuum cleaner he still held. 'That's a good sign. One's associates should be able to work on their own without continual supervision,' she continued, with the ghost of a smile that betrayed irony and interest in equal measure. 'It looks as if he has made a good job of the place in your absence. Has he been with you long?'

'About twenty-four hours,' Helena said with a straight face.

Margaret crossed the room to take a closer look at Richard. He heard the faint silken rustle of nylon as she approached him, and he found himself wondering if she was wearing stockings. Her faint perfume smelt expensive. Richard felt his cock grow stiffer and tried to avoid looking down at himself. He kept his eyes on Margaret's face, in particular her eyes, which were a startlingly deep shade of green. Like a cat's, he thought. She moved with a feline grace as well, unusual in a woman of her size. In her high-heeled shoes she stood as tall as Richard, so that their eyes were on a level. Richard imagined a canary might feel the way he did under the steady gaze of those cat's eyes.

In order to make the bizarre situation more normal, he set the vacuum cleaner on the floor and held out his hand to her. Instead of shaking his outstretched hand, Margaret reached out and grasped his cock, enveloping him with the warmth of her hand. He felt a shock pass through his body as she took him. His first reaction was to jerk away, but he managed to stand his ground and even to look again at her face.

He thought Helena might be feeling jealous or angry,

but then he remembered she had brought Margaret back to the apartment knowing he would still be there and in the nude. The only thing she couldn't have anticipated was Margaret's intimacy. Or maybe she had, and had relied on it as part of her plan to interest this tall, beautiful woman in her business. Richard could see a certain logic in that. If Margaret liked what she saw and held, as she evidently did, then she might like the rest of the plan as well. He wondered fleetingly if prostitution, of which this was a form, should make him feel like an object, as many women had argued. Instead he felt excited. Maybe he wasn't a prostitute.

Still holding Richard's cock, Margaret asked Helena, 'Would you consider lending him to me for a while? My house is in need of a good cleaning too. I would be able to return him to you even better trained than he is now.'

Although Margaret could not see Helena's face, Richard could. He caught the spasm of anger in her glance, followed by the mute appeal to him. Helena gestured pleadingly at him behind Margaret's back before she replied, 'Of course.' Obviously she dared not ask Richard what he thought about the bargain.

He thought it might be impolitic to deny her, for reasons he would have been hard put to explain had an explanation been demanded of him just at that moment. Such a refusal might even be considered impolite in some circles. He imagined his acquiescence would make the matter of starting-up capital easier for Helena. Also, he reflected, it is hard to refuse the request of a beautiful woman who has hold of your cock. Let's see where this goes, he told himself.

'Thank you,' Margaret said. Still holding Richard's cock, which she seemed to regard as her personal property now, she asked Helena to show her the rest of the proposition.

Helena led the way into the workroom, and Margaret followed, pulling Richard along in her wake. Even leading him by the cock, Margaret lost none of her feline grace.

Helena began setting out her drawings for Margaret's inspection. To Richard she looked nervous, moving quickly and jerkily around the drafting table she used as a work surface. Once she snatched a drawing so hastily the corner tore off. Richard could see the effort it took to control herself. Even with Margaret holding him so intimately, he had enough wit left to wonder if Helena was feeling jealous at the way Margaret had moved in so quickly to make him her own prize.

When the drawings were laid out, Margaret led Richard over to the table to inspect them. When she squeezed his cock he shuddered with excitement. She noticed, and smiled at her power over him. Then she turned her attention to Helena's designs.

Richard admired them as well. Helena had a good deal of skill and imagination, he decided. If these designs were made to measure, rather than merely bought off the peg in a sex shop like those on the *Reeperbahn*, they would be truly stunning. At the same time, he couldn't help noticing that all of Helena's designs incorporated some degree of restraint for the wearer. She must be deeply into bondage, he thought with another flare of excitement. Margaret squeezed him again, believing no doubt that he was reacting to her touch.

Richard saw again the sketches of chastity belts that Helena had shown him, but there were other sketches too, as well as many fully executed drawings, of full face masks, helmets both with and without eye and mouth holes, gags, leather belts and straps for restraining one's partner, even some hastily drawn designs for custom-made high-heeled shoes, most of them with exaggeratedly high heels and many with straps going around the ankles and insteps.

Margaret picked up one and then another design,

considering and then rejecting them, before she came to a drawing of a pair of leather pants. In the margin of the drawing there was a note, which read, 'Can be made with one or two dildoes. Laced on or zipper fastening, lockable, with or without reinforced waist and leg bands. May be made in rubber as well.'

'I'll have one of these,' she said decisively, tapping the paper with one of her immaculately shaped and polished fingernails. 'I want two dildoes and the reinforced waist and leg bands. Zipper fastening. I think I'll enjoy being able to wear this secretly all day at work. And I'll be better able to evaluate your product before making a decision.'

Helena made a note of the design. Somewhat diffidently, she asked, 'Do you want me to take your measurements here? Now?' She gestured at Richard, as if suggesting that Margaret might want more privacy while she was being measured.

'Of course we can do it here. And now. But he will have to be restrained during the process. You have the facilities, I believe.' Margaret squeezed Richard's cock once more and released it. She turned away and stood looking out of the window, leaving Helena to deal with Richard as she thought fit.

Helena walked across to the table and looked at his face with an expression of doubt and mute appeal. 'Please,' she mouthed silently.

Richard looked down at her, vulnerable in her anxiety. He nodded silently, knowing she didn't want Margaret to suspect that she had to ask him. He liked Helena a great deal, despite the situation she had landed him in. And, he told himself, he was already too far into the situation to back out gracefully. Or maybe his acquiescence had as much to do with his lack of clothes and the possessive way Margaret had handled him.

He wondered what 'facilities' she had referred to. He watched, fascinated, as Helena opened one of the desk drawers and withdrew a bag of short, wide nylon cable ties. He didn't resist when she pulled his arms behind his back and looped one of them around his wrists. She pulled it tight, the locking device purring along the strap until it could go no further. With a pair of dressmaker's shears she cut off the protruding end.

When she moved around to face Richard she mouthed 'I'm sorry,' with an infinitesimal nod of her head to where Margaret still stood with her back to them. She shrugged her shoulders resignedly. Richard shrugged his own shoulders in reply.

Helena turned to Margaret and said, 'Are you ready now?'

Margaret moved away from the window to stand near Richard and Helena. She turned him slightly by the upper arm so she could see what Helena had done. She nodded slightly, but looked unsatisfied. She picked up her handbag from the drafting table and produced a chain-type dog collar, with a larger ring at each end. She took a second cable tie from the bag and threaded it through one of these rings. Then she knelt before Richard and passed the cable tie around his scrotum, pulling down on his balls to ensure both were below the nylon band. Then she tightened the tie snugly around his scrotum.

She motioned for Helena to hand her the shears. Richard stood very still as she cut off the end of the cable tie. When she was done, he was left with the chain hanging down between his legs. Margaret stood up and handed the shears back to Helena with hardly a glance in her direction. She grasped the chain and tugged sharply on it. Richard was pulled slightly off balance. As he recovered, Margaret gave a smile and said, 'That won't slip off now. Come along.'

She led Richard towards Helena's industrial sewing machine standing near the wall. He followed perforce. Margaret looked for some way to fasten the end of his lead to the machine. When she discovered no ready way of anchoring him, she frowned and reached for her handbag once more.

While Richard was wondering just what else it might contain, she produced a dog lead with a leather loop at one end and a swivel snap at the other. She passed the lead through the lattice work on the machine's leg and threaded the end through the loop. She then snapped the lead to the end of the chain dangling between Richard's legs, and he was tethered to the machine. With his hands fastened behind his back there was no way for him to reach the snap and free himself.

Margaret grunted in satisfaction as she stepped away from him. Without further ado, she began to strip off her clothes, revealing her body progressively and provocatively to him as she wriggled out of her dress and her pale-green slip. Her legs were long and full, and yes, Richard saw, she wore stockings and suspenders. He approved, but could do little else.

Richard supposed Helena could take the necessary measurements over what Margaret now wore, but he nevertheless hoped she would take everything off. She did, slowly and with all the art of the striptease dancer. When Margaret was nude, she stood erect before Richard to allow him to see all of the body he could not touch.

Then, unexpectedly, Margaret turned to Helena and ordered her to strip as well. Helena went red and stuttered in her embarrassment. 'Please . . . I don't like to. Not here. You know why.'

'I said, take your clothes off. Now. I will not say it again.' Margaret stared hard at Helena, until the younger woman dropped her gaze and began to fumble at the fastenings of her dress. When it dropped to the floor at her feet, Richard was once again amazed at her beauty. Now that he was seeing her in full daylight he realised he had only half-seen her the night before.

Margaret was beautiful too, but in a remote fashion. She dressed stylishly but severely, wearing her suit almost as a badge of defiance: don't tread on me, don't even approach me.

Helena, on the other hand, appeared the more vulnerable and hence the more appealing. Now that she had gone so far, she squared her small shoulders and faced Richard full on as she took off the rest of her clothes. Today, he saw, she too wore stockings and suspenders. And he saw why. Under her outer clothing, Helena wore a chastity belt. She had not been wearing it last night, nor when she had left the apartment that morning. Ergo, she must have put it on – or been compelled to do so – at Margaret's home. The suspenders that held her stockings up were clipped to the metal of the belt that imprisoned her. When she was naked save for the belt and her stockings, she faced Richard with a look of there-now-you-know-it-all, that nevertheless included a silent appeal for his understanding.

He looked at her long and intensely before he nodded. The look of relief on Helena's face was his reward.

Margaret must have seen the exchange and resented it, for she said, 'How very touching young love can be. Now show him your back, my dear,' she said contemptuously.

Even emboldened by Richard's understanding, Helena was still embarrassed. But she turned her back slowly at Margaret's orders. Richard saw that she had been beaten, again sometime between this morning and this afternoon. Once again it must have been at Margaret's hands. Anger made him step forward, until the tether around his scrotum reminded him of the limitations to his power of intervention.

Margaret seemed both gratified and displeased by his reaction. 'I had my chauffeur give Helena a short lesson in obedience this morning. Silence was enforced by a gag during the actual discipline, she being sadly unable to contain herself under the stimulation of the lash. And afterwards I ensured her chastity by the means you now see.I could leave the two of you alone now with perfect peace of mind. That would be amusing.'

Helena's back, from her neck to her knees, was striped with a series of light pink stripes, none of which broke the skin. It must have taken considerable skill to whip her so thoroughly without drawing blood. Nevertheless, it must have been extremely painful. While he had been confined to her apartment, she had been suffering this.

Margaret spoke again. 'We use a medieval whip on Helena when it is time to beat her. I was fortunate enough to secure an antique whip at auction. The provenance, I was assured, was impeccable. It had been used by one of the nuns in a Carmelite convent near Avila to flagellate herself according to the peculiar discipline the good sisters submitted to. In fact the whip itself was called The Discipline by the nuns. Twelve thin, waxed thongs – one for each Apostle, I understand – fixed to a short wooden handle. The Discipline was kept in a special black cloth bag when not in use, always in sight to remind the nuns of the weakness of the flesh and the necessity of daily penance. When you come to my house tonight, you will see it in the place of honour on my mantel shelf. We almost always fetch it down when Helena comes to visit: she is sadly in need of constant discipline, and must be reminded again and again of the consequences of disobedience.

'Did she tell you last night that she actually enjoys her whippings? No? I thought not. Perhaps she would have told you in time. But the sad truth about our little Helena is that she is a practising masochist. At first we have to use force on her. But once she is stripped naked and tied to the whipping frame, she has to be gagged in order to prevent her screams of pleasure from rousing the neighbours. At my country retreat, noise is not such an attracter of unwanted attention, so there she can shout to the rooftops. And she does.'

Helena had meanwhile turned back to face Richard. Her face was red with embarrassment, but at the same time he could see that Margaret's revelations were exciting as well. Helena's breathing was harsh and irregular, and her nipples were erect. A deep flush suffused her neck and breasts. She was clearly excited by the narration of her ordeal.

Richard was excited too. He could feel his cock stiffen as he imagined Helena writhing in pleasure as she was beaten. He could even imagine himself wielding the lash, although he had never done anything like that in his life. But – think of the sense of power.

Margaret's sudden laugh cut across his fantasies. 'Look, Helena, he's got a hard on.' To Richard she said, 'And do you want to beat our little Helena until she shrieks in ecstasy? I think you do. Well, I may let you do that one day.' Turning again to Helena, she asked, 'And would you like him to beat you, this handsome man you chose on the streets last night? And to fuck you senseless afterwards? Yes, I can see the idea intrigues you. You have chosen well. Richard will fit nicely into our little ménage. He can be the necessary third side to the triangle, keeping us both happy in our separate ways.'

Richard saw a flare of hope light Helena's face at Margaret's suggestion that he become a part of their 'ménage'. The look disappeared as quickly as it came. Margaret didn't see it.

'But let us return to the business in hand,' Margaret said. 'Helena, get out your tape measure and notebook.'

Helena did as she was bid, taking Margaret's details down in her notebook. 'Do you want the legs cut high, bikini-fashion,' she asked, illustrating the detail on her own body, 'or long, like short trousers?'

'High cut,' Margaret replied. 'But make the waist and leg bands tight. I would prefer a strong hook and eye fastener at the waist band, and a zipper below that, to the crotch.' She drew an imaginary line from her navel to her pubic mound. 'The dildoes must be removable, both for comfort and for sanitary reasons,' she directed. 'And be sure there are loops or tabs for suspenders.'

'Colour?' Helena asked.

'Red,' Margaret replied. 'Everyone has boring black leather pants. I will be different.'

'Will there be anything else?' Helena asked.

'Not in the clothing line,' said Margaret, seating herself on the edge of the worktable.

As Helena approached, Margaret looked directly at Richard. 'Watch this. I am sure you will enjoy the show.' She scooted back on to the top of the table and placed her feet flat on the work surface. She bent her knees and spread her thighs so that her sex was fully displayed.

Helena obviously guessed what was coming next, and she tried to dissuade Margaret. 'Please. Not that. Not in front of . . .' She indicated Richard with a hopeless gesture. Her flush this time was from embarrassment rather than excitement.

Margaret didn't reply. She simply lay waiting for Helena to take up a position between her legs. Helena looked hopelessly again at Richard as she moved between Margaret's thighs. She bent down and began to use her tongue and teeth in an attempt to arouse the other woman.

Richard remembered a similar performance from the previous evening. If that was any indication, Margaret would soon be aroused to fever pitch. From where he stood, Richard could see her breasts, slightly flattened as she lay on her back, but still very firm. The nipples were slowly becoming erect. She turned her head so that she could look at Richard while Helena worked away between her thighs. She smiled at him and then closed her eyes, surrendering herself to the stimulation of her labia and clitoris. Her knuckles whitened as she gripped the edges of the table, and there was a short, stifled moan from her as she came.

Richard thought that either it was a short orgasm, or that she was fighting to keep from showing her pleasure. He wondered why she might want to do that. Perhaps, like many dominant people, she equated pleasure with weakness, and didn't want to appear weak. That was one argument against dominance, Richard reflected.

Nevertheless, he felt his cock throbbing as he watched Margaret's arousal. A large part of the excitement came from the sight of Helena's bottom moving enticingly between the older woman's legs.

Margaret gave another short cry, instantly stifled. But it was clear that she had come again. Her eyes were open again, but she was no longer looking at Richard. Her eyes were unfocussed, as if all her attention was on inner matters. Her nipples were erect now, stippled with tiny bumps like gooseflesh. Her hips jerked once or twice, as if she was unable to control her body quite as well as she would have liked.

As the arousal went on, Margaret lost more and more of her self-control. Richard saw her reach for Helena's head, her fingers twining in the short, dark hair and holding the younger woman against her fiercely. Her body arched in a sudden spasm, and the cry she gave this time left no doubt that she had finally been driven to the brink and over it. Her eyes were screwed shut and her breath rasped in her throat as she climaxed again and again. She was out of control, bucking and shuddering as Helena used her tongue and teeth on the older woman. She was holding Helena tightly against her, as if she would never let her go. Her cries were loud in the small room. Her legs closed, trapping Helena's head.

The sight of Margaret's arousal excited Richard immensely. His cock was stiff and slightly red, and he knew he would like to bury it inside Margaret if he could. He understood now why she had had him restrained. He had never played the spectator's role in sex as he was now forced to.

After what seemed like a very long time, her body relaxed on the table and she let go of Helena's hair. Her legs parted and she seemed somehow smaller and much less dominant. She let her arms drop to the table top. There was a smile on Margaret's face as she lay back after her exertions. Her pubic hair was damp with her musk, and her labia were still erect, suffused with blood and very pink. Richard stared at her exposed sex with a certain degree of frustration.

The younger woman stood up and stretched her cramped muscles. She was very red in the face, whether from embarrassment or as the result of her exertions Richard couldn't tell. Nor did he feel inclined to ask. He felt a reticence in Margaret's presence, as apparently did Helena. He stood where he had been tethered and waited for the next development. Helena looked once at him but made no move to come closer.

Margaret took a long time to recover. Her breathing slowed, but there were still occasional spasms that shook her. Her face and neck were red, and Richard still caught the smell of her from time to time. That was exciting, but there was nothing he could do about it. That was why Margaret had insisted he be restrained before she made herself vulnerable in his presence. He imagined she enjoyed arousing him by forcing him to watch as she was brought to climax. His cock was still stiff, and he didn't like the idea of Helena seeing the strength of his response to what he had witnessed. But there was nothing he could do about that either.

She seemed to understand his feelings, for when she next risked a glance in his direction she silently mouthed, 'It's all right.' That made him feel a bit easier. It was more evidence of a welcome conspiracy between the two of them against Margaret.

But there was no time for more than that. Margaret sat up on the worktable and looked directly at him, as if gauging his reaction. His cock, standing at attention, was all she needed to see. With a smile, she stood up and crossed the room to him. Taking his cock in hand again, she stroked the underside with her fingers before scratching it sharply with her fingernail. His cock leapt in her hand with a life of its own.

'Poor Richard. Would you like to put that inside me? Or would you prefer our little Helena?'

There was no satisfactory answer to that question, so he remained silent.

Margaret, however, did not insist on an answer, and her next act relieved him of the need to say anything that would anger either of the two women. She moved closer to him and slid his cock between her thighs, squeezing her legs tightly together. He could feel the warmth of her cunt against him, and the slickness of her fluids, still flowing after her climaxes. She began to rock her hips backward and forward, causing his cock to slide between her thighs. At the same time she arched her back and thrust her breasts almost into his face, as if mocking his inability to touch them, or her.

And he responded. He couldn't help it. If he had been asked at that moment whether it was against his will, he couldn't have answered. Luckily, there was no one there – not even himself – who was interested in asking that question. He knew he was going to come, or be made to come, as soon as Margaret took him between her thighs. It was merely a matter of time before the inevitable happened. It turned out to be a short time. Witnessing Margaret in rut had excited him more than he knew, so that when he came it was suddenly. Margaret had no time to move back, if that was what she had intended, before he spurted down the insides of her legs. But even after that had happened, Margaret made no move to withdraw. She gazed steadily at him with an amused half-smile. Richard tried to out-stare her, but in the end he had to look away.

Margaret released him and moved away, calling for Helena to bring warm water and towels from the bathroom. She then had Helena clean her legs and dry them. Once more she caught Richard's eye. With a gesture at the younger woman cleaning her, she said scornfully, 'Sometimes I have her lick me clean, but this time I'm in a hurry.'

Helena flushed at the words but did not look up. Richard, perforce, stood in place. The younger woman moved from time to time as she worked, giving him the opportunity to study the chastity belt she wore. It appeared to be made of brass. Logical, he thought. Steel would rust and leave nasty stains. There was a narrow band that fitted snugly to Helena's waist. It had been carefully shaped to her contours, dipping at the back as a more conventional belt would do. It was hinged on her left side, and there was a flat lock with a keyhole on the right. To the waist band in the front a V-shaped piece was hinged. The solid part covered her pubic mound, and a narrower band passed between her legs and up over her bottom, joining a short band that descended from the waist belt, to which it was secured with a similar flat lock.

The device was evidently designed to be worn for long periods, even under normal clothing, for it was lined with leather to avoid chafing or pinching the wearer. It was cleverly made: Margaret must have access to a highly skilled metalworker. He wondered what else he – or she – might have made for the tall blonde woman who stood before him.

When Helena had dried her long legs, Margaret began to get dressed. Helena made no move to resume her own discarded clothing. Richard, of course, was unable to dress himself even if he had had his clothes. He wondered what had been done with them, and when they would get around to releasing him. He wasn't particularly worried about what Margaret might do to him. Torture and mutilation did not seem to be on the menu. Though taunting and humiliation might well have a central place on it. And bondage, of course, if his present situation was anything to judge by. He was interested.

Margaret ordered Helena to get dressed, to Richard's mild regret. When she was clothed, the younger woman was told to go down to the car and fetch Richard's clothes. He gathered from that that some change in his situation was imminent.

When Helena had departed on her errand, Margaret turned to Richard. 'I'm glad to see that you aren't in the habit of asking stupid questions, like what we might be planning for you. Though I'm sure you are thinking about that. Here's what we're going to do. When you're fit to be seen in public once more, we – you and I, that is – will go to my country house, passing by your guesthouse to allow you to pay the bill and collect your belongings. Little Helena will remain here for the time being, a hostage to your good behaviour, if you like. I may allow you to be reunited when I judge you are ready.

'At my country house you will be given obedience training. There's no point in saying more than that just now. You'll find out soon enough what is involved. Not all of it will be unpleasant. In fact, some of your predecessors even found parts of it very pleasurable. I hope you will make a similar discovery, because happy servants are the best kind. I will be your principal, though not your only, tutor. You will meet the others in due course.'

'And what if I don't like your plans for me? I've never

been asked what I might like,' Richard said. They were the first words he had spoken since Helena and Margaret had returned to the apartment. His voice sounded strange in his own ears after the prolonged silence, thin and somehow strained.

Margaret's gesture included both Richard and his restraints. 'What choice do you think you have? I could have you taken to my house exactly as you are – minus the sewing machine, of course. Our little Helena will be needing it in any case. But I'd much prefer you came without any undue reluctance. It would be so much easier on everybody. Including Helena,' she added menacingly.

Richard believed her. He had never met a woman who seemed as self-assured and decisive as Margaret. She was what could be called a natural leader. Or a dictator. The undercurrent of excitement he had been feeling ever since this woman had come into his life stirred in him again, urging him to see where else she might lead him. 'All right,' he heard himself saying, as if from a distance, or as if a stranger had taken over his voice and body, and he had become merely a spectator. His throat felt tight.

Margaret nodded. 'Good. I'm glad that's settled. Now we will see about getting you loose.' She picked up the dressmaker's shears from Helena's worktable and snipped the band that held his wrists behind his back. 'Unsnap yourself and give me the lead,' Margaret ordered.

Richard did as directed. Margaret stowed the lead in her handbag. He gestured at the chain that dangled between his legs. Margaret said, 'We'll leave that for a while. If I cut it off now I'd only have to replace it later this evening. And besides,' she said with a mischievous grin, 'I might accidentally cut you in a very sensitive place.'

Richard doubted that she would make such a

mistake. Her acts were much too carefully calculated. But he said nothing more.

Helena came back a few moments later, saving him from the strain of making small talk. He put on his clothes, tucking the chain down one leg of his trousers. He saw Margaret extract a large wad of Deutschmarks from her handbag and hand over some of them to Helena.

'Use this to buy whatever you need to get started on my order. Anything left over can be applied to running expenses. I'll be around to see you again in a few days, and I'd like to see some progress on the design. Now I will allow you a few moments to say *auf Wiedersehen* to Richard.' Margaret left the room.

There was an awkward silence between Helena and Richard, then both began to speak at once. Helena stopped in confusion; Richard told her to go ahead. He wanted to hear from her what he was getting into.

'I'm sorry for what's happened, Richard. I had to do it. One day – soon, I hope – I will be able to tell you all about it. For now, please go along with Margaret. For my sake. I don't think she will hurt you. She has never done any serious or permanent harm to anyone else she took in hand.' Helena stopped and blushed at her gaffe.

Richard smiled and nodded for her to go on.

'Margaret likes to have people obey her. Especially men, but as you see she likes women to follow her orders as well. It can be unpleasant at times. Even humiliating. She enjoys humiliating people. And there is a certain amount of pain. But I can tell you from personal experience that it is not unbearable.'

Richard compared Helena's understated description of the whipping with Margaret's own more forthright one. But he nodded once again. 'All right. I'll go along, for your sake.'

Helena smiled in relief and gratitude. 'Soon, I hope, we will be able to talk more freely. And maybe to escape from Margaret's influence.' She leant forward as if to kiss Richard but pulled back abruptly at the sound of the opening door.

'Time to go. Come along, Richard. Helena, I will see you on Friday.' Margaret summoned him as she dismissed Helena.

They went down the stairs and out into the soft light of early evening. Margaret led the way to a large BMW with darkly tinted windows that was parked at the kerb across the street. She unlocked the doors and motioned for him to get into the passenger seat. 'Buckle up,' she said.

Two

They stopped at the guesthouse where he had been staying. Richard paid his bill and collected the rest of his luggage. Then they left Hamburg and drove south on the autobahn towards Hanover. Margaret said nothing. Presumably having given him all the information she thought necessary, she left Richard to consider it and to make whatever plans he could to face the obedience training he had been promised. Or maybe she felt her position as tutor imposed a duty on her to maintain her dignity and distance from the 'trainee'. At any rate, they drove for something over two hours at a speed which ensured there were few drivers able or willing to overtake them, and in total silence. Somewhere in the Luneburg Heath area, Margaret took an exit marked 'Soltau'.

They passed through the town centre and continued on into the outskirts. Soon cows became more numerous than cars, and fields more frequent than either. Margaret slowed and stopped before a pair of tall wrought-iron gates set into a high stone wall. The wall was lined along its top with razor wire and what looked like electrical insulators, no doubt carrying a discouragingly high electric charge. It was a wall that said plainly, 'no trespassing', if one was on the outside. From the inside it meant no escape.

With a remote control, Margaret caused these

forbidding gates to admit them. She then drove along a private road for ten minutes or so before the house came into sight. Richard saw what she meant when she had spoken of allowing Helena to scream as loudly as she liked in the country house. No one was going to hear anything short of a very loud explosion from the road.

What Margaret had described as a 'country house' was in reality more like a manor. It was constructed of stone on the ground floor, while the first floor exhibited the fanciful ornamental woodwork so popular on Alpine chalets. Like those distant chalets, the large house had extensive flowerbeds on all sides, and Richard could see window boxes and hanging baskets in the lights from the veranda that ran across the entire front of the building. Margaret's country retreat looked as if it could easily house three families.

As the car drew up, the front door opened and an attractive young woman in a maid's costume came out: black satin dress that came only as far as mid-thigh, a white frilly apron and cap, black stockings or tights and black high-heeled shoes. She was blonde like Margaret but shorter and slighter of build. She approached the car with curiously short steps, and Richard saw with a thrill of surprise that she wore leg-irons.

The maid opened the door for Margaret, who tossed the keys to her with a terse order to put the car into the garage and to bring the packages in the boot back to the house. She gestured for Richard to follow her into the house. The maid got awkwardly into the driving seat, hampered by her leg-irons. She seated herself and then swung both legs together into the car after her. Richard saw a flash of white flesh as her short dress rode up her thighs. Evidently she wore stockings rather than tights. Carrying his bag, he followed the tall blonde woman towards the front door.

In the hall another maid awaited orders. This one was

taller and somehow less willowy, but wearing the same sort of uniform as the one who had come out to the car. Unlike her, the maid in the hall was not wearing leg-irons. Richard wondered why.

Margaret handed her coat to the woman to hang up and asked for drinks and a snack to be served in the drawing room in ten minutes' time. Then she led Richard down the hallway and into a large, high-ceilinged room with comfortable-looking furniture arranged in two groupings. Each group consisted of a long couch with armchairs facing it and a coffee table in the centre. Above each group was a chandelier that shed a soft glow from many candle-shaped bulbs over the thick, light-blue carpet. Margaret sat on one of the couches and waved Richard to one of the armchairs.

He set his bag on the floor and sat down across from her. He waited for the next move, which had to be hers.

Realising this, Margaret began to speak. 'This is where you will stay during your training period. I do not mean this room. There are attached quarters for the trainees, and you will have your own assigned to you. But before we begin there are some things you need to know. House rules, you might say.'

Richard interrupted her before she could get into the details. 'What makes you think I'll abide by your rules, or even that I'll stay here? I'm on holiday now, but I have obligations back home which can't be shrugged off.' Even as he spoke, he was aware that his words sounded feeble.

Margaret was undeterred by his objections. 'The answer to your question is that you are already here. If you need any further convincing, just think back to what happened this afternoon at Helena's apartment, and to your less than active participation or objection. You have not said anything since then either, even though you could have spoken at any time as we drove here. Your silence is admission enough that you are interested in what will happen. So you need not bother to deny it. Nor,' she added with a tone of finality, 'should you interrupt me again. After I have finished you will be permitted to ask questions, but for now you need only listen.'

At that moment the maid came in with a trolley laden with bottles of liquor and a tray of sandwiches. She said, 'We have had another delivery, Madame.' Margaret nodded but didn't speak. The maid began to arrange the food, the glasses and the dishes on the coffee table. Richard watched with interest as she deferentially placed the drinks trolley near the couch. The woman was stockier than the other maid, with a thicker waist and more muscular legs, but she moved lightly and easily about the room. Her hair was cut short so as to frame her face, and was a soft brown shade. When everything was arranged, she asked, 'Will that be all, Madame?' in a husky voice and with a French accent.

Margaret dismissed her with a negligent wave of the hand, and the woman withdrew silently, closing the double doors behind her. Margaret gestured for Richard to help himself.

He made a drink for himself, a scotch over ice, and looked questioningly at Margaret, the bottle still in his hand. She nodded, and he poured the amber liquid into a glass, added ice and handed it to her before resuming his seat. Yes, he was interested to see where this would lead. There was a stirring of excitement in him that kept his throat tight.

Margaret spoke into the silence. 'I train servants here,' she said. 'You have seen two of them already. There are several others here now, and more trainees may come at any time. When their training is over, I recommend them to anyone who applies to my employment agency in Dusseldorf, Hamburg or Stuttgart. Several of them have found employment with the top executives at a top car manufacturer. One has even been taken by a vice-president of a multi-national company. She accompanied him back to London when his appointment here ended. As far as I know, she is still with him.'

'If you are only training domestic workers, servants if you prefer, then why was the one who came to meet us wearing chains? Is that part of the training?' Richard asked.

'Yes, it is, in several ways,' Margaret answered, with a disapproving glance at Richard. 'I just told you not to interrupt me,' she reminded him, 'but since you have already done so I will answer the question. Marie is Swiss, from a German-speaking canton near Zurich. She was sent here by her employer, one of the negotiators with a leading bank, for further training before being taken on a series of business trips to the United States. She had been – how shall I say? – remiss in her duties, and he felt she would benefit from further instruction before travelling with him.

'She wears those leg-irons to remind her that she is here to obey. They are also handy in preventing her from running away, which she has threatened to do once or twice after being disciplined. Since she speaks German, it would be very easy for her to escape by fading into the local population. Hence the chains. She will continue to wear them for the duration of her stay, and they will be sent to her employer when she goes back to him, in case she is in need of a further reminder. Many of the women and men who pass through here need to be prevented from running away during their first days here, and they too are placed in leg-irons. There are other methods of restraint for the more intractable, or for repeat offenders, of whom I trust you will not be one.' Margaret glanced at Richard as she spoke.

'I will not try to explain all of the rules at once. Some are best learnt by the example of others. And some from one's own experience after breaking them. The basic idea is to get everyone here accustomed to taking the orders of their trainers, and of their future employers. Some of the men and women who pass through our programme are not seeking employment, but merely enjoy the thrill of learning obedience through rigorous training and discipline. And we have our share of bondage devotees. We never know who will show up next, so the routines are always changing. It is only the rule of obedience and subservience that never changes.

'You fall partly into the latter class: that is, you are here for the thrill of it. Of course you may later seek employment as a servant if you find the training to your liking. At the same time we will be training you to act another role: that of confidential courier. You'll be told about that when the time comes. And what you learn may come in handy in other ways. One never knows what the future will bring. We – I – have no intention of keeping you here indefinitely. As you have said, you have other obligations at home. But I will probably recall you from time to time as conditions dictate.

'Since there is always the chance that you will seek to escape during your first days with us, we will take precautions in case you should try. Even though you are not being trained for future employment, never forget that the rules apply to you as well as to the ones who are seeking domestic work.'

'Like wearing leg-irons?' Richard asked, forgetting Margaret's injunction.

'No,' she said with asperity. 'Until we can find a maid's costume like the one worn by the servant who brought these –' she indicated the snacks and drinks '– we will keep your clothes under lock and key. Running away in the nude is not an attractive prospect. After we have got the maid's costume for you, you will of course wear that. Running away while dressed in women's clothing will not be so attractive either. And of course I have little Helena in my care. I don't think you would like to have her hurt by running away. You are fond of her, are you not?'

Richard nodded, not wanting to provoke Margaret further by speaking. As he went over what she had said, he felt the stirring of excitement again. This was something he had never tried, and now he had got over the initial surprise, he found himself strangely eager to begin.

As if reading his thoughts, Margaret summoned the maid with a small silver bell. The same one who had brought the refreshments appeared a few moments later.

Margaret said, 'Richard, I'd like to introduce you to your new colleague. His name is Raymond, but since he is French the final letter is silent.' Addressing Raymond, Margaret directed him to take charge of Richard's clothes, both those in the bag and the ones he was wearing, and to treat them 'in the customary manner'. To Richard she said simply, 'Strip and give your clothes to him.'

Richard looked at his colleague, and all at once he understood why the maid's waist and legs, indeed 'her' whole figure and way of moving, seemed so strange. It was hard to believe that the person wearing the maid's costume was male, but he didn't doubt it now. He would have to learn to move and act as Raymond did. As he rose to take off his clothes, Richard remembered Margaret's half-promise to answer his questions after she had finished explaining his new regime. There were a hundred questions he could have asked: everything was new about the fantasy he had fallen into. But he could think of only one clearly just then.

'When will I see Helena?' he asked.

'When you have got through some training I may bring her to visit you. She will be due for more training herself, and I think she might enjoy seeing you in your new costume. You could show her how well you can walk in high-heeled shoes,' Margaret replied.

Richard felt a flush of embarrassment at the idea of appearing before Helena in women's clothing, but he never thought of backing out. In for a penny, he told himself. As he took off his clothes, he caught sight of a black cloth bag lying on the mantelpiece. That must be The Discipline which had been used on Helena. Once again there flashed into his mind the image of himself wielding the whip while she writhed and screamed under the lash. So vivid was the mental picture that his cock grew stiff, so that when he came to take his pants off he had to manoeuvre them around a full erection. The chain dangled down between his legs, and he was suddenly aware again of the nylon band around his scrotum. He had almost forgotten its presence during the ride from Hamburg and the conversation with his new mistress.

'Look, Raymond,' she said to the maid. 'I think he likes us!'

Raymond said nothing as he took Richard's clothing and folded it into the bag containing his possessions. Silently, obeying some rule of which Richard wasn't aware, he extracted the small bag containing Richard's toilet articles and laid it on the coffee table. From this Richard gathered that at least something would be left him.

Margaret looked on approvingly. 'You will need your razor to shave your legs in a few days,' she informed Richard. She gestured at the maid's legs, and Richard noticed that they were as bare as a woman's under the sheer black tights. Or were they stockings? What was the protocol about that here? He shrugged mentally. He would know soon enough.

At Margaret's gesture of dismissal the maid withdrew, taking Richard's clothes with him. She rang the bell once more and another maid came in. There was little doubt that this one was female. It would have been impossible to give a man that hourglass figure. Her movements were subtly different from Raymond's: more natural, not so studied. And she smelt like a woman, with just a hint of perfume. Her voice was a pleasant contralto. He found it hard to place her accent. Dutch, maybe?

Trying, and failing, not to look at his erection, she asked what it was that 'madame' wished her to do.

Instead of replying, Margaret strode across the room to a low cabinet along the far wall. Bending down, and allowing Richard to see her legs all the way up to her bottom, she rummaged among the contents and selected a pair of handcuffs from the collection inside. Straightening up, she moved behind him. Richard didn't need to be told what she intended. Wordlessly he brought his hands behind his back, and stood still as she locked the cuffs around his wrists. This tacit acceptance of whatever Margaret wished to do to him was yet more proof, if more were needed, of his complicity in his own transformation.

'Take him to his room, and leave him chained in the usual way,' she ordered the maid.

The girl picked up his shaving kit and took the chain attached to his scrotum like a lead. She tugged gently on it, and Richard followed her out of the room and down the hall towards the rear of the house. On the way they passed the maid who had come to the car. She was carrying two medium-sized suitcases into what appeared to be a dining room. At any rate there was a long table inside, and on the table were four more of the same kind of suitcase. The maid – Marie, Richard recalled – moved carefully lest she trip over her leg-irons, but she took time to smile briefly at Richard and his escort. Richard smiled tentatively back. His escort stopped before a set of lift doors. She pushed the button and waited until they opened. She led Richard inside by the chain. She pushed a button, and the lift went slowly downward. Apparently the house had a cellar, not visible from the outside.

When the doors opened, his escort tugged again on the chain, and once more Richard followed her down another hallway, this one lined with doors that gave it the appearance of a hotel corridor. The girl led him about halfway down the corridor before stopping in front of a door that stood open.

'This is your room,' she told him. Once inside she dropped the chain, and Richard felt it, cool against his leg. The girl faced him with her finger on her lips. She signalled for him to stand still while she made a circuit of the room. Richard followed her with his eyes as she checked the ensuite bath, the wardrobe (empty, of course), the bed, the television set and the stock of videos and paperback books with which the room was supplied. There were rugs on the floor, colourful islands in the stone sea. Reading lamps were arranged near the armchairs and over the bed. The room looked comfortable enough, even though it was windowless.

She came back to where he stood with a faint look of relief on her face. 'I don't think they're listening to us now,' she said, speaking softly nevertheless.

Apparently trainees were not supposed to speak to one another, although Richard couldn't see why not. As with most places with strict regimes, there was an obsession with keeping the inmates from forming relationships with one another.

'I'm Heidi,' the girl told him.

'Richard,' he replied. 'How long are you in for?' he asked, thinking this was just the sort of conversation they would be having if they were in jail.

'I've been here four months, with two more to go,' she told him. 'I'm supposed to be getting trained as a governess and housekeeper. Why are you here?'

'I'm not sure,' Richard said. 'Call it curiosity.'

'You came here of your own free will?' Heidi asked.

'Practically,' Richard replied. Seeing the look of

bewilderment on Heidi's face, he added, 'There was some coercion, but I suppose I could leave if I insisted.'

'I don't think so. None of us can leave without permission from the Mistress, or unless we are taken away by our employer. Even you would find it hard to get out, I think.'

'Well, yes, I suppose that's why they took away my clothes. But I think they would give them back and let me go if I made a fuss.'

Heidi looked dubious. 'Then why have you been handcuffed?'

'As you saw, I allowed Margaret to handcuff me. I could have refused.'

She still looked doubtful, but said only, 'When I go, I am expected to leave you chained by your . . .' She hesitated, as if groping for the polite word, before continuing, 'your chain. To the ring there by the bed.'

She pointed to a heap of chain attached to a ring set into the stone floor near the foot of the bed. Richard also noticed other rings set into the walls and the ceiling. The room suddenly looked less comfortable and more penal. He walked over to the bed to look more closely at the ring to which he was to be fastened.

There was a heavy padlock, open, waiting to be used. There was no key in evidence. 'And what will happen if you don't leave me chained as you were ordered?' Richard asked the girl.

She looked startled, as if the thought of disobeying had just occurred to her. 'I would be beaten, of course. They would be very angry with me.'

'Have you been beaten before, then?'

'Oh, often.' Heidi shuddered as if the memory was painful.

'Why?' Richard wanted to know.

'Once I dropped a stack of dishes and broke them. That was not very serious, and I only had twenty-five lashes. But when I spoke without permission, Madame was very angry. I cannot remember how many lashes I had that time, I lost count, but I hurt for days after. And several times just because I had not been beaten recently: to keep me in line, Madame said when I cried.'

'So why don't you run away?' Richard asked. 'You should be able to get outside and then just make for the woods.'

'You don't understand. You have just arrived, so you don't know about the wall. It goes around the whole estate. We call it the Berlin Wall, and it is impossible to get over. It is electrified. And there are alarms, just like the ones they had in Berlin.'

'Are there minefields and armed guards who shoot on sight?' Richard asked half-jokingly.

'Oh, no. No mines. Guards, yes, but they do not shoot. They just bring you back, and then you get a beating, and they make you wear leg-irons, like Marie. She tried to run away and they caught her. They made us all watch as she was whipped. And then they locked those chains on to her ankles. They are only removed when she has to dress and undress, and then only with one of the trainers in attendance. She has to sleep in her chains. I would not like that.'

Richard had a sudden thought. 'Heidi, do you know Helena? Short, pretty face, dark hair, about twenty-four or twenty-five?'

Heidi nodded. 'I have seen her come for visits to Madame. And once I watched as she was stripped and beaten. She seemed to like the beating.' Heidi sounded puzzled at the idea.

'Do you wear a chastity belt like hers?'

'Oh, yes. All of the women do. I have got used to it. Now I hardly know it's there.'

Heidi lifted her short skirt and Richard saw her belt resembled Helena's. She wore stockings. Her legs were rather fuller, but very nicely shaped. Richard felt his erection growing as he looked at her.

Heidi let her skirt fall and looked at him shyly. Then she caught sight of his cock standing at attention, and she blushed down to the tops of her breasts. 'Oh, I wish I were not wearing it now,' she said. Nevertheless she came closer to him, her eyes fixed on his erect cock. She stroked it, shyly at first, and then, as if coming to a sudden decision, she knelt before him and took his cock into her mouth.

'Heidi, you don't have to . . .' he began.

'Shhhh. I want to. Please let me.'

As before, in Helena's apartment, he could do nothing to stop her. And as before, he had no wish to do so. Her lips and tongue sliding along his cock, and the teeth that nipped him gently, made his blood pound in his ears. He felt himself sway on his feet, and Heidi steadied him while she continued to work on his cock. When he looked down he could see the top of her head, her long hair falling about her face and over his thighs in a heavy curtain. Once she moved back to reposition herself, and he could see her erect nipples through the satin bodice of her dress.

He wished that his hands were free, and that she were not locked into the chastity belt. He wished . . . Then what he wished ceased to matter as he came. Heidi swallowed and kept working her head back and forth until the spasms ended and he felt shaky on his feet.

She looked up at him with a smile. There wasn't anything either of them could say. Heidi stood up slowly and faced Richard. Abruptly she put her arms around him and kissed him on the mouth. He could smell his own musk on her breath as she embraced him. It was a new experience to him. None of the girls he had known in England would have done what this stranger had done to him.

His thoughts were interrupted by the sound of a door opening in the corridor. Heidi jumped away as if stung. Hurriedly she picked up the chain with its padlock. Richard stood still as she approached him.

'Please understand,' Heidi said softly. 'I have to do this or –'

'You'll be beaten,' Richard finished for her. He looked at her for a moment and then nodded. Heidi looked immensely relieved. She looked at him for a moment longer and then looked down to fit the padlock through the ring on the chain that dangled from his balls. The lock closed with a heavy snap, and she let it fall between his legs. He felt the weight of the lock and the longer chain dragging at him. Not painfully, but definitely there.

'I'll just put your case in the bathroom,' Heidi called a little too loudly as she moved away from him. She dropped the case in her haste and alarm. When she came back into the main room, she had herself just barely in control. She was frightened and trying to look normal.

'Heidi,' Richard said softly, 'wipe your mouth and take a deep breath.'

She did as he directed, and looked at him once again with more composure. She even managed a shaky smile.

'Who keeps the keys to my handcuffs, and to the lock and your own belt?'

'I don't know,' she replied. 'I have to go now.'

'Try to find out,' he told her as she disappeared. The door closed behind her with a heavy thump, and Richard saw that there was neither handle nor keyhole on the inside. He knew without further exploration that he was locked in. Since there was no immediate escape, he decided to make the best of things. The bed looked comfortable enough.

He woke from his doze at the sound of the door opening. This time it was an older woman, perhaps forty or forty-five years old, Richard estimated. She was still an attractive woman, one who had obviously taken pains to combat the signs of ageing. Her body was still firm, and she carried herself well. She was stylishly dressed, not in the ubiquitous maid's uniform. He concluded that she was somewhat higher up the pecking order here than Heidi. As she came closer, he thought he detected the signs of cosmetic surgery in the firmness of her chin and the lack of wrinkles around the eyes and mouth.

'You are Richard,' she announced. She looked at him for a long moment before nodding her approval. 'Margaret has asked me to take your measurements. Will you please stand?'

Richard got awkwardly to his feet. 'Since you know who I am, might I not know who you are?' he asked.

'My name is not important,' the woman replied.

'It is to me,' Richard retorted.

The woman shrugged and said, 'Very well. I am Ingrid.'

'And are you one of the trainers here?' Richard asked her.

'No. I own a small dressmaking and tailoring shop in the village. But I am often asked to make things for those here, at what we in the village call *Schloss Margaret*.' Smiling at what she thought of as a small joke, Ingrid produced a tape measure, a small leather-bound notebook and a pencil from her handbag, which she laid on the bed. She looked once more at Richard, then said, 'May I use your bathroom before we begin?'

She was already turning towards it as Richard said, 'Of course.' He continued to stand beside the bed as she left the room. When she returned, Ingrid smiled her thanks. Richard liked her. She was an outsider in what was, to him at least, a bizarre setting, and she was treating both it and him naturally, without embarrassment or awkwardness. He felt more at ease with her.

Ingrid held a key in her hand. 'I am allowed to remove your handcuffs, Richard. Indeed, I must do so in order to measure you. I hope you will conduct yourself correctly.' She unlocked the handcuffs and laid them on the bed beside her handbag.

'And the other lock?' Richard asked, indicating the one dangling between his legs. 'Are you allowed to remove that as well?'

'No. I am sorry. I was not given the key.' And she did sound regretful. 'Now, if you will just stand naturally, we will begin.' Ingrid unrolled her tape and began to measure Richard: around the waist, around the chest, across the shoulders, sleeve length, height, everything in fact but his inside leg.

But her next measurement surprised him. Ingrid asked him to hold one end of the tape at his waist in front, while she stooped down and took the other end through between his legs. With her free hand she grasped his cock and held it upright against his belly while she took his measurement through the crotch and up to his waistline at the back. He felt himself growing stiff in her hand.

So did Ingrid. With a chuckle, she said, 'Richard, you promised to behave correctly.'

'And it's incorrect to get an erection when an attractive woman is holding your cock?' he retorted.

'So you think I am attractive?' Ingrid asked. 'I am almost old enough to be your mother.'

'And aren't all healthy boys supposed to have a crush on their mothers? Freud said so.'

'Do I remind you of your mother, then?' Ingrid asked him.

Richard, who remembered his mother as a rather plain and very ordinary middle-aged woman, said, 'No. She didn't look anywhere near as good as you do. Nor have I ever wanted her as much as I do you.'

'So. Gallantry too,' Ingrid said, sounding pleased nevertheless. She stood up with a grunt and put away her tape. When she removed her hand, Richard's cock returned to its normal position, and his erection was much more obvious. She looked at it for a long moment before saying, 'Now he tries flattery. Enough already.' But she was smiling. 'Thank you for the compliment, for so I shall take it. But it will have to wait for another time. I have much to do today.'

'So there will be another time?' Richard asked quickly.

'Perhaps. We shall have to wait and see.' Ingrid gathered her things together and picked up the handcuffs from the bed.

Richard wondered if she had been instructed to re-apply them, but she was moving towards the door. There she paused to smile broadly back at him.

'*Auf Wiedersehen*, Richard.' She opened the door and stepped into the hallway.

Before she closed it again, he caught a glimpse of a strange man passing with a suitcase in his hand. It was the same type of case he had seen earlier in the hall upstairs. Was it part of the same delivery? He wondered what it might contain. But the door closed and locked behind Ingrid, and he was alone again.

Although his hands were now free, he was still chained to the ring in the floor. He took the chain in his hand and walked towards the bathroom. There was enough slack to allow him to get inside. There was a toilet, hand basin and shower stall, all within reach. There was also a bidet. For female trainees, he assumed. He caught sight of a white card on the side of the basin. When he picked it up, he saw that it was Ingrid's business card. He learnt that she was also a Wagner. Was she related to Margaret? Possibly, but Wagner was a common name in Germany. He saw that her dress shop was in the village. There was a telephone number too. But on the back there was another, written by hand. Her personal number? Why had she left the card for him?

There was no way to find out. He would have to wait

and see, as Ingrid had suggested. He put the card away into the side pocket of his case and returned to the main room.

There was no clock in the room, so Richard had no way to measure how long he had been there. He thought of turning on the TV to get the time, but when he did so, he found it only worked for viewing videos. So he looked through the video collection for something to pass the time while he wondered how Helena was doing.

Richard woke again when the door opened. He still sat in the armchair in front of the TV, which displayed only a grey and white pattern. The video had ended and the machine had shut itself off automatically. He didn't realise how hungry he was until he smelt food. Heidi entered the room with a trolley from which the tantalising smells were coming.

'Good morning. I hope you slept well. I have brought some breakfast, and when you have finished I will take you up to see our Mistress. She has told me that your training must begin immediately, so hurry up. She does not like to be kept waiting.'

'Then she should send breakfast along sooner,' Richard retorted, even as he felt a knot of excitement tighten in his stomach. He ate breakfast, while Heidi sat on the bed watching. When he had finished, she produced a key hanging on a thong around her neck and unlocked the padlock. The short chain once more dangled freely between his legs.

'Please take a shower and get ready to go upstairs now,' Heidi told him. She cleared away the breakfast things while Richard went into the bathroom. When he came out, he saw that she had left his clothes on the bed and had withdrawn, locking the door behind her. Richard shrugged and got dressed. Then he sat waiting for Heidi, or someone, to come let him out.

Presently she came back, beckoning him to follow

her. She conducted him back along the hallway and to the lift. They travelled up to the main floor with only smiles between them, hers shy and his enquiring. Margaret was waiting for him in the drawing room, pacing impatiently backward and forward over the thick carpet. There was no one else in sight.

'We are going for a short drive. I have many things to do today so I will leave you at Ingrid Wagner's shop while I attend to them. She will outfit you and I will collect you this evening. Raymond or Heidi will tell you what to do next. Come along now,' she said, as she gathered her coat and handbag and headed towards the door.

The BMW was waiting at the front door. Margaret drove back down the long driveway to the gates, where she again operated the electronic control to let them out of the grounds. This time she drove more slowly towards the village. Richard saw that it was a fairly large one, with a new shopping centre on the outskirts. The centre of the town was older, the streets narrow and cobbled and the buildings crowded together, a typical European town of the sixteenth or seventeenth century.

Margaret drove into a covered alleyway and turned into a minute car-parking space behind Ingrid's shop. It was walled, and had gates. Richard noticed that there were no windows overlooking the small courtyard. Nor were there any streetlights that he could see. This would be a dark and private place at night.

Margaret led the way through the rear door and into the shop. The storeroom they entered was empty, but voices were audible in the shop itself. Richard recognised Ingrid's voice, and at least two others – customers, presumably. Margaret glanced impatiently at her watch. She looked annoyed. Eventually the front door opened and closed as the customers left the shop, and Margaret led the way through the doorway. They met Ingrid coming back towards them. She smiled briefly at Margaret and Richard.

Margaret began speaking at once. 'Ingrid, I am running late. I need to leave Richard here so you can start on him. I will be back around five in the evening to collect him.'

'Margaret, you know I need more time with him. He is just getting started and will need a lot of work. You should plan on collecting him sometime tomorrow evening if you expect a good job of preparation,' Ingrid said.

Margaret looked even more annoyed. Apparently she hated having her plans altered. But she said crossly, 'Oh, very well. Keep him here until tomorrow. Just be sure to take the customary precautions.' She produced a pair of handcuffs from her handbag and handed them to Ingrid. Then she ordered Richard to strip. She stood impatiently while he took off his clothes and Ingrid folded them into a plastic bag with her shop's logo on it. This she handed to Margaret, who left immediately.

'Is she always this cross and abrupt?' Richard asked when she was gone.

'Not always, but often enough. She is difficult to please. Always has been. But you will find that out for yourself soon enough,' Ingrid replied. 'But I'm glad she didn't insist on a hurried job. I do need some time with you.'

'What are you going to do with me?'

'Transform you into a woman, at least outwardly. That is what Margaret wants, for reasons she will tell you when she's ready. But we can talk as I work. The more I know about you the better job I can make.'

'And will I also learn about you as we work?' Richard wanted to know.

'We'll see,' Ingrid replied with another smile. 'But now, will you promise not to run away if I leave you for a moment?'

'Like this?' Richard asked, gesturing at himself. 'What would the good burghers of Soltau think of a naked man running out of your shop and down the street?'

Ingrid smiled at the idea. 'I only meant that I have to go through into the shop and fetch some things for you. Will you be good?'

Richard nodded, and Ingrid disappeared into the front of the shop. She came back after a few moments holding a plastic bag with the legend *Bergers Herrenmode* on it. She handed it to Richard without comment. He reached into the bag and came out with a pair of trousers, a shirt, underwear and socks. There were shoes in a separate box.

He looked questioningly at Ingrid. 'Won't Margaret be displeased?'

'She would if she knew, but we are not going to tell her, are we?' Ingrid replied with a conspiratorial wink. 'Go on, get dressed. We have several things to do before closing time. If anyone comes into the shop you will be my nephew, visiting me from Berlin. You *do* speak German, do you not?'

'*Ich habe meine Deutsch auf der Universität gut gelernt*,' Richard replied.

'Your accent is awful,' Ingrid said, laughing. 'Try not to talk if you can avoid it.' She motioned for him to precede her into the shop. 'Margaret wants me to dress you as a woman, so we need to spend some time picking a wardrobe for you. I think you would be about a size sixteen,' she said, as she showed him a rack of dresses in that size. 'You need to pick out at least three dresses, plus the same number of skirts and blouses. I will help you with the lingerie and accessories afterwards.' She pushed Richard towards the dresses.

Now that the moment had come he felt both excited and embarrassed. He remembered one or two occasions when, as a boy, he had dressed in his mother's clothes. Even then he had known instinctively to keep it secret. Now he was being made to do the same thing in public. He felt himself flush hotly.

Ingrid noticed. 'Do not feel embarrassed. I have done the same thing many times for the men who pass through Margaret's establishment. I am here to help you follow her wishes, not to laugh at you, or to judge you. Margaret is a forceful woman. She is accustomed to getting whatever she wants. And just now she wants you.'

Richard began diffidently to sort through the clothing. Ingrid moved away to allow him to make his choices in private. He chose three dresses he imagined would look good on Helena, and then turned his attention to the skirts and blouses, using the same principle of selection. When he was done he started to call Ingrid. But at that moment the shop door opened to admit two ladies of about Ingrid's own age. She turned to serve them, while Richard tried to appear inconspicuous. The two women seemed to take for ever to make their selections, and Richard wondered why he had been able to choose in such a short time. Perhaps there was some fundamental and unfathomable difference between the shopping habits of men and women.

When the two women left, Ingrid came back to inspect Richard's choices. 'I see you have chosen the modern equivalent of Dior's "little black dress". That was wise. The other two, not so wise.'

'What's wrong with red and green?' Richard wanted to know.

'As colours, nothing,' Ingrid replied, 'but for someone who is trying to masquerade as a woman they shout for attention – attention which you should avoid until you have had more practice in acting the part. You would stand out like a peacock on a lawn.' She put back the two bright dresses and chose a pale beige and a pale blue one in their place. 'Protective coloration,' she told him. 'Now try to make similar selections from among the separates. And look for long sleeves and high necklines, unless you want to shave your chest and arms.' Ingrid left him alone again, moving about the shop and hanging up again the things her customers had tried and rejected.

Eventually the selections were made and approved. They moved on to the underwear section. Here Richard had to confess he was at a complete loss. 'You choose,' he asked Ingrid, and watched with a growing sense of excitement as she chose three panty corselets, three slips and several pairs of dark tights for him.

'Why these?' he asked, pointing at the corselets.

'Because you need something firm underneath to prevent your pretty cock from bulging too conspicuously and giving the game away. Not many women can manage an erection. Now, take all this through into the back and go upstairs. I'll come as soon as I close the shop for the evening. And if you really want to make me happy, make some coffee and something to eat for us both.' Obediently Richard went up into Ingrid's living quarters with the clothing. He set it all down on the sofa in her front room, which looked out over the street. For a while he watched the people coming and going about their business. He heard the shop door open once or twice more, and the muffled sound of voices from the ground floor. But eventually he became bored and began to explore the apartment. He found where Ingrid kept the broom and the vacuum cleaner, and, just as he had done in Helena's apartment, he set about tidying up.

He decided to leave the kitchen for last, and turned into her bedroom. There he saw her 'facilities', as Margaret called them. There was a ring set into the floor with a chain and padlock, just as there was in his room back at the country house. But the chain was considerably shorter. He saw that anyone fastened there would be unable to reach the bed, and he wondered if he was going to spend the night on the floor.

There were only a few of Ingrid's things lying about. She was apparently a much neater housekeeper than Helena. As he began to put the underwear into the proper drawers on the bureau, he noticed a framed photograph of Ingrid and Helena. It looked recent, and he picked it up to examine it more closely. On the back was written, 'Kiel. Summer holidays.' The date was two years ago. He set the photograph down thoughtfully and continued clearing up. How did Helena and Ingrid come to know one another?

Back in the front room, he listened to the voices from downstairs, and decided he could take the risk he knew he was going to take anyway. He opened Ingrid's writing desk and began to search for more photos. In the middle drawer, placed casually, not hidden, he came across a thick and well-thumbed photo album. He opened it and found more photos of Helena. They ranged in age from toddler stage through to the present. In some of them she was alone. In others Ingrid and a strange man smiled out of the picture with her. In still others Helena and Ingrid were together.

The obvious conclusion was that the two women were mother and daughter, or at least aunt and niece. Richard thought he heard a step on the stairs, and he hurriedly put the album back in the desk and closed the drawer. But no one came, and with a huge sense of relief he stood up and went into the kitchen to prepare something for the two of them. While the coffee percolated, he tidied away the few dishes and cups on the draining board. He had made a platter of sandwiches by the time Ingrid finally did come up the stairs. She found him sitting in an armchair in the front room with the food ready on the coffee table.

Ingrid looked with surprised pleasure at the room and the food. 'I think I will have to keep you permanently. Thank you for tidying up.'

Richard motioned for her to sit down and eat. She

kicked her shoes off and curled her legs – quite nice legs, he saw again – under herself on the sofa. Women seemed to feel comfortable in that position. He knew of no men who could even get their legs into it.

They ate in companionable silence. Richard judged the time was not right to ask Ingrid about Helena – not least because it would reveal he had been snooping.

At last Ingrid set down her cup and said, 'Another sandwich and I'll begin to get middle-aged spread. They were very good. But now, if you are finished, it's time to begin on you.' She stood and led the way into the bathroom. There she ran water into the tub, added bubble-bath salts and filled it about halfway. 'Take your clothes off and see if the water temperature is comfortable,' she directed.

Richard got undressed and stepped into the tub. The water came up over his ankles and was pleasantly warm. He smelt the faint perfume from the bubble bath.

Ingrid motioned for him to sit down, and he did so. His legs were just that little bit too long to allow him to lie down fully with the water up to his neck. Ingrid began to wash him. He had never been washed by a woman since he was a little boy. It was soothing, and brought back pleasant memories of Saturday-evening baths in his parents' home.

All that changed abruptly when Ingrid said, 'Now let me soap your legs well so I can shave them. Watch closely so you will be able to do it next time without cutting yourself. Razor cuts on a woman's legs look so unsightly.' Expertly, she soaped first one leg and then the other. She used a disposable plastic razor and gently shaved the hair from his legs, moving from bottom to top. 'Go against the grain,' she advised Richard. When his legs were bare, she pulled the plug and let the water drain away. There was a tidemark around the tub, and a clump of hair in the drain hole.

'Always clean the hair away,' Ingrid said. 'Next time

there will not be nearly so much, but it builds up. Try to be neat.'

The air was cold on his newly bared legs as he stood in the empty tub. 'I thought for a minute you were going to shave my pubic hair too,' Richard said.

'No need for that,' Ingrid replied. 'If anyone gets that far up your skirt, it will not be the hair that gives the game away. Besides, it itches terribly when it starts to grow back. Once I shaved mine for a date with the boy of my dreams. He was surprised to feel me bare down there when he got his hand in my pants. And it was a wonderful weekend we had in an Alpine chalet. But by the next Wednesday I could not bear to wear pants. I was prickly and sore all over. After it grew back, I vowed never again. But now stand still while I shampoo your hair.'

Ingrid turned on the shower and washed Richard's hair thoroughly. 'You will need to shampoo regularly. Hair gets awfully dirty under a wig, especially when it is worn for long periods, as you will be doing.'

'Anything else, Mother?' Richard joked.

'Yes. A thousand things you will have to learn – and unlearn. This is not something you can run through just once. Pay attention to everything I do. Now shave your face very closely, and be careful not to cut that either.' She handed him the razor and watched while he shaved. 'Do all men pull such faces in the mirror?' she asked.

Ingrid led Richard into the front room again. Outside in the streets, evening was falling. The first streetlights were appearing, with that garish yellow sodium glow characteristic of European cities. She drew the curtains. 'It would not do to have the world and his brother peering in at us,' she observed. 'Now pick up all those things –' indicating the dresses and other clothing they had chosen for him '– and bring it all through into the bedroom. I want to use my make-up mirror for the next stage.'

In the bedroom, Ingrid placed a chair before her bureau. Arranged on the top were her cosmetics: everything from lipstick through eye shadow and on to foundation and cleansing creams. 'I know you must have watched a woman put on her war paint,' she said, 'and I guess you were asking yourself why it took so long. Well, the answer is just that it does take time. You will see just how much time in the next few days. I will do it the first time to show you how. Then we will wash it off again before bedtime, and you can do it yourself in the morning. Now sit there and be still,' she directed, indicating the chair in front of the mirror.

Richard sat quietly as Ingrid began opening various jars and tubes. The draft under the door felt cool against the bare skin of his legs.

Richard, on the verge of this transformation which he both welcomed and wanted to avoid, felt the need to prove something to himself: perhaps that under it all he was unchanged, that all this was happening on the outside. When Ingrid turned back to him with a tube of foundation cream, he stood and put his arms around her waist. She didn't resist when he pulled her to him and kissed her on the lips. Her mouth was soft and fragrant, slightly open. She was waiting for him to decide what to do next.

What he did next was to put one hand on the back of her head, twining his fingers in her thick brown hair and gently rubbing her scalp as he held her face still for the kiss. It lengthened, until he could feel himself stirring against her belly, and Ingrid's breath grew harsh and short in her throat. Then he pulled back and looked into her face.

Her eyes were closed and a faint flush reddened her throat, where he could see a tiny pulse just below the fine texture of her skin. Ingrid still held the tube in one hand, but she put her free arm around Richard's waist. When he bent to kiss her again, she sighed and opened her mouth to him. Finding herself unable to hold him tightly enough with her one arm, Ingrid groped behind her and dropped the tube of make-up on to the dresser. Then she could hold him as she wished. They stood locked together for an endless time, while each explored the other's face, mouth and throat.

Richard felt he could have stood there for ever, but not Ingrid. She appeared to reach a decision. She pulled slightly away so that she could look up into his face. 'It truly does not bother you that I am so much older than you?' She searched his face for a sign.

'Don't you remember what I told you the last time you brought up the matter of age?'

'Yes, but I still wonder if that was not just something you were saying – a compliment you did not mean. You see, when a woman gets older, she must always ask herself these questions. Women age so much more quickly than men. And we are judged much more harshly. Youth is the same thing as beauty to us, you know.'

Words would not answer her, so instead he brushed her hair aside gently and caressed her face before kissing her again. This time he was slow and thorough: his mouth explored her eyes, her nose and forehead, her cheeks, her ears, her throat where the tiny pulse beat, until her eyes closed and he felt her sag against him.

'Unzip me, please.' Ingrid's voice was low and tense. He turned her away so he could pull the zipper down the back of her dress. As the material parted, he kissed the nape of her neck, then the tops of her shoulders, the hollow of her spine. Finally the dress lay in a pile around her feet. She stepped out of it and turned to face him. In a voice that shook slightly, she said, 'Would you like to undress me completely now?'

Richard nodded wordlessly, but before beginning he put his arms around Ingrid and drew her to him once again, holding her tightly.

With a low moan, Ingrid embraced him, pulling him fiercely against her as she turned up her face to be kissed again. She darted her tongue into his mouth, and her breath mingled with his as they clung to one another. It seemed as if her doubts were gone.

Finally she pulled away and gasped, 'Take my clothes off, quickly.' She took hold of Richard's cock as he lifted the slip over her head and unsnapped her bra. Her full breasts sprang free, the nipples erect. Richard paused to touch them, then bent to kiss her breasts. Ingrid drew in a tremulous breath as his lips touched her. He worked her pants off while the kiss went on, his tongue circling her swollen nipples and his teeth nipping gently at her.

Ingrid pulled away with an effort and sat on the side of the bed wearing nothing but her stockings and suspenders. Reaching for the chain that dangled from his scrotum, she pulled him closer. She took his cock in her hand once more, stroking it and cupping his balls in her other hand. She seemed fascinated by it, teasing and tugging at it. Richard stood still for a long moment, allowing her to do as she wished with him. Then he pushed Ingrid gently back on to the bed. She lay looking up at him for a moment, and then stretched her arms up to him.

He lay down beside her and they embraced, their bodies fitting against one another effortlessly, oblivious of all else. Richard stroked Ingrid's legs, relishing the electric feel of her sheer stockings under his hand, and enjoying the change in sensation as he reached her bare skin. She held him tightly as he caressed every part of her he could reach, breasts, thighs, bottom, crotch. Her breath was loud in his ears, and she moaned softly as his hands roamed over her body, touching, moving on, touching her again, until she was wild with desire. Then he moved over her.

Ingrid spread her legs and guided him inside. She was

wet and parted, ready for him, and she gasped with pleasure as he slid home. Richard felt her vaginal muscles close around his cock, enveloping him in warmth and softness. When he began to thrust, Ingrid matched his rhythm, her hips rising and falling to receive him, and then almost to lose him, before he plunged into her again and again.

Ingrid's mouth was close beside his ear, and Richard could hear her little gasps as she became more excited. Then she was making small, incoherent sounds of pleasure as she began to climax in short, sharp spasms that rippled through her and that he could feel in his cock as her vaginal muscles gripped and loosened, gripped and loosened. She held him fiercely against her as she was swept by her ecstasy.

Ingrid abruptly relaxed, her breath sawing in her throat as she lay beneath him. Richard looked questioningly at her and made a move to withdraw. She caught him again.

'Stay inside me,' she gasped.

Richard lay atop her as her breathing slowed. Finally Ingrid spoke. 'Please raise yourself for a moment and let me look at you. This feels so good I am beginning to think I have died of pleasure.' She pushed gently against Richard's chest.

He lifted himself and looked down into her flushed, happy face.

'You are real enough,' she said softly. 'I wonder why I was so worried about making love with such a young man.'

Richard covered her mouth with his own. 'Don't talk about it,' he breathed into her. Then he kissed her lips, feeling them open to him. With one of his hands he stroked the back of her neck, while the other twined in her long hair, holding her mouth against his own. Then he began once more to move inside her, and felt her muscles clamp down on him again. As he moved in and out, in and out, he could hear her breath quickening in little, sharp moans.

Her hands were holding his bottom, keeping him inside her as if afraid of losing that delicious penetration. He felt her begin to climax, and then she was bucking and writhing beneath him. Muffled sounds of pleasure escaped her again, and Richard felt himself go over the edge. He held tightly to her as he emptied himself into her body, and Ingrid's cries were loud in the room.

Afterwards they lay side by side. It was dark in the room. He felt drained but glad that they had been able to share such pleasure. Ingrid's hand lay on his thigh, as if she were still afraid to lose contact with him. At length she sat up and turned on the bedside lamp.

'I want to look at you,' she said in explanation.

'And I will look at you,' Richard replied.

'No. Please. Now that it is over I am afraid you will see an old woman again.' Her face was sad.

But he stared into her face, refusing to look away, until she smiled again.

'You told the truth,' she finally said. 'It doesn't matter.'

Richard pulled her down on top of him, liking the feel of her breasts firm against his chest and the feel of her warmth along his body. He wrapped his legs around hers and pulled the quilt over them both. Ingrid sighed gently and relaxed in his arms.

When he awoke, he was alone in the bed. Richard turned his head and saw Ingrid sitting at the dressing table looking at him. 'How long have you been awake?' he asked her.

'Not long. I was going to wake you, but you seemed to need the sleep.' She continued with a smile, 'After that, I can see why.' Ingrid rose and wrapped herself in a dressing gown. Then she said, 'Come on, get up,

Richard. We have much work to do on you. I shouldn't have let you seduce me into bed with you.' But her smile at once gave the lie to her words.

Richard rose too, kissed her on the corner of the mouth and went in search of the bathroom. The cool air on his bare legs reminded him once again why he was there.

Back in the bedroom, Ingrid was waiting for him. The dressing gown was belted about her waist now: back to business.

'Are you naked under your gown?' Richard asked her, with a smile of his own.

'Don't start again, please. I don't think I can take much more of that,' she said with a smile. Ingrid retrieved the tube of make-up from the dresser and motioned for him to sit in the chair again. 'Look in the mirror and watch carefully what I do,' she commanded, as she began to spread the make-up gently over his forehead.

Richard watched as Ingrid gradually covered his entire face and neck with the foundation. Then she dusted a lightly scented and tinted powder over the cream.

'To take away the shine and feel of the cream,' she explained. 'I won't do anything elaborate. You will not have the time to learn how to use eye shadow and eyeliner and all the other things women use. You will have to be content with just the basics.'

'The basics' still seemed to require a lot of skill, Richard concluded as he watched her work. Slowly his face began to take on a feminine appearance. It was still his face, but now it was softer, with highlights and emphasis where before there had been none. Ingrid used mascara to darken and lengthen his eyelashes. Next his eyebrows received the same treatment. Subtle touches around the eyes, a light shading. Then lipstick, a pale rose shade.

'Use neutral colours,' Ingrid advised. 'Just as I told you in choosing dresses, you do not want to call attention to yourself with a too-bright make-up.'

Richard nodded.

Ingrid stepped back to examine her handiwork.

'Not too bad,' was her verdict, 'but your eyebrows are too thick. Tomorrow I will thin them slightly, and give them a more definite arch.'

From the mirror a different person stared back at Richard. He stared at the transformed face in fascination. Ingrid stood beside him, a hand on his shoulder, gauging his reaction.

But even she was surprised by it. Richard took her wrist and pulled her down on to his lap. Ingrid settled herself and put her arms around him. Her dressing gown parted to reveal her long, full legs, but she made no move to cover herself. Richard felt himself stir and grow stiff as she lay against him.

Wordlessly, Ingrid shifted until she was straddling him. She opened her gown and let it drop to the floor. Then she guided him inside her quickly. Richard began to thrust at once, and she cried out as his hands cupped her breasts. When his fingers touched her taut nipples, she moaned and pressed herself down on his cock. Ingrid seemed to be affected by the same feverish haste, for she came at once, a shudder passing through her. She matched his rhythm, and came again, his cock sliding quickly in and out as they set one another afire. It was over almost before it had begun. Ingrid let out a low scream as she felt him stiffen and then spurt inside her. She ground her hips against his pelvis and shuddered again as her climax took her.

They sat for long minutes, locked together, tense, before he felt her relax her hold on him. She lay against his chest as their breathing slowed to normal and their heartbeats ceased to shake their bodies.

Ingrid was the first to move. She sat up and looked

at Richard's face under its layer of make-up. Then she brushed her hand lightly over his face and hair, a feather touch. 'Don't speak,' she said, when she saw he was about to. 'I understand. You had to prove that the change you see is only outward – that you are still the same man you always were: not lost, not changed.'

Richard nodded silently. 'So you do understand. I'm sorry I took it out on you.'

'Don't be. I know you were quick, but it was wonderful for me too.' And this time she kissed him. 'I know you are still the same, so you shouldn't worry about that,' she said, standing up. 'Now, come to bed with me.'

And they lay under the quilt holding one another tightly through the dark, quiet hours.

Three

Richard woke first in the morning. He looked at Ingrid for a long time as she lay beside him, her face softened in sleep. Then he bent and kissed her eyelids softly.

'That is the best way to wake someone,' she said.

Richard got out of bed and went through the apartment into the kitchen, where he made coffee. He brought Ingrid a cup and returned to the kitchen to boil some eggs and make toast – his standard breakfast. In the mirror hanging on the door he caught sight of himself. The make-up Ingrid had so carefully applied the evening before was mostly still there, though there were smudges. But the face that looked back at him from the mirror was quite strange.

Ingrid came into the kitchen as he was regarding himself. Like Richard, she was nude, seemingly having cast aside her reservations sometime during their lovemaking the night before. She came up behind him as he stood at the mirror and wrapped her arms around his waist, pressing her firm breasts against his back. 'You really should scrub off your make-up before going to bed. It is bad for your skin if it stays on too long. And, more important, it gets all over my nice pillows.' Her smile robbed the words of censure.

He turned in her arms and kissed her laughing mouth. He felt his cock stiffening against her belly as they embraced.

So did Ingrid. 'Not now. We have a lot of work to do before Margaret comes back for you. But I am looking forward to this afternoon.' Disengaging herself, Ingrid sat at the table. 'Come and eat now. Then we must begin.'

They ate, and then she told him to wash off the make-up and shave while she cleared up in the kitchen. She pushed him towards the bathroom.

He took a shower and scrubbed his face, then shaved. When Richard got back to the bedroom, he saw that she had laid out the clothes they had chosen yesterday.

With a pair of dressmaker's shears, Ingrid cut the nylon strap around his scrotum and let the chain fall to the floor. 'Margaret can put another on you if she wishes, but now it would be useless. Start with the tights,' she directed.

Richard sat on the edge of the bed to put on the sheer black tights she had selected. They slid up his bare legs easily, and he stood to ease the top into place. But Ingrid gestured for him to wait. She cut a long strip from a roll of surgical tape and made him hold his cock vertically against his belly while she taped it to his skin. Then she helped him to pull the panty part of the tights into place.

'You can leave the tape off when you're moving around Margaret's house,' she told him, 'but you must use it when you go in public. Now reach inside and pull your balls up from between your legs. Let the tights contain them. Otherwise you will be very uncomfortable in a short while.'

Richard did as she commanded. Then she helped him ease himself into one of the panty corselets. She pulled it up tightly into his crotch and smoothed the top part over his body. His cock made only a slight bulge in the tight garment. The cups of the brassiere were, of course, empty, but Ingrid produced several breast-shaped foam-rubber pads. 'Falsies,' she told him as she stuffed them into the cups. 'They will give you the necessary shape. And if you want to be bigger, you can always add another set. Size sometimes matters.' She pointed to several more pads on the bed.

'Now the slip,' she directed. And when he had put it on she handed him the black dress. 'It goes on over the head,' she told him.

It fitted well enough, but he couldn't reach the back zip. Ingrid had to help him with that. She turned him towards the mirror so he could see the result. The old familiar face was there, but the body now looked like a woman's. He stared at the unfamiliar shape for a long moment. Ingrid handed him a brunette wig from the bureau and helped him settle it on to his head. Like Raymond's, it was short and framed his face much more closely than his own hair. 'Unless you plan to learn to style hair, I suggest you use a short wig. It is easier to manage. Now sit down before the mirror so I can do your eyebrows.'

Ingrid used a small pair of scissors and a pair of tweezers to thin and shape his eyebrows. When she had finished they were more arched than they had been: more feminine, he would have said.

'Now put on the make-up. Do what I did yesterday,' Ingrid told him. She produced another towel and draped it over the top of the dress to prevent his getting cosmetics on it.

Richard applied the make-up under her watchful eye: foundation, powder, lipstick, eye shadow, mascara. He made only a few mistakes, which Ingrid corrected for him.

'Now I will look at your nails,' she said.

He showed her his hands, the nails blunt and with traces of dirt under them. She made disapproving noises and went to get a hand basin and nailbrush. She scrubbed his hands and cleaned the nails, then with a file she shaped them.

'There's not much I can do with them until they grow a bit more,' Ingrid said. 'But I can make them appear narrower by making the ends more pointed.' After wielding a nailfile, she showed him how to apply nail varnish: first a clear lacquer coating, and then a pale rose shade that matched the lipstick she had chosen earlier. 'You can do your toes yourself if you want, but no one is likely to see them.'

As she spoke, Ingrid handed Richard a pair of black high-heeled shoes and indicated he was to put them on. When he had done so, she motioned him to stand. 'Be careful,' she advised. 'You will have to learn to walk in high heels, and it takes time.'

When he stood, Richard felt off balance, his weight thrown forward on to his toes and the balls of his feet. The unnatural elevation of his heels made him think he was falling forward. He took a few tentative steps, and very nearly did fall. Ingrid caught his arm and helped him regain his balance. Then she released him and told him to walk across the room. He did so, slowly and unsteadily, and stopped near the door.

'Now give us a twirl,' Ingrid told him. Richard turned slowly so that she could see him from all angles. He walked several times across the room, feeling a bit surer of foot and of himself with each moment.

Ingrid produced a 35mm camera and asked him to hold still for a moment. 'We need some photographs for your new passport.' She took several exposures and then told him, 'That will do for now. I have to go down and open the shop. I will come back here when I have some free time. You should practise walking and sitting and get used to acting like a woman. If you are going to please Margaret, you will have to become much better at these things.'

'Why do you think Margaret wants me to dress and act like a woman? And why a new passport?' Richard asked.

'I think I know why, but the answer will take more time than I have now. I will come up here for lunch with you. Make something nice, and we will talk about you and Margaret and what she wants.'

Richard practised sitting and standing and walking about, until he got more accustomed to moving around the apartment. He even went down the stairs without mishap. While he was downstairs, he looked into the shop and saw Ingrid serving a customer. He almost plucked up the courage to let someone else see him, but couldn't quite manage that yet. He went back upstairs and began to prepare lunch for them both.

Ingrid came up again at midday, and they ate sandwiches and salad. When they had finished, she began to talk about Margaret. 'Margaret and I are half-sisters,' she told him. 'Her father married my mother when I was ten years old, and she was born about two years later. From the time she could talk, she always tried to get her own way, and since she was so pretty both my mother and stepfather indulged her. I suppose I did the same. As a result, she grew up believing everyone should obey her wishes. By the time we noticed that she was becoming tyrannical, it was too late to do anything about it, so I suppose we were all at fault. We all helped her become the domineering woman she now is.

'As she got older, I realised she must have been badly frightened about sex by someone, because she had a hard time with boys, even though she was a beautiful young woman. I don't know what happened, but even now she has difficulty in letting herself enjoy a normal relationship with any man. I know she is not a virgin, because I walked in and caught her and some boy at it one afternoon. She was on top, which I now know is her position of choice in all matters, not merely in sexual relationships. It was an accident, and I tried to apologise, but she was very angry, as if I had seen her doing something shameful.

'She never saw the boy again. I suppose she could not bear to face him after I had seen them together. There were not many other boys as she grew up. And she made certain I never caught her having sex again – not that it mattered to me what she did.

'At university she spent all her free time studying. No one could persuade her to join in the social scene. Margaret graduated in just two years with an honours degree in business studies, and she got a job in one of the big banks in Stuttgart right out of university. That was when she adopted her favourite dress style: severe suits, always in a dark colour. Even so she looks attractive, but she almost always rebuffs any advances. She began to make some high-powered contacts in her years in Stuttgart. She was promoted again and again, and finally became a travelling negotiator for the bank. Not many women get that far even now. But she was not satisfied. She said she resented working for men, who got the best jobs and the best salaries.

'So she quit. She became an independent operator. But she kept her contacts, and now these men come to her for huge money transfers and business loans. And she has done very well for herself. That is how she bought the house. And she continues to do well. She even manages to finance her hobby from the proceeds of her deals. I mean the business of training servants. As I said, she likes to dominate people, and what better way to do so than to train servants?'

'Do you mean all of the people there are servants?' Richard asked.

'No. Most of them are quite genuinely being trained to work for real people, although their employers tend to share Margaret's views about having power over others. But there are others who are there for the thrill of being dominated. Many of the men come for that reason, men like Raymond, whom you have met. And there are people like yourself, whom I suspect Margaret will use in the other side of her business. I think she is cleaning money, which may not be strictly illegal, but it is not always above board.'

'Do you mean laundering money?'

'Yes, I think that is the correct term,' Ingrid replied. 'I do not know where this money comes from. Nor, I think, does Margaret: at least, not always. She does not ask any questions, but those who come to her for this service are either the same men she helps in their everyday financial dealings, or people recommended to her by her business associates.'

'Then why does she need me?' Richard asked. 'I have no experience in this kind of thing.'

'She does not need you specifically, but she needs someone like you. Someone who is on holiday, who has a bit of spare time, someone who is not going to be missed for a while, someone who is susceptible to her offer of training and domination. I believe she will use you as a courier. If you can pass as a woman, she will use you in that way, and no one will know who you are. Later she may decide to use you under a male identity: perhaps when your disguise as a woman becomes too well known. She always needs couriers. I mean, there is always a turnover. You may not be doing anything illegal – merely clandestine. And you will be well rewarded, both in cash and in kind. Margaret is not tight with money.'

'How do you know all this?'

'Oh, I keep my eyes and ears open, and I talk to many of the people she sends to me as she did you. And I sometimes do a little of the work myself. The extra cash always comes in handy, and the travel is always first class. I manage several holidays a year in that fashion. When I go, I merely take along an extra suitcase filled with cash, and I deliver it to the bank she designates anywhere in the world.'

Richard suddenly remembered the 'delivery' that had come yesterday, the sudden appearance of those identical suitcases. He asked Ingrid what the suitcases were like, and her description matched what he had seen. Several pieces of the puzzle fell into place at once.

'But what I would like to know,' Ingrid was saying, 'is how Margaret happened to choose you. Did she find you in England?'

'No,' Richard answered. 'In Hamburg. And it wasn't Margaret who selected me. It was Helena. The same girl in the photograph with you. How did you come to know her?'

'So you have met my foster daughter,' Ingrid said. She paused, then continued, 'I am glad you did. Did you like her?'

'Very much. It's because of her that I've come here. She seemed to believe Margaret would be angry with her if I refused.'

'Then maybe you can help her. Margaret has some sort of hold over her and makes her do many things she dislikes. I would like to see her free to go her own way. Would you try to find out what Margaret knows about her? Helena will not tell me. Please help her – us.'

Before he could reply, the telephone rang. Ingrid answered it. It soon became clear that it was Margaret calling. Ingrid didn't say much, mostly 'yes', or 'all right', but towards the end she managed to tell Margaret that he would need some more instruction before he was ready to be seen in public. Most especially, he would need some practice in visiting public places.

'Yes, I know you plan to do your own training, Margaret,' Ingrid was saying, 'but you are busy, and anyway you tend more to the stick than the carrot. Both kinds of training are needed. Yes, all right. I will see you in an hour or so. Richard will be ready to go with you.'

She hung up and turned back to Richard. 'She will come to pick you up in one hour. You will be going back to her country house, but I have managed to persuade her that you need to come to me for some further training.' Ingrid smiled slightly at the last word.

'I have had good reason to change my mind about younger men,' she told him. 'But will you also help me with Helena's problem? I need to know why Helena fears Margaret. She may tell you what she will not tell me.' Ingrid had a slightly desperate look as she spoke of the problem of her foster daughter and her half-sister.

Richard nodded. 'But I don't know when I'll be able to see Helena again. Margaret keeps me locked up in the servants' quarters.'

'I will find a way to help,' Ingrid promised. 'I can come and go as I like at Margaret's estate, and I will get you out when I can – when Helena is here. I think that will be in one or two days, so be ready. Now that Margaret thinks you cannot run away dressed like that, you will find you have more freedom to move about the house than before. You must try to convince Margaret that you like her training. She will then allow you even more freedom. And who knows,' Ingrid said with a half smile, 'you may really enjoy it. Others do.'

Margaret came up to Ingrid's apartment, where Richard was waiting for her. He had grown accustomed to being with Ingrid, but he felt terribly embarrassed when Margaret saw him for the first time in his new dress. At the same time, he was aware of an excitement which made his cock stiffen inside the tight corselet which confined it. He stood uneasily when Margaret came into the room. Ingrid had told him she liked to see that show of deference. She looked him over, and then turned to Ingrid, who also showed signs of uneasiness.

'He will do for now,' Margaret announced, and Ingrid relaxed a bit. 'I will take him with me now, and you can start making his maid's uniform. Can you be ready with that in three more days?' The question was more of a command than anything.

Ingrid nodded. 'Bring Richard back then, and everything will be ready.' She changed the subject abruptly: 'When can I see Helena again?'

At first Margaret seemed inclined to ignore her half-sister's demand but, finally, she said, 'Next week. I'll bring her here at the same time I drop Richard off. She might enjoy seeing him outfitted.' Margaret smiled scornfully, and continued, 'Speaking of being outfitted, Richard will need a handbag. No woman would be seen without one.'

Ingrid nodded. 'I think he should have a shoulder bag. He is not accustomed to a handbag and he might forget it somewhere, until it becomes more a part of him. I have selected one that will go with almost anything.' She indicated a black bag with a shoulder strap on the bureau.

Richard picked it up and Ingrid showed him how to sling it casually. 'That will do for now, but he needs to have his own make-up and the other things a woman carries in her bag,' she said.

Margaret nodded. 'We will go shopping now.' She beckoned Richard to follow her and left without another word to Ingrid.

Richard cast one look of appeal over his shoulder, which she caught. Ingrid mouthed, 'Don't worry. I'll see you soon.'

Then he turned to follow Margaret. The high-heeled shoes tapped loudly on the stairs as he went down, and he was holding on to the handrail in case he fell.

Four

Richard spent the next week learning what Margaret meant by submission and obedience, a not altogether painful experience. He discovered that he enjoyed the role he was coerced into more than he had anticipated. Perhaps that was due as much to Margaret's skill at blending pain and pleasure, submission and humiliation, reward and scolding. Whatever had led Helena to select Richard for Margaret to train made him respond to the regime imposed on him. He began to look forward eagerly to the next time Margaret would come to him with her demands.

He was locked into his room at night, when he was expected to take care of his personal needs and look after the wardrobe Ingrid had selected for him. This mainly meant hand-washing the lingerie, corselets and tights he wore during the day, and shaving his legs whenever they began to get rough. The dresses were taken to the laundry by Heidi, and returned to him ready to wear the next morning. On the first evening, she had come in when he was taking the dress off. She had watched silently as he struggled with the back zipper, then had helped him with the task. 'You must learn to do this on your own,' she warned him. 'When Margaret sends you on a job, there will be no one to unzip you.' And she had shown him the proper contortions to accomplish the job.

By the end of the third day he was able to walk in the high-heeled shoes without fear of losing his balance, and Margaret began to coach him to move more naturally and unselfconsciously about the house, so that he would not call attention to himself when he was in public. She used a bamboo cane to reinforce her instructions, and to correct any mistakes he made. So whenever he stumbled she was likely to crack him across the bottom, or the backs of his legs. Similarly, when he failed to stand erect, she lashed him on the back or across his stomach. It was an effective method, and Richard found himself wondering with a curious excitement what it would be like if Margaret decided to use the cane for more than the occasional corrective blow.

Perhaps that was why he was clumsy with the tea things when called upon to serve Margaret and an unknown man, to whom she was more than usually deferent. They had been discussing some financial transaction, when Richard entered the room without knocking. Margaret looked up in annoyed surprise, and he stumbled and spilt sugar on the floor. The visitor took no notice of the accident, but they both stopped talking at once as if unwilling to have their conversation overheard. Richard noticed one of the same suitcases he had seen earlier. He guessed that another cash transfer was being arranged. Margaret glared at Richard and signalled for him to withdraw. From the hall he heard their voices resume in the sitting room.

When Margaret sent for him later, Richard saw that she was still angry. He thought her anger made her more exciting. Wordlessly, she beckoned him into the long dining room and closed the door behind them.

He had never been inside the room properly, only catching glimpses of it through the open door in passing. Now he saw that it contained a long table with seats for perhaps sixteen people. One wall was entirely of glass, allowing the sunlight to enter the room whenever the heavy drapes were pulled back, as they were now. French windows opened on to a patio, and there was a long view across the side garden to a distant line of trees. There was no one in sight in all that open land.

But it was not the view that held Richard's eye. In the corner farthest from the door was a whipping frame. That was obvious to him, even though he had never seen one before. It consisted of three wooden upright posts joined at the top, their feet resting on the carpeted floor. There were horizontal poles just above floor level fitted into the uprights in order to prevent them shifting. The device had been made with some care. The joints were carefully fitted, and the wood had been polished so that it was almost a part of the room's furnishings. But it stood apart from the table and the chairs, its purpose entirely different from the rest of the furniture.

Margaret rang a bell, and presently Marie appeared at the door. She still wore her leg-irons, but seemed unselfconscious about them. Margaret ordered her to fetch rope from the basement. When she had gone, Margaret turned to Richard and ordered him to take his clothes off. He managed to unzip the dress on his own this time, and he stepped out of it to stand before Margaret in slip, tights and corselet. She motioned him to hang the dress over a chair and to get out of his underwear as well. Soon he was naked before her angry gaze.

His cock, taped to his belly as Ingrid had shown him, nevertheless began to stiffen. Margaret noticed but said only, 'We'll see how it feels after you've been disciplined.' They both stood silently until Marie came back with a coil of rope and a kitchen knife. She handed these items to Margaret and withdrew silently, but not before she had caught Richard's eye and made a mock grimace of sympathy for him.

Margaret closed the door and beckoned Richard to follow her to the whipping frame. She tied his hands together in front of him and had him stand on one of the horizontal base bars so that his feet were off the floor. Then, standing on another of the same bars, she lifted his bound wrists and tied them to the apex of the triangle. She spread his ankles and tied them to adjacent poles. Richard found that he could stand comfortably enough but of course could not free himself.

Only when he was secured did Margaret offer any explanation for her anger. 'I never allow the servants to overhear my business affairs. You should have knocked before entering the room. The man I was entertaining is very important to my business, and he wishes to remain anonymous. You will not do that again.'

Richard started to say that he had not known the importance of anonymity, but in the end remained silent. Ignorance was no defence in Margaret's eyes. Nor was anything else, once she had decided to assert her dominance. This much he had learnt from casual conversation among his fellow servants.

Margaret left the room and returned shortly with the bamboo cane she often used to emphasise her instructions. Richard glanced once over his shoulder as she approached him, admiring once again the feline grace of her movements. He would never be able to learn to move as she did. Then he looked away, out to the garden and the tree line as he waited for her to begin.

He didn't cry out as she struck him. That was his way of letting Margaret know that there were some things she couldn't make him do – an assertion of his own essential independence, even as he submitted to her will. His silence may have prolonged the beating. But he didn't think so. If he had cried out or begged her to stop, she would only have struck him harder, he believed. He had learnt from the others that Margaret was never moved by pity. Heidi told of being beaten harder the louder she screamed. She also gave it as her opinion that Margaret enjoyed making others beg her to stop.

Yet even as she whipped him he was conscious of a stirring of excitement. His cock, stiff before she began, remained so throughout the beating. He even felt he was on the verge of orgasm at several points. What was the protocol about that, he wondered? Would Margaret regard it as a victory if she made him come? He wondered if he would be able to stop himself, or if he wanted to. In the end, Margaret decided the issue by stopping before he came.

Richard hung from the ropes that bound him to the frame. His back, bottom and legs felt as if they were on fire. But he had remained silent. Despite her best efforts, Margaret had not been able to break him. When she moved around to stand in front of him, he saw that she was breathing heavily from her efforts. He raised his head and looked into her eyes before lowering it again. She knew that inside he was still untouched. He knew that she would have to try again.

But when he looked at her again, he saw that she was excited too. Margaret's face was flushed and her breathing more rapid than her exertions warranted. Clearly, she got a sexual thrill from hurting and dominating others, as Heidi had intimated.

Nevertheless, what she did next took him by surprise. Ingrid had said that her sister was very private about her sexual indulgences, but Margaret moved directly in front of Richard and raised her skirt around her hips. She wore no pants, and Richard wondered how much planning had gone into that.

Margaret's legs were long, full and shapely, accentuated by the soft sheen of the stockings she wore. Richard felt his cock move against his belly where the tape held it.

Margaret noticed his erection too. She prodded his

cock with the cane, enjoying his sharp intake of breath. But she was more interested in her own reaction. Satisfied that she had Richard's attention, she moved her feet apart so that her thighs were parted. Margaret moved the cane between her own legs, touching her crotch with the stiff bamboo and running it back and forth against her labia. As she did so, her breath became more ragged and rapid. Clearly she was arousing herself and enjoying his inability to take part in the act, very much as she had done in Helena's apartment.

Richard watched her autoeroticism and did indeed regret his inability to join in. A waste of a beautiful woman, he thought. And he wondered what had made her this way.

Margaret removed the cane and held it towards Richard. He could see that it was wet with her juice. She moved the cane under his nose, and the scent of her arousal was unmistakable and very strong. She smiled at his reaction.

'Would you like to make love to me?' she asked with a distant smile.

This time Richard allowed his feelings to show. He nodded, not trusting himself to speak.

Margaret's smile grew wider, but she made no move towards him.

'Well, you can't,' she told him. 'But you can watch,' she taunted him. 'I imagine you won't be able to look away.' She put the cane back between her legs and continued to arouse herself.

Richard watched as she moved the rod faster and faster between her thighs, pressing it harder against her cunt as she did so. The flush deepened and spread down her neck, until it was hidden by the neckline of her blouse. Margaret used one hand to cup her breasts, teasing herself through the fine silk.

Richard could only watch helplessly as her excitement mounted. He knew that much of it was due to his presence and his obvious desire to have her. He wondered what she would be like if she ever allowed him – or anyone else – to make love to her.

Margaret's excitement grew. She breathed more rapidly. The rod moved faster between her legs, and her fingers now squeezed and twisted her breasts as she approached climax. Her hips moved slowly, sinuously, in time with the thrusts of the cane between her legs. Her eyes lost their focus. She seemed to be looking through Richard. Abruptly she jerked her hips and moaned loudly. Her back arched as she came.

Richard was excited by her display. His breath was short, and he felt the familiar tenseness in his groin and cock. But he could do nothing about that.

Margaret clearly had no need of any help. She was lost in a series of shattering orgasms. She moaned continuously now, her hips moving and her thighs quivering as she came. He might as well not have been there for all the attention she paid him.

Margaret's excitement fed on his presence and his helplessness. She needed an audience to reach these heights of pleasure. Too bad she didn't seem to need his active participation. Involuntarily, he thrust his own hips towards her.

Margaret opened her eyes at the same moment, and she smiled as she recognised the signs of his arousal. She moved the cane from between her legs and regarded him with flushed face and heaving breasts. She lashed his cock lightly, and he felt it leap from the blow before the pain struck him. Margaret enjoyed his reaction, leaning against the frame to which he was bound as excitement ebbed. She smiled slightly at him as she allowed her skirt to drop back into place. 'You are learning,' she said, as she turned away and left the room.

Richard looked out at the trees in the distance as he waited for the fire in his back and in his cock to die down. Then he closed his eyes and dozed.

* * *

The cool breeze woke him. He saw that the French windows were open, and that both Heidi and Marie had come to him. Marie told him that they didn't dare untie him: Margaret would only find out, and they would be beaten.

He nodded his understanding.

She offered him a glass of wine, and he took it gratefully. Then she told him that they had come to offer what comfort they could, knowing what Margaret was like. She raised her short skirt to let him see she was still locked into her chastity belt. Heidi made a 'me-too' gesture. Then Marie knelt before him and freed his cock from the surgical tape. The two women, one blonde and the other dark, then took turns caressing and arousing him. Perhaps it was their way of demonstrating their power over him. Everyone here seemed to be playing the power game.

But after a while that didn't matter very much, as the two women vied with one another to arouse him. They seemed to enjoy giving him pleasure after the suffering. Kneeling before him, Marie took him into her mouth, and he was engulfed in the warm wetness, in which her tongue was a magical serpent winding itself around and around him. Heidi stood behind Marie and toyed with the other woman's breasts, unbuttoning the top of her maid's outfit to expose them. Heidi unbuttoned her own top as well, so that Richard could see her rounded breasts as he was aroused by Marie.

He could only stare helplessly at her nakedness as Marie used her mouth on his cock. Heidi cupped Marie's breasts in her hands, as if offering them to him. Marie groaned, the sound muffled by the cock in her mouth. When Heidi squeezed the taut nipples between her thumb and forefinger, Marie arched her back with a loud moan of pleasure. Her hips began to thrust slowly backward and forward as her orgasm built.

Richard too was thrusting as Marie's tongue teased

his cock. He felt himself sliding in and out between her lips, his cock alternately warm and then cool as he moved in the slow dance of arousal and pleasure. Marie followed him, never letting him slide out completely, her groans counterpointing his own deeper grunts. He was pulling involuntarily against the ropes that bound him to the frame, wanting to use his hands to hold Marie against him as his excitement grew. Some part of him realised that his added excitement was at least partly due to his helplessness.

Marie held him steady with her arms around his waist, trapping almost the entire length of his cock in the warm wetness of her mouth. She nipped him sharply with her teeth as another orgasm racked her. That was too much for Richard. He could hold back no longer, and with a low groan he came. Marie gasped with her own pleasure but managed to swallow his semen. None escaped to stain her uniform or the carpet.

When Richard had spent himself, the women turned to one another. They began to kiss and rub one another's breasts. Had it not been for the chastity belts each wore, he was certain they would have gone straight for one another's cunts. In the aftermath of his own orgasm, Richard wondered idly if they were lovers. Each seemed to know what would arouse the other. For a long time he watched the play of hands and fingers on breasts, the teasing and pinching of engorged nipples, and the kissing and sucking of eager mouths, as they took what pleasure was allowed them. After what seemed hours, they were done. Both women kissed him as they left the room. Once more he stared out at the distant trees as he waited for Margaret to release him.

Night was falling when she came for him. Wordlessly she untied him from the frame and watched as he stretched his cramped muscles. She ordered him to get dressed and then go help in the kitchen with the evening meal. After Margaret had eaten, the servants gathered in the kitchen for their own meal. Richard ate standing up. Marie and Heidi said nothing, either about the beating he had received or about their later visit to him. The cook was not reliable, he had learnt, and was apt to carry tales to Margaret. Raymond was absent, and Richard learnt that he was away. Probably carrying a suitcase full of cash, Richard guessed, and wondered when he would be sent on a similar errand. The idea of travelling disguised as a woman excited him.

When he got to his room that night, he saw several parcels on the bureau. There was no address on any of them, and it appeared they had been hand-delivered. Inside were three long-sleeved maid's uniforms in black satin. They were similar to those worn by Heidi and Marie, but where theirs were cut away to reveal the tops of their breasts as they served about the house, these all had high necklines and even a narrow collar. He remembered Ingrid's remark about keeping the hair on his arms and chest hidden. These uniforms would do that well enough. The white lace aprons were in a separate package. In the others, he found a supply of opaque black tights of the type worn by the other maids, and several pairs of high-heeled shoes. There was also a pair of high-heeled knee-length black leather boots.

As he was unpacking all this, Richard thought one of the shoes seemed heavier than the others. Inside he found a small grey steel box with a lens and several buttons. There was also a key and a note from Ingrid.

She wrote, 'This control will allow you to open and close the front gates to the estate. The key is for the front door of the house. If you can manage to get out of your room, try to get to the main road. Helena is coming to visit me, and she will be waiting in my car about one kilometre away from the gates. She will pick you up and bring you to the shop. Try to get out two days from now. Good luck.'

She had signed it, 'Love, Ingrid.'

He was pleased at that. He had tried to give her pleasure. Evidently he had succeeded. At the same time, he wondered how he was going to deal with Helena and Ingrid at the same time. There might well be some awkward moments.

The smallest package contained a British passport made out in the name of Pamela Rhodes. The photo Ingrid had taken of him had been used in it. Richard guessed that obtaining a false passport would be a small matter for someone with Margaret's connections. He was impressed by the ease of it all. And it would work, so long as there was no reason for a body search. From this he guessed Margaret was planning to use him as a courier soon. He would have to learn as much as he could from Helena and Ingrid.

The next two days seemed to drag along. On the first day, Richard appeared in the maid's uniform, guessing that Margaret wanted him to wear that in the house and to save the other dresses for his public appearances. The guess proved correct. Margaret nodded approvingly when he appeared. He felt more at ease now that he was dressed more or less as the other servants were.

His only real occupation was in devising some way to escape from the room once he was locked in at night. The lock was strong, and there was no handle on the inside. The door opened inward, so he would not be able to force it open, even if he dared risk the noise. In the end, the problem was solved by enlisting Heidi's aid. She had taken a liking to him, and the idea of thwarting Margaret's rules appealed to the element of mischief in her. Richard never said why he wanted to get out, telling her that the less she knew, the better for her if he got caught.

On the appointed night, Richard waited in his room for Heidi to let him out. He wore the maid's uniform with the opaque tights so that he would appear more normal if he were seen by any of the other servants. Of course, if Margaret saw him, the game was up. He hadn't seen her around the house all day, and there was talk that she had gone to Stuttgart on business. He hoped that was true. Richard had taped his cock as Ingrid had suggested, since he would be going out in public. He was conscious of it under the tight corselet. He was excited both by the feeling of constriction and the sense of embarking on an adventure.

When Heidi came to let him out, he was keyed up, but he remembered to smile at her and give her a kiss of gratitude. 'You must be back before daylight,' she warned him. 'If Margaret knows you've been out, it will go hard for both of us.'

Richard nodded as they went up in the lift. It wouldn't be fair to earn Heidi a beating when he was having all the fun.

The hallway was deserted when Richard passed to the front door. He took a long belted coat from the rack by the door, recognising it as one of Margaret's. He opened the door, stepped out into the darkness and closed the door behind him. The lock clicked into place, and he was committed. He hurried down the drive, stumbling once or twice in the high-heeled knee-length boots he had worn against the cold. Once away from the front door, he breathed easier. There had been no alarm, and he guessed he had got away unseen.

The gates looked taller tonight than they had ever done, seeming to tower over him. But they opened readily enough when he used the control box Ingrid had sent. Once outside, he closed them and hurried along the road, hoping that Helena had not forgotten their rendezvous. At the same time, he also hoped that no other car would pass him. Anyone seeing a woman struggling along the road after dark was likely to stop, and there would be awkward questions.

After what seemed like miles, he saw a car parked alongside the road, facing towards him. Helena? It was. She smiled happily as she opened the door for him.

'Oh, Richard, I have missed you so much!'

Helena leant over and kissed him as soon as he had closed the door. She still smelt clean and fresh, reminding him of country air and long walks in the woods and fields. And she felt good against him.

She drew back and with an impish grin squeezed his falsies. 'You've changed so much since I saw you last. I wish I were that big. Feel how small I am,' she invited him.

He touched her breasts, feeling the nipples taut under her clothing. Yes, she was glad to see him. Just as he was glad to be with her again. But this wasn't the place for a reunion.

Helena seemed to realise this as well, for she drew back and started the engine, saying, 'We'll be more comfortable in Ingrid's house.'

Richard abruptly remembered where they were going. 'But won't she be angry – jealous – if we . . .?' The sentence trailed off.

'Why should she be?' Helena asked with a grin. 'You have not been – how do you say? – shagging her, have you?' She burst into laughter as he flushed hotly. 'Oh, but you have! How could you? She is like my mother. She is older than you and me.' But Helena was still smiling. 'Of course I know what you two have been doing. Ingrid told me as soon as I arrived. She does not mind what we do. Neither do I mind what you two have been doing, so long as you try to make her happy. She says you did, so everything is all right. Besides, she will not be there tonight. She has plans of her own.'

Richard was relieved.

They drove back past the gates to Margaret's house and continued into the village. Helena parked in the shadowy courtyard behind Ingrid's shop and let them into the same back door he had arrived at with Margaret. She closed the door and led him up the stairs to the apartment over the shop. This time he didn't have any trouble climbing in high heels. Practice was all it took.

Helena turned on the lights and looked at Richard as he took off the coat that covered his maid's outfit. When he hesitated, she told him, 'Go ahead. Don't be embarrassed. I want to see what you look like. I know you are doing this for me.'

Richard took off the coat and stood while she looked him over.

'If I didn't know you,' she told him, 'I wouldn't know you are not a woman. I mean that as a compliment. And thank you for going into this for someone you hardly knew.'

'For someone I want to know better,' Richard corrected her, and felt gladdened by her smile.

But Helena said, 'Enough looking for now. Now I want us to get undressed. I want to get into bed with you, and I want to feel you inside me.'

That was not the kind of invitation Richard was going to resist. 'Unzip me,' he said, turning his back to Helena. It was an interesting reversal of roles for him. There had been many women in his life who had issued similar requests. Now he stood as Helena unzipped the maid's outfit and helped him out of the tight dress. She paused to touch the bulge of his cock, held against his body by the tape and the tight corselet. He felt himself grow harder as she stroked him through the elastic material.

They undressed one another and climbed into bed. There Helena took charge, caressing his cock and smiling as she felt him grow stiffer in her hands. At the same time Richard saw her face flush with excitement. Her nipples grew taut, and she began to breathe rapidly. When he reached to touch her breasts, Helena told him to lie still. 'I want to do this,' she said. So he lay on his back, while she continued to arouse him.

Finally Helena straddled him and guided his cock inside her, sighing with pleasure as he slid home. She lowered her body until her breasts were pressed against his chest, and put her arms around his neck, holding herself tightly against him and rocking her hips gently. Richard put his own arms around her waist, pulling her down on to his cock. 'Hold me for a while,' she said. They lay quietly for a long time, joined but not moving, neither one wanting to break the spell.

Helena was the first to move, raising her hips and sliding up his cock until she almost lost him. When she slid back down, she gave a gasp of pleasure. At once she began to move more rapidly, and Richard felt her hot, slick cunt tight around his cock. Being on the bottom was best, he thought. He watched her face as she began to lose control. Her eyes were open but not focused on anything. Her mouth too was open as she gasped for breath. She came suddenly with a gasp of surprise and pleasure, hunching herself up as if to contain the orgasm within the smallest possible area. She moaned softly, her mouth almost touching his ear, a wordless cry of pleasure, broken by the waves of sensation flooding through her.

She gradually grew still, then lifted herself up to look into his face, as if to reassure herself that he was still there. 'Oh, Richard, that was wonderful.'

'Don't talk now,' he told her, as he pulled her down once more against his chest. He began to thrust slowly, and she matched his rhythm. Helena moaned softly, and he felt her muscles clench around him as she began another series of orgasms. Once, twice, three times. Her spasms of pleasure seemed to go on for ever.

But Richard couldn't hold back for ever. The slow, deliberate thrusts were more exciting than Helena's quick, sharp motion. When he spurted inside her,

Helena gave a loud cry and increased her frenzied movements, gasping and shuddering in time with his own orgasm.

As she lay warm and fragrant on top of him, Richard thought back to Helena's intense response to his lovemaking, so much more intense than that of any other woman he had slept with. Is it me, or something in her? he wondered. It was very flattering to believe she had responded to him, that he had awakened emotions in her that she had never felt with anyone else before. But that was a question he would not ask her. The answer might not be as comfortable as the fantasy.

Helena seemed to be asleep as she lay there, and Richard felt himself becoming drowsy in the aftermath of their lovemaking. But just when he thought he might fall asleep, Helena stirred and sat up, slowly disengaging from him.

She looked serious, almost solemn, as she said, 'Richard, it has been so long since I could enjoy sex like that. Margaret does not like me to enjoy sex, except maybe when she is whipping me. That's why she locks me in that chastity belt. That's why we have to meet here in secret.'

'Why do you allow her to have so much power over you?' Richard asked.

Helena sighed. 'It is such a complex thing. I would rather not talk of it so soon after our lovemaking, but I suppose we have to talk about what is happening with us and with Margaret. There are some things you should know about me before you decide to go along with her plans for you.'

'This sounds serious,' said Richard. 'Are you sure you want to talk about it?'

'I must tell you these things, because I am on the verge of falling in love with you, and you must know what you are getting into.'

'All right. Talk. I'll listen,' Richard said. She had said,

'falling in love', he thought. No one had said that to him before. It was going to be a new experience.

'I thought you would be different from the others as soon as I saw you on the *Reeperbahn*. It was a sudden feeling, an instinct, not rational. But I was right. Now I must tell you that Margaret sends me out every now and then to recruit a new courier for her. Some stay with her. Most will not tolerate her insistence on obedience and training. But I did not choose you for Margaret's sake. I need someone to help me. I hope you will do it. Will you?' Helena looked serious, even worried as she spoke.

Even without knowing what she wanted from him, Richard's first impulse was to agree. 'I already promised Ingrid that I would,' he told her.

Helena's smile was his reward. Her face changed from solemn to happy in an instant. She leant down to kiss him. 'I am so glad. Margaret can sometimes be nice, but mostly she wants people to do what she says. Even though she is my aunt, she can be very cruel and demanding. I want to be free of her. I want to be able to see whomever I wish. You, I mean, whenever I wish. And I want to be independent and self-sufficient. I would like to be able to develop my own life and my own business. Margaret will not allow that.'

'Why don't you just move away, disappear? She can't follow you all over the world, can she?' Richard asked.

'Perhaps not by herself, but her contacts can. Through them she has influence and resources to do almost anything she wishes.'

Margaret was beginning to sound like a formidable and manipulative tyrant. Richard's instincts were all for helping Helena to escape her clutches, even though a part of him knew his motives were less than noble and pure: namely, that part of him that was still inside Helena. But then, the hero usually got the girl as part of the reward for being heroic, didn't he?

Helena continued, 'Margaret has certain documents that could get me into a lot of trouble. She threatens to turn them over to the police if I don't do as she wishes.' She paused.

Richard asked the natural question, 'What kind of documents, and what kind of trouble?'

'The going-to-prison kind,' Helena replied.

'You'd better tell me about it,' he said.

Helena began at once, as if she had been waiting for this moment. 'When I was a student, I knew someone who had been planning a bombing incident. You have probably heard of some of the things he and his kind did. I mean the firebombings of Turkish *Gästarbeiters'* houses. Some people got killed, though I swear I did not know what he was doing. We were lovers. I did not want him to do these things, but he would not listen. He thought he was going to save Germany from being swamped by inferior races.'

'Like Hitler,' Richard interjected.

Helena nodded. 'But of course I did not think of that at the time. He was just my lover. And afterwards they caught him and made him tell about the people he knew. The police came looking for me, but Margaret warned me and let me hide at her country house. She found out what the police knew through her contacts, and she had the documents stolen so that there would be no evidence to link me with him in any way. I thought she was doing me a great kindness, until she told me how I would be repaying her. But until now I thought going to prison would be worse.'

'And now?' Richard asked.

'Now you are involved with her. She is making you dress as a woman and punishing you and making you serve her as a slave. And soon you will be transporting money around Europe and taking risks of your own – risks that could land you in prison. And I got you into this. I would not blame you if you hated me for that.'

The line was as old as time, Richard told himself, but it was nonetheless effective. He was going to help her. 'What do you have in mind?' he asked.

Helena said, 'Steal the papers from Margaret and burn them. Then I will be free of her. We could go to England and start a new life.' She halted abruptly. There was a long silence. Then she resumed, 'But maybe you don't want that. I was not thinking of you, only of myself.' Her face became sad.

At that moment Richard knew he wanted nothing more than to take Helena to England. His aunt's house at Bacton had been good enough for him, but he had been lonely without realising it. Helena would brighten the old house – and his life.

'Of course that's what I want. I want you with me.' As soon as the words were out, he knew he had said the right thing, both for him and for Helena. Her face lit up with a smile, and he knew it was for him.

'Oh, Richard, you make me so happy. I am so glad I found you.'

And so was he. He gave no more thought to the rights and wrongs of the matter. But he did have one important question. 'Where does Margaret keep the papers?'

Helena answered, 'I do not know where exactly, but they must be in her house. You must be on the lookout for a safe of some sort. I am sure she would not just leave the papers lying around for anyone to find. She is most careful about such things. I am coming to the house in a few days' time, and I will help you by looking around myself. I have much more freedom there than you have. But keep your eyes open all the same. Now that you know there is something to look for, you might notice something that will help us.'

Just like that, 'me' had become 'us'. Richard felt very good about that. But Helena was bent on making him feel even better. She put her arms around him and urged him to roll over so that he was lying on top of her. Then she raised her legs and crossed them behind his back, opening herself for him and pulling him down into her. Richard felt her vaginal muscles clamp down on his cock, and he began to grow hard almost at once. This time their lovemaking was more frenzied than before. Helena urged him on ever faster, moaning beneath him as he thrust into her, matching his rhythm with an urgency that almost overcame his self-control when she had her first orgasm. He managed to hold back, but he knew he wouldn't be able to last very long. Helena seemed a woman possessed, bucking and writhing as she strove to take all of him inside her. She cried out again and again as she peaked, but she never slackened the pace. Her legs were clamped around his waist, and she was rearing and plunging as she clung to him. At last he let himself go and felt another shattering orgasm claim him as Helena screamed in ecstasy. Then once again they lay quietly, catching lost breath, cooling slowly from the fever heat of their lovemaking.

He rolled on to his side, looking at Helena. Her eyes were closed and a damp tendril of her hair lay across her cheek. She looked contented, and he was glad he had been able to give her pleasure. Richard could have stayed there for ever, but time was passing. It would soon be dawn, and he had to be back inside the house and in his room, dressed in the maid's uniform and ready for the day's work when the servants came to let him out.

Helena too seemed to realise the situation. She opened her eyes and looked at him with a wistful smile. 'I wish you could stay with me, but we have to get you back before Margaret misses you.' But she brightened at once. 'Once we get the papers from Margaret, we will be able to do as we wish, all day and every day.' She looked happy at the idea.

They got out of bed and began to dress. After the

lovemaking, the assertion of his maleness, Richard felt much more conscious of the change as he put on the tights and corselet, the slip and the tight, black satin maid's uniform. He was conscious of the tight clothing on his body, and felt anew the excitement he had experienced the first time he was dressed in women's clothes. He liked the sensation of being enclosed, restricted, by the tight-fitting corselet. He had lost the earlier self-consciousness. Helena had taken his transformation in her stride, even thanking him for making the effort for her. He was glad she had not made an issue of the dress.

He put on the high-heeled boots and the coat and was ready for the trip back. Helena led the way downstairs silently. She checked the courtyard, and then they both stepped out into the pre-dawn darkness. There was not much conversation during the drive through the town and out to Margaret's country estate. Once Helena rested her hand on Richard's leg, stroking him lightly through the opaque tights. Just as I have done with other women, he reminded himself. It felt strange to be on the receiving end, but not unpleasant.

When she let him out on the roadside, Helena leant over and pulled him down to her window. She kissed him lingeringly and then let him go. 'It will not be long, Richard. Please be patient.'

'When will I see you again?' he asked.

'I do not know exactly. Margaret is supposed to come to Hamburg sometime next week to pick up the leather gear she ordered the day you met her. She usually wants me to come out to her house for discipline when she visits. The last time I escaped. She took you instead. I hope you did not suffer too much in my place.'

Richard shook his head, remembering the whipping he had received, and its aftermath, and this night with Helena. He would do it all over again. He told her so, and was rewarded again by her smile.

'I will suggest to Margaret that she bring me out next week, if she does not suggest it herself. I will stay the night there – I usually do anyway – and I will come to you that night in your room. I have the freedom of the house and can come and go where the servants cannot. Even though Margaret sometimes has one of the servants whip me, I am still more free than they are. Freer than you are, too,' she added with a rueful smile.

'Never mind,' Richard told her. 'I'll manage until I see you again, but don't be too long. I want to be with you.' The words were out before he realised what he was saying, but he didn't regret them. The prospect of days, weeks, years with Helena suddenly brightened his future.

'I'm glad. I feel the same, my darling. Soon. I promise.' She kissed him once more, and they parted. She put the car into gear as Richard went in through the tall, iron gates and up the drive to the house. He saw the sky brightening in the southeast as he crunched up the gravel path in his high-heeled boots. He realised he was becoming accustomed to them, and to the other clothes he wore. It could become a habit, he told himself with an inward smile.

Richard let himself into the house with the key, being careful to lock the door behind him. He hung the coat on the rack in the hallway and quietly made his way back to the lift, intending to slip back to his room. As he passed the dining-room door, Heidi stepped out.

'I was worried you might not get back before Margaret. I couldn't sleep, so I have been waiting here.' She wore a carelessly belted dressing gown which fell open to reveal her breasts. She didn't seem to mind that, but she was insistent that he get back to his room at once.

Richard was relieved when he saw that she was wearing her chastity belt. After the evening with Helena, he didn't think he would be much use to someone else.

Only in sex fantasies does the stud get hard every time he sees a naked tit. He was also relieved to see that Heidi didn't seem to expect anything more from him than she was asking. They went to the lift together and descended to the basement.

She hurried him along to his room and almost pushed him inside. He heard the lock click as she hurriedly shut the door. He undressed so he could take a shower and perhaps get an hour of sleep before the new day began. He knew that he would have to dress again and do his make-up in order to pass Margaret's scrutiny. There must be no hint that he had been anywhere but in his room all night – for everyone's sake.

[illegible]

[illegible] what

Hers didn't seem to expect anything more from him

than she was asking. They went to the [illegible] together and

[illegible] in the basement.

She hurried him along to the [illegible] and started pushing

[illegible] inside. [illegible]

[illegible]

[illegible]

[illegible]

[illegible]

[illegible]

room all night [illegible]

Five

The next day Richard cleaned and tidied around the house, helped in the kitchen with the cooking and washing-up, and looked around for signs of the safe Helena had told him about. He looked furtively behind pictures and mirrors and behind books in the library. By now, wearing women's clothing felt normal. He practised walking like a woman, swinging his hips more than he was accustomed to, becoming more adept at walking in high-heeled shoes and in dressing himself and applying make-up. He even attempted to restyle the wig he had been given. He thought he had done well enough, until Marie told him otherwise. She came to his room as he was brushing the wig and peering into the mirror.

'You will never be a hairdresser,' she said, taking the brush from him. 'Sit down there and watch.' With a few deft strokes, she changed the style. 'Now you look like a different person,' she told him. 'Madame will be pleased that you can change your appearance so easily. It will be very handy when you go on a job.'

Richard had to admit she was right. He did look different. Casually he rested his hand on Marie's waist. He felt the steel of her chastity belt beneath her clothing. 'It's a pity you have to wear that all the time.'

'Yes. A great pity,' the girl sighed. 'I have not had a man inside me in a long time. I miss it, but there is nothing to be done. Madame insists I wear the virgin's basket and these –' she pointed to her leg-irons '– all the time.'

'Where are the keys kept?' he asked. 'I might be able to get them, and then I could unlock you whenever you wished.'

'Yes, that would be nice. I would like to be free for you, but Madame keeps them safely out of our reach.'

'Where?' Richard persisted.

'She has a safe in the dining room beside the fireplace, but only she and the cook have a key to it.'

As simple as that, Richard thought. All I had to do was ask the right person. 'And where does the cook keep her key?' Richard asked.

'On a chain around her neck. She keeps it with her even when she sleeps. And she sleeps very lightly. I know, because I have tried to get it myself. She woke up and caught me. Of course she told Madame, and I got a beating for my pains.'

'Maybe we can think of some way to make her sleep more soundly,' Richard said. 'Does she drink at all?'

'She likes brandy. She usually has some after dinner has been served and she wants to relax. But she never takes much.'

If I can get a message to Helena or Ingrid, he thought, I'll bet they can get some kind of sleeping draught to slip in her brandy. It was the only plan he could think of, and it would depend on waiting until Margaret was away. The first thing was to get the message out. The best time for that would be when Helena came to the house, as she had said she soon would. He felt better now that he had some idea of how to get at the place where Helena's papers were probably kept.

Marie sighed as he patted her again and briefly explained his plan. 'It will not be easy,' she said. 'But we will try. The reward will make almost any risk worthwhile. You really want to try?' She looked at him intently.

'Yes. Let's do it,' he said decisively. 'We must both be on the lookout for a chance to get a message out to Ingrid. We need something to put in the cook's brandy. Try to think of something we could use, and I will do the same. I will also ask Ingrid to help us the next time she comes to the house.' They smiled at one another, conspirators against the tyrant.

Marie was smiling still as they left the room to begin their day's work.

Margaret came home late in the afternoon, as Richard was cleaning in the dining room. He thought he had spotted the safe, and was about to look closer, when he sensed he was not alone. Margaret had come in silently and was regarding him levelly as he turned from the fireplace. Luckily he could use the duster and tin of furniture polish as an excuse for his presence.

Without preamble, Margaret announced that she would see him in the morning, causing Richard immediately to wonder just what she might know or suspect about him.

'I have been told of your progress, Richard. The reports say you have been doing well in perfecting your disguise. Continue to do so.' She left as abruptly as she had appeared, leaving Richard too shaken to make any closer investigation of the safe. But he knew that there were several bricks in the hearth that looked loose. He would look more closely the next time Margaret was away.

He couldn't remember ever being as nervous with any other woman. More and more he was accepting Margaret as the arbiter of his behaviour. He obeyed her because he wanted to please her, and because he was becoming more accustomed to obedience. It was a new way to order his life.

In the morning Heidi came to his room with breakfast. She told him that he should remain there until Margaret came for him. He should also dress with extra care. She would stay, she said, to help him get ready. Richard was left with a sense of uneasy anticipation. He had little appetite for breakfast. The prospect of a close interview with Margaret unsettled him.

Heidi seemed to sense his nervousness, moving to stand beside him. She seemed uneasy too, but her unease came from a different source. She was sexually excited. Richard saw that as soon as he looked closely at her. She looked distracted, and her breasts rose and fell agitatedly. When she brushed against him, he felt the hard steel of her chastity belt as he had felt Marie's. Richard wondered if she too was frustrated by the enforced abstinence. There was not much he could do about her condition until he could get the keys from the safe, but he might be able to relieve her somewhat.

Swallowing his own nervousness, he said, 'Come here, Heidi. Sit on my lap.' The alacrity with which she obeyed told him he had judged correctly.

Without further ado, he unzipped her maid's uniform and pulled the top down to her waist. He bent to kiss the tops of her breasts, hearing the catch in her breathing as his lips touched her flesh. Through her sheer brassiere he could see her nipples becoming erect. He touched her through the filmy material, and she moaned aloud.

'It's been so long,' she said softly, echoing Marie's words of the evening before.

Richard wondered why Margaret made such a fuss about keeping the women from sexual gratification. He concluded that it was a natural consequence of her need to control others. He had long ago decided that any institution which strove to make others fear sex and abstain from it under duress was unworthy of his support. Yet he found himself excited by being forced to wear women's clothes, and by the way Margaret teased him without letting him reach orgasm.

He was eager to help Heidi (and Marie, and Helena, and Ingrid) to evade 'Madame's' restrictions. At the same time, he was honest enough to acknowledge that his efforts ensured his own sexual gratification. No one, he told himself, ever acts from wholly selfless motives.

But here was Heidi, sitting on his lap and panting with desire. He reached behind her and unfastened her brassiere, allowing her full breasts to fall free. Her nipples were taut and crinkly with her excitement. He touched them, and Heidi gasped with pleasure. Although it was a bit like the groping sessions he had once enjoyed when younger, Richard nevertheless concentrated on giving Heidi pleasure. For her part, she seemed to enjoy his manipulation of her breasts and nipples. Her eyes were closed and her breath was short and rapid, and she squirmed in his lap as she became excited.

Her hands, which at first had rested on his shoulders, migrated down to his cock, imprisoned inside the tight elastic material of the corselet. Heidi rubbed and stroked him through his clothes. Although it was less satisfactory that way, nevertheless he felt himself grow hard under her hands. She was doing her best to help him as he continued to tease and kiss her swollen breasts and nipples. She raised herself slightly from his lap, so that she could slide the tight skirt of his maid's outfit up to his waist, leaving only the corselet and tights between her and his stiff cock. Richard began to breathe rapidly in his turn as his excitement grew.

He could smell the clean scent of her as she was shaken by her first orgasm. Either her breasts were more than normally sensitive, or she had been deprived of all sexual contact for too long. At any rate, Heidi came repeatedly, writhing against him and moaning with her own pleasure. Her body shook and her head was thrown backward, the sinews of her soft throat taut beneath her skin. Richard could see the pulse at the base of her neck beating rapidly. But even in her highly excited state, he noticed that she strove to be as quiet as possible. He guessed that she was afraid they would be overheard and thus bring Margaret's wrath down upon themselves.

His hands moved to raise her short skirt until he could touch the bare flesh of her thighs where her stockings ended. He tried to worm his fingers under her tight belt, but there was no room, even though Heidi tried to help him. Margaret had designed a very effective chastity belt. She was nevertheless excited by his efforts to reach her cunt, gasping and shaking as she felt his hand on her. Richard wondered what she would be like if she could be penetrated in the usual fashion.

But then he had no more time to wonder about anything. His own orgasm took him by surprise. He felt the warm fluid soaking his tights and corselet as he spent himself inside the tight clothing. He shuddered in his turn, and heard Heidi's sharp intake of breath as she realised he was coming. She moaned in his ear as he surrendered to his own pleasure. Afterwards he wondered at the strength of his response. Was it due to being forced to wear the maid's outfit, the novelty of the tight clothing constricting him as his own clothing never did?

At length they both subsided, Heidi resting her head on his shoulder as she recovered her breath and the flush of excitement ebbed from her face, neck and breasts.

She broke the silence first. 'Oh God, how I needed that!'

'Me too,' he replied, glad that they had been able to pleasure one another.

As Heidi stood up, Margaret's voice broke the spell of their intimacy. 'Very touching. I hope you both enjoyed that, because you are not likely to enjoy what comes next. Heidi, you know the rules well enough. Richard might be excused partly because of ignorance, but you will both have to learn what happens when people break the rules of the house. Stand up, both of you,' she ordered.

Margaret, standing in the open doorway, looked both distant and stern. When she spoke again the impression was heightened. 'Richard, I have been away for several days on business and have had to neglect your training. I see you have formed the mistaken impression that you can do whatever you like in my absence. I will have to correct that now. I must be able to rely on your unquestioning obedience when you go out on a job.'

Heidi would not meet Margaret's glance. She was transformed from the abandoned lover into the cowed slave in just the time it took to realise Margaret had caught them. She began to pull up her dress, but Margaret stopped her. 'Don't bother to get dressed. Take off your clothes and wait for me in the hallway.'

Heidi looked back once more at Richard before leaving the room.

Richard looked directly at Margaret. Her anger made her even more attractive. She looked dangerously beautiful, and he wondered briefly what she would be like if she ever abandoned her stern demeanour. Quite a handful, he guessed. But she didn't allow him time to dwell on that fantasy. 'Wait here for me,' she ordered. Margaret left the door open as she left the room, certain that her order was enough to restrain him from following her or trying to escape.

And she was right, Richard reflected as he sat quietly, the hard sound of Margaret's high-heeled shoes receding into the distance. The room, the hallway, the entire house was unnaturally quiet, as if awaiting the onset of a storm. And yet it was only one woman's displeasure which made the stillness seem ominous. I'm beginning to see how Margaret can make others obey her, Richard thought. Helena's submission, Ingrid's acquiescence, the fear so evident in Marie and Heidi, all made sense to him at that moment as he waited for Margaret to return and pronounce his own doom. He felt the damp patch in his lap cooling against his skin, the scent of his own semen strong in his nostrils.

From time to time there were distant sounds, doors closing, footsteps, and once, startlingly, a woman's scream. Richard wondered if Heidi was being beaten for her part in their encounter. It might not be fair, but Margaret had never said anything about her regime was. He heard more footsteps, approaching. The tapping of high-heeled shoes. Margaret?

Raymond entered the room. Like Richard, he wore the maid's outfit. Richard noticed that his dress had a high neck too, doubtless to conceal the hair on his chest. His wig was dark, like Richard's. Otherwise they were dressed identically. He carried a coil of rope.

'Margaret has ordered me to tie you up while she deals with other matters. She seems rather angry with you,' Raymond said by way of explanation. He indicated the rope he carried.

Richard shrugged resignedly, but asked Raymond where he had been these last few days.

'On one of her errands,' he replied laconically.

Richard got the impression Margaret did not encourage idle talk between her couriers. Keeping the operation secure meant no one being told more than they needed to know. But the policy of secrecy also ensured that no one would learn anything useful from anyone else. And he wanted to know what he was facing in the way of travel and risk, as well as what it was like to be out in public on one's own, disguised as a woman.

He pressed Raymond further. 'Where did you go? And how did you carry the money through customs without being caught?'

Raymond looked over his shoulder in case Margaret, or anyone else, were present. Then he said, 'I went to Basle. To one of the many Swiss banks so renowned for their discretion. The name hardly matters. There are so many of them she uses. I carried the cash in an ordinary suitcase. There is no law against entering Switzerland with large amounts of cash. In fact, I imagine they would like all visitors to come so burdened. I also imagine they would prefer them to leave behind as much of their burden as possible. But it would be awkward to have to open one's suitcase for customs' inspection and let everyone see what you are carrying. Dangerous too, I would say. Large amounts of cash can sway even the most law-abiding citizen to transports of greed. But I imagine she has an arrangement with the customs to ensure the bags are never opened. I was waved through in a very perfunctory fashion.'

Raymond's information sounded reassuring, but, Richard reflected, there was nothing like going through it for real to show what it was like.

But there was no more time for talk. Raymond approached with the rope. 'Madame gave orders for you to get undressed,' he said diffidently.

Again Richard shrugged. He unzipped the dress and laid it over the armchair. Next came the slip, the corselet and the tights. The wig he set carefully on the seat. Then he stood waiting.

'It might be a good idea to go to the toilet before I tie you,' Raymond suggested. 'One never knows how long it will be before another opportunity comes. Madame is quite capable of leaving you here for hours.'

Remembering how he had been left after the whipping, Richard saw the sense in Raymond's suggestion. He went into the toilet and emptied his bladder. He also took a drink of water, just in case. When he came back into the bedroom, he saw that Raymond had cut several lengths of rope from the coil. All was ready.

Richard stood quietly while Raymond tied his hands behind his back. He was surprised when his bound wrists were lifted into the small of his back and tied there with several turns of rope about his waist. At Raymond's direction, he sat on the side of the bed while his ankles and knees were bound together.

'Try to enjoy the anticipation of a visit from Madame,' Raymond said, as he gathered up the rope and made his exit.

Richard sat on the bed where he had been left and wondered what Margaret would do when she returned. It was probably going to be painful, but he had endured the earlier whipping, and he could probably endure this one. In any case there was nothing he could now do to influence the course of events. His thoughts turned to Helena and Ingrid. The memory of the time he had spent with both of them was pleasant. He thought of the earlier whipping, and of the later visit of Heidi and Marie, and he found himself developing an erection.

Margaret walked into the room, startling him. He had not heard her approach. She still wore her high-heeled shoes, so he guessed she had made an effort to walk silently, perhaps to surprise him. She looked at his erection with a sardonic smile. Perhaps that was the point: to let him excite himself in preparation for her return. If so, the ploy was successful.

'Pleasant fantasies, or were you just looking forward to another whipping?' Margaret asked.

The guess was too accurate. He didn't trust himself to speak, so he said nothing.

Margaret carried a leather strap with several small knotted tails. It was obviously a whip, but not of any type Richard had ever seen. He wondered why it appeared to be so light in construction. He doubted that Margaret had had a sudden access of concern for her victim. In her other hand she carried a bag with what looked like a bicycle pump protruding from it. She set her burdens down near the bed and approached Richard. His eyes followed her progress, and he felt another surge of excitement as she came nearer. He responded to the menace in her. His cock reminded him once more of its presence.

Margaret looked at his cock as if judging the extent of his arousal. She must have been gratified that she could have this effect on him merely by being near. She reached out to touch his cock, and smiled as it leapt in her hand. 'You seem to believe the next bit will be enjoyable,' she said. 'And who knows? You may be right. Lots of other people find it so.'

Margaret turned to the bag she had brought with her. She extracted the bicycle pump and a leather harness from it. There was a black rubber bag fastened to the harness on a wide strap. As she began to buckle the harness around his head and neck, the bag hung loosely on its strap. Richard couldn't imagine what its purpose was, until she put the bag into his mouth and fastened the wide strap in place with a buckle behind his head.

This was obviously a gag, but not a very efficient one. He managed to ask, 'What's going on?' despite the obstruction in his mouth. Margaret didn't reply. She simply continued to fix the harness, adjusting the buckles that held it in place. When she was satisfied, she picked up the bicycle pump and screwed a short tube to the hose.

Richard recognised the tube as the type used to inflate footballs, and he realised what was coming next even before Margaret inserted the end in the small hole in the centre of the strap that went around his mouth and held the rubber bag in place.

She began to pump, and Richard felt the rubber bag growing inside his mouth. Margaret continued to pump until the bag filled his entire mouth, trapping his tongue and forcing his jaws open. At first he thought he could bite the rubber any time he wanted, but when he tried he found that his jaws were held open by the air pressure in the bag. Margaret pumped the bag up hard and full, and when Richard next tried to say something, he could only manage a low grunt.

Margaret had never found it necessary to gag him before, and he wondered why she had done so this time. She must have something quite painful in mind if he had to be silenced beforehand. Margaret's expression gave no hint of her purpose, and in any case it was far too late to protest. He could only wait helplessly for her to get on with whatever it was. He felt he was trapped in a dream that was both frightening and terribly exciting.

As it turned out, he didn't have to wait very long. Margaret felt his distended cheeks to satisfy herself that the air pressure was right. Then she pulled the tube from the inflation orifice of his gag and laid the pump on the floor beside the bed. She put her hand against his shoulder, pushing him back until he lost his balance and fell helplessly backward on to the bed, his bound wrists under him. Margaret lifted his legs and manoeuvered his body until he was lying wholly on the bed. She sat down beside him, resuming her manipulation of his cock.

He was helpless to interfere with her handling of him, and he felt his excitement grow as he thought of her complete domination of the situation. He shuddered with pleasure as Margaret lifted his balls from between his legs and cupped them with her free hand.

She stroked his cock until he thought he must come. As if sensing the imminence of his release, Margaret let go of him and sat watching as he struggled to make her go on. Soon it became obvious she had no intention of continuing: she was enjoying his arousal and his inability to do anything about it. His breath was short and rapid, and he felt as if he were burning up. Margaret watched coolly until he showed signs of subsiding. Then she once more grasped his cock and balls and resumed his arousal, stopping once more just short of orgasm.

Richard had read of such teasing, but had never

experienced it – nor had he expected to. It was not the sort of thing the women he had known enjoyed. And until now, he had not known what he had been missing. Margaret was an expert at keeping him forever on the brink, but never going that last little bit that would push him over. He was oblivious of everything except those hands touching and stroking him.

Suddenly Richard felt a stinging pain across his abdomen. He jerked convulsively and opened his eyes. He was just in time to see Margaret raise her arm for another blow. In her hand she held the leather strap with the knotted tails he had noticed earlier. He had forgotten about it after Margaret had begun her expert manipulation. She struck him again, this time directly on his erect penis. He jerked as the pain shot through him, but at the same time he felt a sharp stab of excitement. Margaret continued to lash him, the blows landing on his stomach, his belly and his cock, and as the torture progressed he became more aware of the excitement. His body was translating what should have been pain into the sharpest of sexual sensations. His cock tingled as if he were on the verge of orgasm. This was something he had never suspected about himself. Margaret had uncovered a streak of masochism in him, as she had done in Helena.

Abruptly the blows stopped, and Richard felt lost, excited beyond anything he had ever felt before, and then deprived of the stimulus which had driven him to this pitch. He tugged wildly at his bonds, grunting behind the gag. His back arched as he tried to present his cock to Margaret for more of the sharp pain that he suddenly needed.

She smiled at this demonstration of her power to arouse him so far and then deny him fulfilment, but she was breathing heavily too, and not only from her exertions. Her breasts rose and fell, outlined under her tight-fitting dress, and her face and neck were flushed.

Margaret was staring at his erect cock, swollen and throbbing after being lashed. She tore her eyes away from the sight and looked into his eyes.

Richard saw there her own arousal. He knew that she had been excited by her domination and by the pain she had caused. Ingrid had said that Margaret was frightened of sex, but that wasn't the whole story. This was what it took to arouse her. The power over others was the most powerful of aphrodisiacs to her, Richard now knew. He lay still, holding her gaze, challenging her to go further, to surrender to her own arousal, to use his body for her pleasure. The moment seemed to go on for ever.

Still holding his gaze, Margaret stood slowly and began to remove her dress. She seemed to be in a trance. Her hands moved slowly as she groped behind her back for the zipper to her dress. The sound of the zipper as it purred down her back was loud in the silent room. She stepped out of the dress and let it fall to the floor, then stood before him in her underwear, inviting him to stare at her.

Richard saw a beautiful woman standing beside him, her body outlined by the filmy clothing. He couldn't tear his eyes away as she unclasped her lacy bra and allowed her full, rounded breasts to fall free, rising and falling to her rapid and shallow breathing. The nipples were hard and crinkly with excitement. When she stepped out of her pants, the crisp blonde curls of her pubic mound seemed to be charged with electricity. He heard the static hiss as the pants slid down her legs. Then she stood erect again, clad in nothing save her stockings and suspenders, once again inviting him to stare at her, flaunting herself before him, knowing that he was helpless and that it must be she who did anything, if anything was to be done. She stood so long that Richard began to believe that this was just another demonstration of her dominance, that she would walk away from him, leaving him aroused but helpless.

Margaret broke the tableau, moving to the bed. She knelt on the bed, straddling him, then sinking down until her weight rested on his thighs. Richard felt a thrill as the sheer nylon of her stockings brushed his legs, and the warmth of her flesh touched him. He felt her pubic hair against him like an electric shock. Margaret slowly sank forward, so that she was lying on top of him, her breasts crushed against his chest, the full length of her touching him. The scent of her was in his nostrils, the warm salty smell of her arousal strong in the air. He shifted and felt his cock brush her. He couldn't stop the shudder that passed through it, and him, at the contact.

Margaret pressed herself against him, seeking as much contact as possible, shifting her hips so that her pubic hair touched his cock. She gasped at the touch, her eyes opening wide. A faraway look came across her face, as if she were momentarily in another world. Then her look changed, and she smiled down into Richard's eyes.

She rolled off him and turned on the bed so that they lay head to foot. This time when she straddled him, her cunt was raised above his face. He could see the warm pink of her labia hidden between her legs, smell her musk. He groaned behind the gag, wanting to be able to caress that secret place with his lips and tongue, to taste her arousal in his mouth. Margaret raised herself until she could sit down over his mouth. She moved until her cunt was directly over the hard rubber inflation valve, then lowered her body until she could rub her cunt against it. At the same time she took his cock in her mouth.

Richard groaned helplessly as he felt himself surrounded by the heat of her mouth, the slickness of her tongue, the sudden sharpness of her teeth as she first caressed him and then nipped him warningly as he writhed on the bed. He lay still.

Margaret continued to rub her cunt against his gag,

becoming more excited by the moment. Richard could see her labia and the pink flesh between her cunt lips. The smell of her was strong in his nostrils, exciting him even more. It was almost impossible to hold still, but he dared not move. He wished he could at least use his teeth and tongue to arouse Margaret to the point where she could not hold out any longer. He wondered what she would do in that case, whether she could resist her own urges. Or would want to.

Abruptly Margaret broke the impasse herself. With a loud moan she tore herself away and stood up beside the bed, looking down at Richard with agitation. Her eyes were narrowed and her cheeks flushed. Her breasts rose and fell with her breathing, the nipples erect and crinkly with excitement. She appeared to hesitate, as if deciding whether to throw herself over the brink. Richard looked up at her, wanting her, feeling still her mouth, her teeth and tongue on him, but he managed to keep his glance neutral, knowing that he had to let her make the decision, let her see him waiting helplessly for her to come to him. The sight of her arousal sent a powerful message to his cock, which stood erect and seemed to throb with a life of its own.

She decided with characteristic suddenness. She climbed once more on to the bed, this time facing him, straddling his legs as she reached for his cock. Still, at the last moment, she hesitated, as if afraid to carry out her decision, then she settled down against him, guiding him inside her.

Richard held still, although the sensation of being engulfed in the liquid fire of her cunt was well-nigh overwhelming. He clamped down, holding himself back from orgasm by sheer willpower. He knew Margaret would be displeased – to say the least – if, after agonising over her choice, he were to deprive her of the full enjoyment of it. And he knew that it would be an error to let her see that he knew she was surrendering, behaving like any other woman on heat. He didn't want her to break off for his own reasons as well. He wanted her too, even if he could not reach out to touch her breasts, kiss them, pull her down and fuck her.

But Margaret was nothing if not aware of the situation. She lay atop him, her breasts crushed against his chest, rubbing them against him as she aroused herself further. She clamped down on his cock, and he gasped as he felt her strength. Margaret moaned again, closing her eyes as if to blot out what she was doing, to deny her enjoyment of sex as she had been doing all along. Then she began to move, raising her hips and arching her back as she rose and fell above him, riding him, fucking him as he wanted to fuck her but was prevented from doing by his bonds.

Margaret came abruptly, the cry of pleasure seeming to be torn from somewhere deep inside her. Richard, restraining himself from his own orgasm, was studying her face, concentrating on her reactions as a way to control his own. Her saw her face go slack as her orgasm swept through her, her head thrown back as she rode the wave of her pleasure. Then, curiously, a spasm of anger crossed her face, and she flushed with something like embarrassment, having been seen to lose control. To him it seemed that she was still fighting her body's needs.

The moment, and the look, passed. Margaret appeared to make up her mind to go on, having gone this far already. Or maybe she simply didn't want to appear indecisive or weak in his eyes. Or she might just be enjoying his body, enjoying his helplessness and her dominance. Richard thought fleetingly that it might please her if he too appeared to be lost in the experience of sex with his mistress. Not that he would have to pretend very hard. So the question became, how long should he hold out? He didn't want to end this too soon. He was enjoying her too much. And he knew that he dared not show greater restraint than she could, now that she had come this far. She would be angry – embarrassed – and the consequences of that might be painful. But most of all, he didn't want to offend her in her most vulnerable moment. He wanted her to enjoy the experience as much as possible. And, of course, he wanted to enjoy it too.

Margaret, meanwhile, seemed to be having no such complicated thoughts. She was having, instead, a long series of orgasms, moaning and thrashing above him, grinding her hips against him as if she would pound him into the mattress. Richard, seeing her excitement, lost control of his own body, so that he spurted inside her, emptying himself into her as Margaret cried out in her own release, her scream loud in the room. She shuddered as he did, then abruptly relaxed, lying slackly on top of him as if drained of all strength.

She lay for a long time, so long that Richard thought she might have been sleeping. He took that as a sign of her satisfaction and, indeed, of some sort of trust. She had let him see her at the moment when she lost control of herself, so Richard felt as if they had shared something much more intimate than the mere joining of their bodies. But he would never be able to mention it to her. She would not like to be reminded of her surrender. He knew he would have to keep this secret for her. He was strongly attracted to Margaret, had been since the first time she ordered him to be restrained at Helena's apartment, and he didn't want to do anything to cause her to lose face before others, as she would if he betrayed this moment. If his hands had not been tied behind his back, he would have put his arms around her and held her close.

But if his hands had not been tied, would she have surrendered herself to him? Probably not, he thought. Probably her pleasure had come partially from knowing that even when she was most vulnerable, he was unable to exert any control over her, or even touch her body with his hands. This was her way of maintaining control over him. And Richard knew that his reaction to her had been heightened by this very helplessness to influence events.

He knew that when she recovered, Margaret would resume her role as mistress, and he would be under her control as before. He would be made to put on the maid's outfit, the tights and the corselet once more. And he would once more be her servant, subject to her whims, her whip and her unpredictable moods. She might even be more severe than she had been, attempting to re-establish her position of dominance. And he would be excited as before by being made to wear women's clothing, the tight garments reminding him of his position and the whip letting him know who was in control. But they would both remember this moment as well, and things would never be exactly the same between them.

Margaret stirred and opened her eyes, looking straight into Richard's face and seeing there a mirror of her own sexual release. She raised herself on her arms and looked down on him, as if to impress upon him the necessity of keeping silent. Richard nodded, unable to give any verbal reply, and she looked relieved. She stood up, still looking at him. Silently, she began to dress, once more covering the body he would have liked to touch. But the message was clear: she was in control, he was the servant again. Margaret finished dressing and gathered the rest of her belongings: the whip, the bicycle pump, the remainder of the rope. She turned without a word and walked into the hall, shutting the door behind her and leaving Richard bound and gagged on the bed they had shared.

He lay still as the sound of her footsteps faded and died away. The aroma of her perfume and the smell of her musk clung to his body. The air was cool on the damp patches, reminding him of the heat of her as she lay on top of him and rode him so relentlessly. He felt regret that it was over, but nothing was for ever. And he knew that there would be other times. But for now, he could only lie and wait for the next development. It was hours before Margaret relented and sent Marie to untie him.

Six

Richard did not see Margaret again for several days. He wondered if she was avoiding him, not willing to face him after their shared intimacy. He thought that would be a pity, but at the same time he realised that a complete relaxation of her aloofness would remove some of the mystery, and a good deal of the authority, which made the exercise of discipline so exciting to him. Of course, it was also possible that she was busy with her consultancy, meeting her mysterious clients and helping them to handle their affairs. And earning the considerable sums which made it possible for her to operate the training establishment of which he was a part.

But Margaret out of sight was not necessarily Margaret out of mind. Three days after their encounter, several packages arrived for him. Going to his room after lunch, he found them on his bed. Inside he found more dresses, of the type more suitable for public wear. From that he inferred that the time for his first errand in Margaret's courier service (which he had privately dubbed cash-and-carry) was drawing near. Margaret, he guessed, thought him ready to appear in public. Hence the new wardrobe. He was much less sure of that himself, but at the same time he knew that he would have to face it at some time.

The second package contained more underwear for

him: slips, tights and corselets similar to those chosen for him by Ingrid from her shop in Soltau. There was also a note from her. She said that she was keeping busy but thinking of him fondly. She would, she said, be on the lookout for a way to have him visit her again soon. Her note said nothing of Helena, which was a relief. Helena had said that Ingrid didn't mind sharing him with her stepdaughter, but it was a relief to have confirmation from Ingrid herself. Jealousy could lead to unwanted complications.

Ingrid told him to examine the alterations she had made to the tights and corselets on Margaret's instructions. 'The purpose of the alterations to the crotch area will become clear when Margaret returns,' Ingrid had written. Richard didn't know if Ingrid was genuinely ignorant or simply being mystifying. He looked at the corselets and saw that a small hole had been made in the gusset, the edges neatly stitched. He saw the hand of Ingrid the dressmaker in the work. The gussets of the tights had been similarly pierced, the holes here being surrounded by small patches of thin leather, glued to both sides of the material with fabric glue. The holes in both garments had been made to coincide with one another, but Richard had no idea what Margaret might have had in mind when she ordered these alterations. It was typical of her, though, to keep him wondering what she might do next.

Richard laid aside the altered garments and opened the third package. It contained several pairs of shoes in various styles, their only common features being the stiletto heels and the ankle straps. Richard guessed that the former were to keep him on his toes, while the latter were intended to keep him in the shoes in case he stumbled.

Ingrid's note continued, 'Margaret has given me the impression that she will be bringing you to the shop soon, for further instruction, I presume. I am looking forward to that. I have in mind some further instruction she might not have thought of. Hope to see you soon.' It was signed, 'Love and kisses, Ingrid.' The closing sounded almost girlish. Richard wondered if Ingrid was beginning to trust his repeated assertions that age didn't matter to him. 'P.S.,' she had written, 'I know you can't reply to this – house rules. But think of me until we meet.'

Yes. He would. In the meantime, he would put the new wardrobe away and wait to see what plans Margaret had made for him. He wondered, too, if she would be jealous or angry if she learnt of his liaisons with Ingrid and Helena. Best to keep silent, he concluded.

There was also the matter of helping Helena get free of Margaret's hold over her. It might be more difficult to keep that promise now, after what he and Margaret had shared, but he had made a promise to help find the evidence Margaret had hidden somewhere in the house. What better time than now, when he was least likely to be caught by the keeper of all the secrets? Helena would then be free to go her own way, back to England with him. He had imagined taking her back to the lonely old house where he had lived for so many years. So – to work, to make it all happen.

Since Marie had revealed the location of the safe, Richard had checked the information. The loose stones he had spotted in the dining-room hearth had, on closer examination, confirmed it. The mortar was not so even as it was around the other stones. If Margaret hadn't almost caught him trying to examine the stones the first time, he might have found what he was seeking then. He would take the opportunity afforded by her absence to complete the task now. He only had to think of a way to separate the cook and the keys.

Originally he had planned to slip a drug into her brandy one evening so that she would sleep while he searched. But there had been several problems with that plan. For one thing, he had no access to anything resembling a sleeping draught. Maybe in time Ingrid could help with that, but even then he had no experience of drugging anyone. In movies and novels it was always easy, a matter of slipping something into the victim's drink and waiting for it to take effect. Afterwards, they always recovered without any ill effects. But he was no doctor. How much should he use to ensure results without administering a lethal dose?

In the end, the solution had come to him in a sudden flash. While cleaning the dining room, he had seen several bottles of brandy and vodka in the drinks cabinet, along with practically every other kind of drink anyone could want. Margaret must have been keeping it all to entertain clients. Richard simply chose two half-empty bottles, one of brandy and one of vodka. Mixing the vodka with the brandy had nearly doubled the alcohol content of the latter. He need only make sure the cook got the right bottle at the right time. She might wake up with an awful headache in the morning, but people seldom died of hangovers, even if they thought they would.

He took the bottle to the kitchen and substituted it for the cook's brandy bottle, which he knew was kept in a cupboard over the refrigerator. He had nothing against the cook, an attractive woman of about thirty whose only fault, from Richard's viewpoint, was an overzealous attention to her responsibilities as Margaret's deputy warder. This evening, he decided, would be a good time. It was necessary that he avoid being locked into his room. Joining the cook for a drink or two would solve that problem, so long as he managed to get the cook drunk while remaining sober himself.

While substituting brandy bottles, Richard took the opportunity to locate a lump of beeswax which was kept in the kitchen among the cleaning materials. The wax was used to give a soft, polished effect to the furniture that Margaret liked. He had used it himself in his domestic chores. Now it would serve a different purpose.

That evening, Richard volunteered to do the washing-up and to help tidy the kitchen for the evening. Ludmilla, the cook and housekeeper, was glad of the help. It was only a short step to suggesting that they share a drink when they were done. Luck is with me, Richard thought, as they sat down and Ludmilla poured from the doctored bottle of brandy. He hoped that she would not notice the difference, and that he could keep from drinking too much. Accordingly he sipped his drink, while Ludmilla drank more normally.

Richard asked her about her family and background. It was one way to keep her from noticing that he wasn't keeping up with the drinking. It turned out that she was the daughter of an East German woman and a Russian army major who had insisted on naming her after his mother. He was posted back to Moscow and wasn't allowed to take them back with him. The Red Army, Ludmilla said, could be as prudish as any other bureaucracy when it chose to be. So she and her mother had been left alone in Leipzig. Her father had sent money and helped to educate her and support her mother, but that had stopped when he was posted to Afghanistan and was subsequently listed as missing in action. His last letter had contained a large sum of money, almost, Ludmilla said, as if he knew he would not come back. In the same letter he had given them the name of someone in West Germany who could help them escape if they wished.

Her mother had elected to stay, but had contacted the person named in the letter about getting her daughter out. The contact had been Margaret Wagner, and she had got the young Ludmilla across the Berlin Wall and had taken her into her own service. But, she added, it was a bit ironic that it was only a few years later that the Berlin Wall had been converted into rubble.

'If I had waited,' Ludmilla said, 'I could have simply walked over to the West.' Nevertheless, she was grateful to Margaret for the risks she had taken, and loyal to her.

Richard watched as Ludmilla drank the doctored brandy, sipping carefully but nevertheless feeling the first effects himself. Ludmilla's eyes became heavier by the minute, and presently she said she would have to go to bed. She didn't know what had got into her, she said: she was not usually this sleepy at this time of the evening. When she got up, she almost fell. Richard caught her and helped her to stand, and then to walk along the corridor to her room, finding the going difficult in the high-heeled shoes and with the effects of what he had drunk.

Ludmilla became more and more of a weight, until in the end Richard was nearly carrying her. He got her to her room and on to her bed, removing her shoes and loosening her clothes as she passed out. The key he sought was, he remembered, on a chain around her neck. He carefully slipped it off and left the room, the gentle snores of the sleeping woman a reassurance that she was *hors de combat*.

Richard walked openly to the dining room, knowing that he stood a better chance that way than if he was seen behaving suspiciously. At the same time, he wished his high-heeled shoes didn't make such a clatter on the stone floor. But he was not seen. He closed the door before turning on any lights. He felt naked and exposed with the lights on, but he needed to see what he was doing. The whipping frame reminded him of the penalty for being caught.

He went straight to the fireplace and located the loose stone he had noticed before. But he couldn't get it out of its place. Obviously some sort of tool was needed.

The only thing to hand was a knife from the sideboard. It was made of silver, quite soft, and it bent as he levered the stone out. He laid the stone on the hearth and stopped to straighten out the knife as best he could before replacing it in the sideboard, hoping no one would notice the damage. Then he peered into the hole left by the stone. The safe was there. It required only a moment to fit the key into the lock. The lock was stiff and heavy, but it turned.

Inside the safe was a bundle of papers and several small boxes. Richard took the papers first. Spreading them on the table, he saw that they were mainly records of cash transfers and deliveries, made on behalf of several dozen clients. The amounts were staggering. He wondered what commission Margaret took. These records easily explained her affluence and her commanding manner.

Among the papers was a smaller envelope with the marks of the German State Prosecutor's office on it. This turned out to be the evidence against Helena. He had found what he wanted, but how to get it out of the house and into her hands was not so obvious. A sound outside the house startled him. It sounded as if someone were knocking on the French windows that led to the patio. He froze, listening. The sound came again, now softer, now louder. Branches knocking against the glass, he thought, still not believing it.

But when no challenge came, he breathed again and began to think. The papers would have to stay here until he could get them out of the house. He had no idea when that might be. But at least he knew where to look when the chance came. The key would have to go back to the cook, but he used the beeswax from the kitchen to make a clear impression of it.

The making of the impression reminded him of his promise to find the keys to Heidi's chastity belt. The odds were that they were also in the safe. He removed the boxes one by one, opening them in turn to reveal bundles of currency: Swiss francs, Austrian schillings, Deutschmarks, US dollars, British pounds, and others he could not identify. There was a lot of cash lying there. He itched to take some of it, but that would be a mistake. The last box contained several keys, which must be the ones he sought. Hurriedly he made wax impressions of them before replacing everything as he had found it. With a sigh of relief, he closed the door and locked it. The stone went back into place, and he dusted away the traces of his burglary as best he could.

Heidi was standing just outside the door as he opened it to make his escape. Richard was so startled he almost dropped the wax impression he was carrying. He had not seen her since they were caught in the act several days ago. She took his arm and led him back towards the kitchen, where the bottle of brandy and the glasses still stood on the table.

Indicating them, Heidi asked, 'Did you find the safe and take the keys?'

Richard wanted to caution her to speak softly, but there seemed to be no one else about this evening. The big house was quiet. He replied, 'Not exactly. I got a wax impression of them.' He held it up for her to see. 'Do you know anyone who could make keys from this?'

Heidi said, 'No, but why don't you ask Ingrid? She knows nearly everyone in the village, and she will do almost anything for you.'

Was there a touch of jealousy there? It was hardly warranted, Richard thought. He would have liked to release Heidi there and then, but there was no way to explain the absence of the keys. He explained that their lovemaking would have to wait until he could get his own set of keys. Heidi was not pleased, but she nodded as she saw the sense in this course of action.

To change the subject, Richard asked her what had happened to her after Margaret had caught them.

'Come to my room, and we can talk,' she told him.

'First let me get the key back to the cook. She may wake up at any time.'

They walked to the cook's room, and Heidi waited in the hall while he replaced the key where he had found it. Ludmilla stirred but didn't waken, and he left the room quietly.

Heidi's room was much like Richard's, no more than a bedsitting room with an *en suite* toilet. The door could be locked as his could, but for some reason Heidi was not locked in this evening. Or at any rate not yet. Perhaps she was considered secure enough so long as she was wearing her chastity belt.

Richard sat on the sofa, and Heidi took the armchair opposite. She sat carefully, as if there were parts of her that hurt.

'Of course, Margaret was not pleased,' she began. 'She ordered me to bring the rope and two gags, so I could guess pretty well what she was going to do to both of us. She took me into the dining room. Raymond came past, and she made him tie me to the whipping frame and gag me. Then she beat me. She seemed very angry, angrier than I have ever seen her. It hurt.' Heidi grimaced in remembrance, but then she smiled. 'But it was worth it. I can hardly wait until you can get the key to unlock me. Then we can have some more fun.'

Richard was glad that she seemed undaunted by what had happened. He felt less guilty for having been partly the cause.

Heidi continued, 'When she had beaten me, she had Raymond untie me. I thought she was finished with me, but I was wrong. She made him tie my hands again, this time behind my back. I know he was excited by what he was doing. I managed to brush his cock with my hands as he was tying them. I felt his erection. But there was nothing we could do about it. Margaret marched me to my room and had him tie my feet together. They left me on my bed and locked the door. I must have lain there for hours. I had to go to the toilet, but no one came. In the end I had to piss myself. And then lie in that for another eternity. When Raymond finally came to let me go, I was a smelly mess.'

She wrinkled her nose in disgust, but once again didn't seem to mind so much what they had done to her.

Richard took a long shot. 'And did Raymond and you have fun when he came for you?'

Heidi reddened slightly, but nodded, smiling again. Richard knew she had come to no serious harm.

'What did Margaret do to you?' Heidi asked. Richard gave her an edited version of what had happened, leaving out Margaret's sexual activities with him. He was sparing both Margaret's and Heidi's feelings, he told himself, not altogether convincingly.

He stood up. 'Do you know if Margaret is coming back soon?' he asked.

'Tomorrow,' she said.

'Then I suppose we had all better get some rest,' he said.

They kissed goodnight, and Richard went to his room.

Seven

The sound of his door opening woke Richard in the morning. At first he thought it might be Margaret coming to him, but it was only Marie. 'Madame wishes to see you as soon as you are dressed,' she told him. 'She is in the drawing room.' When he nodded, she turned and left the room, the chain of her leg-irons clinking softly.

Richard showered and dressed quickly. Margaret would not like to be kept waiting. He heard two women's voices from the drawing room as he approached. He recognised Margaret's at once. The other voice belonged to Helena. Pushing down feelings of awkwardness and embarrassment, Richard entered the room.

Helena looked bewildered and embarrassed, and she made an abortive move towards him, but quickly stopped when Margaret glared at her.

He could see that she wanted to speak to him, perhaps to apologise for getting him into this bizarre situation, but she bowed to Margaret's wishes once again. At the same time, he saw that she was in the grip of what could only be sexual excitement. All the signs were there: the flushed face, the short, rapid breathing, the abstraction. Her gaze strayed from him to the mantel shelf where the black cloth bag containing her whip lay. He understood her agitation.

Margaret broke the silence, smiling crookedly. 'Richard, we are going to entertain Helena in a few moments. I hope you'll enjoy it as well. I always try to make everyone happy. It's the secret of my success.' To Helena she said, 'Bring the whip and come with me.' She moved towards the door.

Helena moved unsteadily towards the fireplace, where she picked up the black bag with a hand that trembled slightly. She turned back to face Margaret and Richard, the excitement plain on her face. If he had had any intention of protesting, it died as he saw her eagerness. If she was that avid for pain, there was no point in trying to dissuade her. And he felt a stirring of excitement in himself, his cock stiffening inside the tight corselet. Margaret caught his eye and smiled when she saw his excitement. She had counted on it, he saw.

They followed as she led the way down the hall and into the dining room, with Helena carrying The Discipline. Richard glanced at the hearth. There was no sign of the previous night's reconnaissance. But there was no time to feel relief. He saw a coil of rope and a pair of handcuffs on the long, polished table. He felt his cock stir as he saw the instruments of their bondage. And something else: a shiny stainless-steel ring, too small to fit a wrist, too large to fit a finger. There was a length of machine chain and a padlock as well. Margaret smiled as she saw his surprised glance.

Helena laid the whip on the table and went to stand beside the frame. She was breathing in short, rapid gulps, as if she had run a race. She made no move to escape. Margaret seemed to dominate everything in the room. Richard knew he would not make any attempt to escape either. Even if he had been wearing his own clothes, the magnetism of the situation would have held him.

Margaret picked up the ring and beckoned him to her side. He came, mesmerised, while Margaret stared challengingly into his eyes.

'Take off your clothes,' she ordered.

Richard undid the long back zipper of the maid's outfit. He was getting quite good at it, he reflected. He stepped out of the dress, laying it on one of the chairs at the table. Standing before the two women in his underwear, he felt a flush of embarrassment, but he never considered disobeying Margaret. The slip followed. He undid the straps of his high-heeled shoes and stepped out of them. The carpet felt soft and smooth under his feet.

Once again he hesitated, standing in the corselet and tights. This time he looked at Helena. She was flushed with her own excitement, but she saw his hesitation. She gave him a small, tight smile of encouragement, and a small nod.

Richard stripped off the tight garment and dark tights. The wig he placed carefully on the table. Then he looked at Margaret. She returned his gaze steadily, appraisingly, amused at his discomfiture. His cock was stiff and his stomach muscles tight.

'I brought you a present,' she told him, holding the small steel ring in her hand.

Richard could now see that the ring was hinged, opening into two halves. On the side opposite the hinge, two flanges had been welded. A hole had been drilled into each of them.

Margaret knelt before him and grasped his balls, briefly squeezing him before she fitted the ring around the base of his scrotum. It fitted snugly. Margaret closed it, taking the chain and the padlock from the table. Richard couldn't see exactly what she was doing, but he could guess the intent. He remembered the nylon cable tie she had fitted to his scrotum at their first encounter in Hamburg. This seemed to be a more permanent version of the same thing. And indeed it was. He heard the padlock click as it was closed, and felt the sudden weight on his balls as Margaret released the chain to hang between his legs.

She turned to Helena, who was watching intently as she awaited what she had come for. 'Now it's your turn,' Margaret said. 'Take off your clothes. It is impolite to be clothed while Richard is naked.'

Helena began to undress. Her excitement was betrayed by the slight tremor of her hands as she took off her dress and laid it aside. Unlike Richard, she wore no slip, only a bra and pants. She unsnapped the bra, allowing her full breasts to swing free. The nipples were taut and crinkly, and she was slightly flushed, whether with desire or embarrassment it was impossible to say. Still silently, she hooked her thumbs under the waistband of her pants and slid them down and off her long legs. Then she too stood naked before her aunt.

Helena straightened her back, her breasts standing proud. She looked at Margaret almost with defiance. Richard thought she looked magnificent. Even after his bizarre erotic encounter with the aunt, he preferred the niece.

Margaret glanced at the two of them, not unaware of the electricity between them. A frown, almost a spasm of anger, crossed her own beautiful face. She concealed it quickly, but not quickly enough. Richard knew she was displeased by his attraction to Helena. So it might go hard with her, and with him.

Margaret picked up the handcuffs. As before, he stood unresisting while she handcuffed his wrists behind his back. He felt a momentary disappointment at not having been asked to tie Helena to the whipping frame, or to wield the whip. This time he was not surprised by his reaction. He could feel his excitement growing as the drama unfolded.

Margaret stood before him and ran her hand over his cock. He gasped and almost fell. When she felt his excitement, Margaret smiled at him as she continued the caress he was helpless to resist. She was going to take him to the brink of orgasm and stop, as she had done several days ago. But this time, with Helena present, she would probably not mount him as she had done then. Or maybe she would, to let Helena know that she could master him and drive him wild. Richard clenched his jaws as she rubbed and fondled him. When he glanced at Helena, he saw a mingling of concern for him and a suppressed excitement as she waited for the whipping which would drive her to the brink – and over.

Margaret's hand on his cock, soft, warm, insistent, claimed his attention once more. He couldn't help his reaction. What man could, he asked himself. He looked down at Margaret as she continued to kneel before him, and flexed his wrists inside the steel bands, wanting to run his hands over her body, make her react to his touch on her flesh. She seemed more desirable clothed as she was, while he was naked and helpless. Her skirt had ridden up her thighs, revealing her full legs beneath the smooth, shiny blue tights she wore. Her dress fitted her tightly, moulding her full figure and sweeping low in front to reveal the tops of her breasts as he looked down.

Margaret looked up and saw him staring. She smiled secretly at him and squeezed his cock, fully conscious of her power and desirability, and of the effect both were having on him.

Richard felt his knees go weak at her touch. He swayed slightly and regained his balance. Helena watched, excited and eager. Richard didn't know if she was aroused by what was to come to her, or if she wanted to exercise her own power over him in Margaret's place.

Margaret let go of his cock and grasped the chain hanging between his legs. With a sharp tug, she led him over to the whipping frame. There was a ring on the back of the frame, Richard saw. It had not been there before. She fastened his chain to the ring with a second padlock, leaving him tethered as she had in Helena's apartment.

Helena watched as he was secured, flushed and excited still. Margaret turned to Helena and ordered her to bring the rope from the table. She walked unsteadily across the carpet, her breasts swaying slightly as she moved. She came back with the rope and stood waiting for Margaret to make the next move.

Margaret took the rope and tied Helena's wrists together in front of her. She looped the rope over the top of the frame and pulled it taut, dragging Helena's arms over her head and forcing her to move over until she stood under the frame. Margaret pulled the rope tighter, stretching the younger woman's arms above her head. She tied the rope off, and Helena was left standing before Richard.

She looked very appealing and vulnerable, strung up and helpless. Richard, of course, could only look at her, which was exactly what Margaret intended. Her favourite 'look but don't touch' rule was in effect. Margaret gave a small nod of satisfaction as she turned away to get the whip from its black cloth bag. The Discipline had a medieval look of suffering to it. There was a wooden handle a little over a foot long with twelve knotted thongs of cord fastened to it. One for each of the twelve apostles, Margaret had said, in the days when the nuns used it to flagellate themselves in penance.

Helena looked over her shoulder to where her aunt held the instrument of her own, somewhat less devout, chastisement. When she looked back at Richard, she mouthed, 'Don't worry.' Then she closed her eyes and bowed her head, waiting for the beating to begin. She was breathing raggedly, and her body was tense with anticipation.

Margaret drew back her arm, but before she struck her niece she, too, looked at Richard. Her own anticipation was clear in her look. She nodded to him, as if to say, 'Watch, and learn about this girl you are involved with.' There was also a flash of malevolence in her look, as if she was determined to punish both of them for becoming interested in one another, to the exclusion of herself.

The blow fell: the hiss of the thongs through the air, and the crack as they struck Helena's back were loud in the silent room. Helena jerked at the impact, the air rushing from her lungs. Her lips were pressed tightly together to prevent any sound from escaping her. Richard was struck by the similarity between her reaction to being beaten by Margaret and his own. They both strove for silence. In his case, the reason was to deny Margaret the knowledge that she could hurt him seriously: a macho response, he knew, but also important for his own self-esteem. Were Helena's motives the same?

Margaret drew back her arm and struck her niece again. Helena's body jerked once more, and Richard saw the tips of the thongs as they curled around into her right armpit, nearly touching her taut breast. Margaret had only to change her stance slightly to make the next blow reach that sensitive area. When he had seen Helena's stripes after her last beating, Richard had noticed that she had been beaten only on her back and bottom. Would Margaret confine herself to the same area this time? She looked angry enough to lash out at anything. Richard felt his stomach muscles tighten as he imagined those thongs landing on Helena's breasts and belly.

The beating went on for what seemed a long time to Richard, and Helena began to cry out as it continued. He wondered what it seemed like to Helena, but she showed no sign of wanting it to stop. Richard wondered how she managed to transform the pain into pleasure as she was so obviously doing. Margaret supplied the answer. Abruptly, she stopped lashing her niece's back and bottom and thrust the whip handle between her legs and into her. Helena gasped at the invasion, and then began to moan with pleasure as Margaret thrust the handle in and out. Helena began to rock her hips, riding with the thrust of the handle in her cunt, her head thrown back and her eyes closed as she savoured the sensation of mixed pain and ecstasy.

Her breasts were suffused with blood, the nipples engorged and crinkly. 'Ohhhh!' she cried, and again 'Ohhhh!' Her cries were long-drawn-out and shuddery as her body was racked with the orgasm. Her bound hands, high in the air above her head, twisted and tugged against the ropes that held her. Her knees buckled as she lost control, thrashing and jerking in her release, the whole weight of her shuddering body suspended from her wrists. If Helena felt any pain, she certainly gave no sign of it now.

Richard felt a tiny stab of jealousy as he saw the depth of her arousal. Even when they had had the time to pleasure one another, he didn't believe that Helena had enjoyed his lovemaking nearly as much as she was enjoying what her aunt was doing to her now with the whip. At the same time he was excited, watching Helena come and imagining what it would be like to be in Margaret's place, wielding the whip, his power over the girl's body absolute as he drove her wild with pleasure. He knew in that moment he could do it. Would do it, if he and Helena decided to become lovers on a more permanent basis. And he knew that they would, that his turn would come. His cock was stiff with the knowledge and the anticipation.

At last it was over. Margaret withdrew the handle from Helena's cunt and let the instrument fall to the floor. Richard, looking up at her, saw her own agitation in the flushed face and heaving breasts. He wondered then how she would react to a touch of the lash she wielded over others, whether she too could transform the pain to sexual ecstasy. And he imagined as well how it would feel for him to be the one to show her the way of pain she had shown to him and to those many others. I could get a real taste for this, he told himself.

Helena still hung from her bound wrists, flushed like her aunt, her breasts heaving as were those of the older woman, but with much more cause. She appeared to be exhausted by the fury of her release. She looked incredibly desirable to Richard, so that he wanted to close the distance between them and fuck her. The desire for her was almost strong enough to overcome his caution, but at the last moment he realised how Margaret would react. He was in no position to provoke her anger – not that he could reach Helena in any case.

Margaret recovered her breath and some of her usual poise, looking from her niece to Richard as if daring either of them to say anything. At last she spoke, breaking the silence that filled the room. 'You see, Richard, how our little Helena loves her rather twisted version of sex. Do you find her so attractive now?'

Richard didn't venture to answer the question, and luckily, Margaret herself seemed to regard it as rhetorical. She turned and stalked from the room, leaving the two of them to make what they could of the privacy. As soon as she had gone, closing the door behind her, Richard asked Helena if she was all right.

At first she didn't answer, and he was alarmed. He moved towards her, but was brought up short by the tether around his balls. Nor could he touch her, with his hands held behind his back. But at last Helena looked up, opening her eyes and looking back at him. She struggled to get her feet under her once more and relieve the strain on her bound wrists. She was breathing more or less normally too, he saw with relief.

'There's no need to worry,' she said huskily. 'I've done this many times before, and it has done me no harm. Rather, it has given me a great deal of pleasure. You must have seen how I reacted to being beaten and to . . . afterwards.' Helena flushed slightly but didn't look away, as if gauging his reaction. After a pause, she asked the question that set his heart hammering. 'Would you do that to me – what Margaret did?'

'Yes, if that's what you want,' he replied. And he continued, as hesitantly as she, with a question of his own. 'And would you do to me what Margaret has been doing?' He nodded across the room to where the maid's outfit he had taken off lay on the chair.

Helena replied, 'Yes, if that is what you want.'

'A marriage made in heaven,' Richard said with a smile. 'We will have to look after one another. No more hesitation or shame between us. OK?'

Helena nodded, smiling. 'OK. If I could reach you, I would kiss you,' she said.

'If I could reach you, I'd do more than kiss you,' Richard said. 'But are you sure you're all right? For a few moments it looked as if you were having a heart attack. I was worried.'

'Not a heart attack. An attack of lust,' Helena told him. 'We will do it again soon. It's the kind of thing more people should do. And,' she added, nodding at his erection with a smile, 'are you sure it was just worry?'

'Touché,' he said, with a smile.

'Would you like to?' she asked. 'Touch me? Have me, I mean?'

Richard nodded but indicated his difficulties.

'I think I can just about reach you,' Helena said. 'Come as close as you can.'

Richard moved until he was brought up by the chain around his balls.

She moved towards him, stretching her arms and arching her back, and she was right. They could touch. His cock was against her belly, and he could feel the silkiness of her pubic hair as he rubbed himself against her.

'I think we can do even better than that,' Helena said with a wide smile.

She lifted herself by her bound wrists and raised her legs, bringing them around Richard's waist and crossing her ankles behind his back. Her heels dug into him as she pulled herself tightly to him. She wriggled against him until he felt himself slide into her. She was wet and parted from her earlier orgasms, and he felt as if he were dipping himself into liquid fire.

Helena began to thrust against him, raising and lowering herself with her arms while holding them together with her legs. At the same time, she used her leg muscles to pull them together and then allow them to separate as far as possible, never quite losing him as they moved apart, and allowing the delicious slide into her to happen again and again as they moved together.

It was the first time he had ever made love to a woman when neither of them could use their hands. And the sensation was something he had never experienced, not even when Margaret had ridden him. She had been able to use her hands, and she had. This time there was no touch except that of his cock inside Helena's cunt, and it was if all sensation had been concentrated at that point. Hands would have been superfluous.

Helena worked single-mindedly to bring him to climax, thrusting rapidly. Richard could do nothing to arouse her except try to move his cock so that it contacted her clitoris, but he had no way to be sure he was succeeding. Helena's acrobatic gyrations made her breathless, and he could see her nipples were erect. But then he couldn't hold back any longer. He shuddered and came, jerking his hips with his own release.

Helena responded by going suddenly still, holding him deep inside her as he spent himself in great shudders. She was looking closely at him, watching as his climax took him, so her own took her by surprise. 'Ohhhhh!' she said, half wonderingly, her eyes opening wide. Then 'ahhhhhh, ahhhhh God, ahhhhhh,' as she was swept away on her own tide of pleasure.

Watching Helena as she lost herself, Richard was glad she had been able to come with him after her intense orgasms earlier. He wanted to hold her against him as she shuddered. He could feel her vaginal muscles clenching tightly around his cock, warm and wet. And all at once he felt relieved, less jealous, now that she had shown her response to him so unequivocally.

Helena clearly knew nothing of his feelings as she held herself against him. She was lost to everything except the spasms that were rocking her. When at last she subsided, she opened her eyes, and he saw there the light of her happiness and fulfilment. Not many men, he thought, get to see that. Sometimes it is lost in the dark. Sometimes it is ignored. Most often it just isn't there. He thought himself very lucky.

Helena held herself against him for a long time, telling him without words that she was glad to be there, even in these bizarre circumstances. Finally she uncrossed her ankles and lowered her legs to the floor, grimacing as she took the weight off her bound wrists. Richard saw that her body was covered with a faint flush still, and she smiled happily at him.

'It would be nice to be able to lie down with you now,' she said. 'But at least we can talk. And look at one another,' she added.

'What shall we talk about?' Richard asked, grinning. 'Shoes and ships and sealing wax somehow seem less than appropriate.'

Helena frowned in perplexity. 'Why should we talk of those things?'

'Never mind,' Richard replied. 'There's always slaves and sex and mistresses. You know, people like us, and your aunt Margaret.'

'Yes,' Helena said seriously. Then she smiled. 'Oh Richard, stop teasing me.'

'I wasn't teasing,' he said. 'I suppose we need to talk about what to do, both now and in the not-too-distant future. We'll have to get away from here – get away from Margaret's domination, I mean, exciting as that sometimes can be.' He paused, then went on suddenly in a rush, saying the words because he knew that hesitation might spoil everything, 'Would you like to come and live with me in England? My house is much too big for just me. And much too lonely, though I never thought so until these last few weeks.'

Helena hesitated in her turn, and he was afraid she would say no.

He went on, 'You could carry on your business from there. We have our own quota of sadists, masochists, bondage freaks and assorted fruits and nuts. They don't speak of "the English disease" for nothing.'

She didn't answer him directly. 'Is this not a case of pots accusing kettles of blackness, as you say in England?' Helena asked. Then she smiled, and he knew everything was going to be all right. Just as suddenly, she became serious. 'But never mind. I would like that very much.'

Richard felt glad and relieved all at once. He began to imagine Helena's reactions as she explored the familiar old house, discovering for herself the things he took for granted because they had always been there. And he imagined his delight and pride in showing her the place he called home, rediscovering the old familiar things through her eyes.

Though there was still the matter of what to do about Margaret, they talked of their new plans, she with her wrists strung up to the whipping frame and he with his wrists behind his back in handcuffs: of making the journey from Hamburg to England, of their landing, of the trip through the English countryside to Bacton, of walking in the woods and along the beaches of North Norfolk, of the everyday details of shopping and settling into the new relationship.

'I don't know if I could sleep in handcuffs,' Helena

said, looking at his. 'But I want to try it one day, when we are safely in England. Then we will be able to make many new experiments to please each other.' Then, changing the subject, she went on, 'But now we need to talk a bit more. Especially if I am to run away to a foreign land with you.'

'And are you going to run away with me? You're not just teasing me when I'm unable to retaliate?'

Helena became serious at once. 'Of course I will. But do you really want me to come?'

'The old house will be much happier with you in it.'

Helena leant over and kissed him. 'Now tell me more about yourself and this house in England where we will live. I know practically nothing about what you do, how you live, what you want.'

'Well, for starters, I want you.' That got him another kiss.

'But,' he went on, after Helena had moved away, 'I can tell you that I am an unattached, though not a confirmed, bachelor, a man of adequate, though not lavish, means – just in case you had visions of yachts on the Riviera. I work, whenever I choose, at architecture. I draw plans for barn conversions and additions to country houses that scarcely need the room. I take time off whenever I want to. Like now. This is the kind of man with whom you are invited to share an old house in the country. Still want to come?'

'More than ever,' Helena said. 'I will have room to begin my business, as you promised?'

'I look forward to that,' Richard told her. 'You can support me when I grow tired of working. I always wanted to be a kept man.'

It was growing dark in the room when the talk turned back to the immediate problem of what to do. Richard told Helena of his success with the safe, and of the impressions he had taken of the key. She was elated at his success, and said so. She also agreed to take the wax impressions to her stepmother, who knew everyone in the village, including of course the locksmith. He would be able to make the required keys, and in the requisite secrecy. Then, keys in hand, it was only a matter of taking the damning evidence and running away like truants over the sea to Bacton.

And, in truth, it all seemed that easy, until Margaret herself came back to the drawing room to see how her charges were faring. 'This place smells like a brothel on a Saturday night,' she told them. 'What have you two been doing while I have been away? No, do not tell me. I already know. You've been at one another, difficult as that must have been.'

It wasn't a hard conclusion to reach on the smell alone, but, as if that weren't enough, there was a trail of semen down Helena's leg which Margaret noticed at once. And of course Richard's pubic hair and cock were damp as well. Most damning of all, his cock did not come to attention at the sight of her, as it had been wont to do.

Margaret noticed that too. What might have been a smile came out as a grimace, a tightening of the lips and facial muscles. The look vanished as quickly as it had come, perhaps because she didn't want to reveal her displeasure to them.

Richard had feared that Margaret would be angry, but she said nothing more. More importantly, she did not pick up the whip and work out her anger on either of them. Richard thought she might do so later. He would have to worry about that when it happened, and he didn't find the prospect all that disturbing. He was developing a real taste for Margaret's brand of discipline.

Margaret untied Helena and told her to get dressed. She unsnapped Richard's lead from the ring and led him out into the hall. There she turned him over to Heidi, who took him to his room. Acting under Margaret's orders, she told Richard, she fastened him by his chain to the ring bolt set into the floor of the room before she left him alone. He lay on the bed and wondered what Margaret and Helena were doing. He would know sooner or later, he guessed, and so drifted off to sleep.

In the morning, Margaret summoned him to the sitting room. The summons was terse, as usual, and delivered by Heidi: 'Madame wants to see you now.' She unlocked him and waited while he dressed. He put on the new tights and corselet Ingrid had sent, realising that the holes were intended for his newly attached chain to pass through. He threaded the chain through the holes and let it hang. It felt cool as it brushed his thighs under the skirt. The weight of it was always there to remind him of the stainless steel collar around his scrotum.

In the sitting room, Margaret was dressed in her business suit, apparently on the verge of going to the city. She was seated on the long sofa. Richard, in his maid's uniform, was required to stand while she gave him his orders.

'Show me the new underwear Ingrid sent,' she commanded.

Richard raised his skirt so she could see the chain hanging between his thighs. Margaret beckoned him closer, and when he stood before the sofa she grasped the chain and gave it a tug. Richard jumped in surprise, but stood still again as Margaret examined the holes in his underwear through which the chain passed. Apparently satisfied, she let him drop his skirt and step back.

Margaret said, 'This evening you will travel to Basle, carrying a sum of money to Frau Hannelore Bern of the Credit Hoffmann Bank there. You will deliver the consignment to her personally and then do whatever else she asks you to do. You will stay with her for at least a week. In that way you will be less conspicuous in your comings and goings.'

The suddenness of the trip took Richard by surprise. He had been expecting to be sent soon, but had counted on some warning.

'I have provided a wardrobe suitable to a young female assistant, which will be your persona on this occasion. You have your passport, and will travel as Pamela Rhodes. Money for travelling expenses will be made available to you. You need not account for every penny, nor should you travel in the most economical style.'

Richard recalled Ingrid's comment on her own travels as holidays, all expenses paid and no questions asked.

'First-class travellers are less often questioned by customs and immigration officials,' Margaret told him. 'You will have to travel by rail, as you are now marked in a way that would cause an embarrassment if you set off an airport metal detector. I, personally, would not like to have to explain why I was wearing a locked ring and chain on my privates,' she said with a smile.

'Incidentally,' she continued, 'it might not be a good idea to sit with your legs open. Someone might ask why a young woman had a chain fastened just there.' She rose and dismissed him.

[illegible]

[illegible]

[illegible] You will have to [illegible] as you are now [illegible] in a way that would cause embarrassment if you [illegible]

Incidentally, [illegible] it might not be a good idea to [illegible]. Someone might ask why a young woman [illegible] just then? [illegible]

Yes and dismissed him.

Eight

The railway station was crowded when Richard arrived. It was the middle of the morning, but there were people everywhere: mostly housewives, Richard guessed, out for the day's shopping. But among them he saw several women dressed as he was: dark skirt and jacket with light chalk pinstripe, black opaque tights and high-heeled shoes. He felt less conspicuous in the professional-looking dark suit Margaret had ordered him to wear when calling on her colleague at the Credit Hoffmann Bank. Like him, most of these women carried attaché cases, but theirs would be full of business papers, not stuffed with cash as his was. All that cash made him feel both conspicuous and vulnerable, as if he were carrying a sign which informed the world what was in his case. Margaret's instructions as to wardrobe allowed him to blend in well with his surroundings. He was glad of that. Of course, she was concerned only that the case and its contents got to their destination, while his worry was twofold. Not only did he have to deliver the case: he did not want anyone to penetrate his disguise either.

He followed the crowd down the platform and out into the street. It was a clear, sunny day with just a slight chill, enough to make him glad of the jacket and more than ever aware of his legs as the cool air circulated under the skirt. He missed trousers, but

Margaret would never have allowed him to have a trouser suit. 'Unfeminine,' she had said, when he brought up the subject. Richard walked to the taxi rank feeling as if every eye were on him, but no one spoke to him as he approached the first cab.

'Credit Hoffmann Bank, *bitte*,' he told the driver, trusting that he would know the address without having to be further instructed in German. Richard did not feel confident about his German, even though he had studied the language. He was also inhibited by his voice. It was too deep for a woman, and he was afraid that it would betray him, so he had spoken as little as possible on his journey to Basle. The driver, however, seemed to see nothing odd about his passenger. He drove through the crowded streets, and Richard could see many more women in the professional-looking uniform he wore. He relaxed slightly.

The bank was a small but solid-looking building with heavy wooden double doors, shut tightly and guarded by a uniformed guard.

'*Wie viele*?' he asked the driver.

The driver gestured to the meter, where the sum of thirty francs showed. Richard handed him a fifty-franc note with a muttered '*Halten Sie den Wechsel*,' which produced a smile and a '*Guten Tag*' from the driver.

Richard got out and approached the doorman. He bowed slightly to Richard and opened the doors for him. Inside, he looked around, expecting to see the counter layout common to English banks. Instead there were several desks scattered about the floor, at which the employees sat and carried out the mysterious activities that bank clerks busy themselves with when they are not actually dealing with a customer.

There was nothing to indicate who was the receptionist, and Richard was trying to decide whom to approach, when a door behind the desks opened to allow a young woman to step through. She was slim, blonde, attractive, and very efficient-looking in her own version of the suit Richard was wearing. She stood stiffly erect, almost as if she were at attention, her back straight and her head high. Something about her stance, and the preoccupied expression on her face, suggested to him that she might be worried about something. Perhaps, as she was coming from what appeared to be the managerial areas, she had just been given an unpleasant task. Or a reprimand for some error.

Richard was just about to approach the nearest clerk when the young woman saw him. She approached him, holding an armful of file folders, her steps precise as if she was trying very carefully to control her movements. She stopped, facing him, and bade him good morning in German. '*Womit kann ich dienen*?' she continued.

Richard said that he had an appointment with Frau Bern, one of the directors, on business from Margaret Wagner. Could she please inform Frau Bern that he had arrived?

The young woman looked more closely at him, noticing for the first time the case he carried. Her expression underwent a change. The look of preoccupation gave way to one of understanding. She seemed to be on familiar ground. Still speaking in German, she asked his name.

'Pamela Rhodes,' he replied.

She nodded and asked if Fraulein Rhodes would be so good as to follow her. She led him back through the door she had just emerged from and into a long hallway lit only by overhead chandeliers and lined on both sides by rows of oak-panelled doors. Each door, Richard saw, bore a nameplate and a title.

The young woman led him all the way to the far end of the hall and stopped before a door bearing the name H. Bern. His guide knocked on the door and opened it without waiting for a reply. She said, '*Fraulein Rhodes ist hier*,' and stood aside for Richard to enter.

The office was vast. The ceiling was at least twenty feet high, with plaster cornices and tall windows that let in the light of the sunny day outside. The carpet was green with an interwoven gold pattern, covering most of the floor but revealing polished wooden floorboards around the edges. Despite its old-fashioned furnishings and proportions, the room was fitted with the latest in computer terminals and fax machines. There was a conference table along the left side of the room, with ten chairs. Across the room, where visitors would have to make a long approach, was a large oak desk with a leather top. And seated behind the desk was a severely beautiful woman of about the same age as Margaret. She was dressed in the same way as Richard and the young woman who had conducted him here, but there was something in her manner of supreme self-assurance that told the world that here was the real power behind the Credit Hoffmann Bank.

As he approached, feeling like a courtier approaching a queen, Richard knew that he was in the presence of another woman who was accustomed to having her way in all things. She and Margaret might easily have been sisters, save that she was dark-haired where Margaret was blonde. The sign on her desk read: Fr. Hannelore Bern. No title. None was needed. This was the woman he had come to see.

She smiled briefly as she rose to shake his hand. Then she sat down again and indicated a chair across the desk for Richard. 'I trust you had a pleasant journey,' she said in accented English. 'Would you like a cup of coffee, or perhaps tea? No? Then we can get right to the business at hand. That, I take it, is the case entrusted to you by Margaret Wagner. If you would be so good as to place it on the desk and open it?'

Richard did as she asked, opening the lid of the case he had carried from Margaret's house to this city. The money was in large denominations, mostly Deutschmarks, but with a sizeable quantity of French francs and U. S. dollars. Richard had not looked at the contents, knowing that Margaret would be displeased if he had, but now he was startled by the sight of so much money. He looked up to see Frau Bern looking at him. There was a smile of dry amusement in her eyes.

'I am pleased to see that Margaret has chosen an honest courier. So many are not, and the money is often too great a temptation to resist. Some even try to run with it. But they never get away. I am glad that you did not act so foolishly.'

Richard wondered how many had tried to abscond, and what had happened to them. It would not have been anything pleasant, he was sure. Crossing Hannelore Bern would be the same as crossing Margaret. But at the moment the claws were sheathed. She asked again if he would like some coffee or tea. Richard said yes, if she was having some herself.

Frau Bern rang a bell on her desk and a young girl appeared at once. She took the order and departed. There was an awkward silence, which Richard was reluctant to break. He had nothing to say to this formidable woman that wouldn't sound trite. While they waited, Hannelore Bern reached into a pocket in the top of the case and extracted an envelope. She slit it open with a silver paperknife and read the contents, pausing to look at Richard from time to time. Her glance made him uncomfortable. She put the letter down and looked once more at him, steadily, examining his appearance.

Then she spoke. 'Stand up and walk across the room, if you please.'

Puzzled, Richard nevertheless did as she asked, pausing at her command and turning around while she regarded him appraisingly from her desk. He felt awkward and embarrassed while Frau Bern continued to regard him. All his anxiety about being found out came back. What would this woman think, he wondered, if she knew that he was really a man in woman's clothing?

Frau Bern spoke again. 'Very good. If Margaret had not told me all about you, I would never have known for sure that you are not a woman. She has taught you well.' Frau Bern paused, and then went on, 'But she has been doing this for years. She has had a lot of practice.'

There seemed no fitting reply to that remark. Richard merely nodded. He was saved from further conversation by the return of the young girl with the tea things. Both of them waited in silence until she had withdrawn. Richard poured the tea for them both and sat down at a nod from Frau Bern.

'Margaret says you are to stay here for some time before returning. This is our usual arrangement. It looks more natural than dashing back immediately. Someone might become suspicious. She also said that you might benefit from further training while you are here. So you will be staying at my chateau, and I shall try to make the time as interesting as possible.'

Richard nodded, but felt a stab of dismay. He had told Helena that he would be back in only a few days, and she would be expecting him. As soon as he had the duplicate keys, they were going to take the damning evidence and flee to England and a new life. But that would have to wait now. During his time with Margaret, he had become accustomed to taking orders, and this Swiss woman had the same air of expecting to be obeyed. If this was what Margaret wanted, he would do it. And not altogether unwillingly. Frau Bern would no doubt see that the time was interesting, in the sense in which he had come to interpret the word since his meeting with Helena and her domineering aunt.

Before the silence could become awkward again, it was broken by the entrance of the young woman who had escorted him to the office. She was carrying a handful of papers, and she went through the doorway of a small room opening off the main office. Richard saw that it was lined with filing cabinets. She knelt on the floor and began placing the papers in the drawers. Once again he noticed how she kept her back straight and refrained from bending as much as possible. Frau Bern watched him watching her, but she said nothing until the young woman stood up. Then she beckoned her over to the desk.

'Gretchen here is one of Margaret's young ladies. She stayed at the country house where you now dwell for something like two years before she came to work for me. So you two will have something in common.'

Gretchen looked suddenly at Richard as if seeing him for the first time. Her face flushed. Richard felt his own face grow warm as he imagined what she had learnt with Margaret. They looked at one another silently, until Frau Bern broke the tableau.

'Pamela here has been watching you. I think she has noticed how erect you carry yourself. I wonder if you would mind explaining the matter to her?' Frau Bern warned Richard with a glance to remain silent.

Gretchen grew even redder of face. The flush, Richard saw, extended down her throat, where a pulse suddenly beat.

'Come, Gretchen, speak up. I will not ask you again,' Frau Bern said.

The young woman looked once at her employer, and then at Richard, as if to let him know that she had no choice but to obey. 'Very well, Madame,' she said. To Richard she said, 'I am wearing a saddle strap, which makes it very painful to bend or stoop.' Her voice was almost a whisper, and her embarrassment was obviously acute.

Richard looked closely at Gretchen, but could see nothing out of the ordinary about her except her carriage. He looked questioningly at Frau Bern, who spoke again to the young woman.

'Our visitor is not familiar with the terminology. Perhaps you had better show her, please,' she said. The command behind the polite phraseology was clear to both Richard and Gretchen.

Gretchen took off her jacket and let it fall to the floor. Then, carefully looking past Richard, she reached behind her back to unbutton her skirt. Her legs, in the black tights, were long and slender, and Richard was unable to tear his eyes away as she let the garment fall around her feet. She stepped out of it and began to unbutton her blouse. Gretchen wore a pale-green lace bra, sheer enough to see her nipples through the cups. They were not erect, suggesting even more clearly her embarrassment.

Richard spoke. 'Gretchen, you don't need to continue.'

Frau Bern cut in. 'Yes, she does. I give the orders here.'

Gretchen, however, carried on as if neither of them had spoken. The blouse came off, and Richard could see she wore a harness of soft leather that came over her shoulders from behind, crossed between her breasts and became a single strap that continued down to her belly. Richard could see the darker line of the strap beneath her tights. It went between her legs, seeming to be drawn very tightly into her crotch, judging by the way it bit into her flesh. Gretchen hesitated, looking briefly at her employer for further instructions.

'Take it all off,' Frau Bern said.

The young woman again reached behind her back to unhook her bra. The clingy material fell away, allowing her full breasts to spring free. Richard felt his cock stiffen in sudden excitement as he saw the thin red lines in her flesh. He knew enough by now to recognise the marks of the whip. Gretchen had endured having her breasts lashed. How had that felt, he wondered, and how had she reacted? Had it been torture for her, or did she share Helena's ability to transmute the pain into sexual arousal? He shifted in his chair in order to conceal the bump of his erection from the two women in the room.

Gretchen, meanwhile, had begun to peel her tights down her legs. When she stood nude before them, Richard noticed that her flush was an all-over one, her skin pink with it. She stood erect as before, her back straight and her arms by her sides. She was not looking at either of them.

'Turn around,' Frau Bern ordered.

Gretchen turned her back to them, and Richard could see the rest of her saddle strap. It ran between her buttocks and rose up her back to meet the shoulder straps. In the small of her back there was a buckle to adjust the tension, with a small padlock to prevent her loosening the harness. The whole contrivance had the finished look that only a skilled leather worker could produce, and Richard wondered if Helena had made it.

'Turn around and face us, Gretchen,' Frau Bern said. To Richard she said, 'You can see why she stands so straight now. If she bends her back, the strap is drawn more tightly against her crotch. She wears it every day as a reminder to her of who is in charge. In the same way,' she continued, 'that you are reminded by your ring and chain that Margaret is in charge of you.'

Her knowledge of his own arrangements took Richard completely by surprise. He had not given any thought to the possibility that Margaret had told Hannelore Bern about that, yet when he thought of it, it was only logical that she had. It would be one way of identifying him to the person on the other end, and of letting that same person know who was giving the orders to whom.

'Now that Gretchen has shown us her little secret, I think it would be only right for you to show her yours. And I must admit I am rather curious myself. So stand up and take off your skirt for us.'

Richard stood slowly, flushing in his turn at the thought of showing what had been done to him, but never considering a refusal. Margaret would be sure to learn of it if he refused, and would be sure to take steps to punish him on his return. Hannelore Bern might take a refusal badly as well, and she seemed to be the sort of woman who could punish others as easily as Margaret did. He unbuttoned the waistband of his skirt and let it fall to the floor as Gretchen had done. Then he lifted the hem of the black nylon slip to reveal the chain dangling between his thighs.

'Gretchen, go over to Pamela and give her the Crocodile Dundee test,' Frau Bern ordered.

'Which test, Madame?' Gretchen asked.

'Never mind,' Frau Bern said. 'Just go over to Pamela and feel how the chain is secured.'

Gretchen flushed again but did as she was told. Her eyes widened, and she gasped in surprise when she touched Richard's balls. She let the chain fall as if it had burnt her and turned away in embarrassment.

Hannelore Bern laughed quietly at her employee's discomfiture. 'You see now that you are not the only one who has a hard time, Gretchen. Margaret expects her people to do anything she asks.' To them both she said, 'Get dressed. We are going to finish early today and go out to my chateau. There we will have the privacy to get better acquainted with one another.' Hannelore watched as Gretchen put on her clothes.

Richard picked up his skirt, but hesitated before putting it on. 'May I use the toilet before we leave?' he asked.

Hannelore Bern pointed to the file storage room. 'There is a toilet in there. Be quick about it.'

Inside the smaller room, Richard saw another door which had to be the toilet. When he was finished, he readjusted the tights and corselet before putting the skirt back on. As he left the toilet, he saw that the file room also contained a bank of video monitors, which he guessed were part of the bank's closed circuit-security camera system.

When he returned to the office, he saw that Gretchen was dressed again. Hannelore Bern pushed a button and spoke into an intercom on the desk, ordering the chauffeur to bring the car around to the private entrance of the bank and to wait for her. Without another word, she led the way to the door and out into a courtyard which formed a private entrance to her office. There was a chauffeur-driven Mercedes waiting, the motor running and the driver standing by the door to help his employer in. He said nothing about his extra passengers. The gates opened to an electronic signal from the car, much as those at Margaret's estate. They drove out into the streets of Basle and on out of the city.

Nine

The country house of Hannelore Bern was much grander than Margaret's. There was the same high wall and electronically controlled gates, the same long drive from the road, and the same air of a guarded fortress. But there were real guards too, walking through the trees and over the lawns. Real guards with real dogs. It would be much more difficult to escape from this house than from Margaret's. The chateau itself was of stone, a villa with a columned portico, a vast building in the Roman-revival style so admired by Albert Speer. The grounds stretched so far that the enclosing wall could not be seen on the far side. A stand of mature trees, really a small forest, grew down the mountainside and marched almost to the door of a small cottage and a large barn in the distance.

It was towards this distant cottage that Hannelore Bern directed the chauffeur. Richard guessed that these might be the guest quarters, and he was partly right. They all got out in front of the cottage, Gretchen carefully keeping her back straight to ease the strap running between her legs. Richard was once more conscious of the chain dangling between his own legs as he slid across the seat and got out. The chauffeur opened the door for Frau Bern and stood aside as they entered. There was a look of speculation in his eyes as he glanced at Gretchen, but he said nothing.

'Pamela, where are you staying in Basle?'

'At the *Alte Hannover* in Bahnhof Strasse,' he replied.

'Give your key to Gunter here,' she ordered. Turning to the chauffeur, Hannelore said, 'Go to the hotel, collect Fraulein Rhodes's belongings and bring them back here.'

Hannelore Bern dismissed him, and as soon as he had gone she became once more the mistress among her slaves. 'Gretchen, go to the barn and bring back your harness.'

Gretchen nodded and departed silently.

'Pamela,' she went on, with an ironic smile, 'you can make tea for us. Come with me.'

Hannelore Bern led him towards the adjoining cottage. 'We are going to have some sex games, we three,' she explained. 'Margaret says you are quite an interesting person, adaptable, malleable. She says you are learning to submit. We shall see. I like submissive people: they are so much easier to deal with. Though I can deal with almost any kind.'

Richard didn't doubt it.

'Go through into the kitchen,' Frau Bern directed, with a wave of her hand. 'Make some snacks for us, and something to drink. Something to sustain us through some strenuous exercise.'

Richard went through into the kitchen, while Hannelore disappeared towards the rooms at the rear of the cottage. The kitchen was large and airy, with tiled floors and oak cabinets. The ceiling was high, with varnished exposed beams from which hung the cooking utensils. Through the curtained windows, he saw Gretchen walking towards the barn, with her characteristic straight-backed stride. She went into the barn through a side door, and presently emerged carrying a leather holdall. Richard set about making sandwiches. Gretchen came in through the kitchen door, and he could see by the pinkness of her cheeks and the shortness of her breath that she was excited. She was obviously looking forward to what was to come, and he wondered what she had in the holdall to affect her so strongly.

She started to speak to Richard, then abruptly looked beyond him. At the same time, he heard the sound of approaching footsteps: the distinct clack of high-heeled shoes. A transformed Hannelore Bern entered the kitchen from the house side, and Richard forgot about Gretchen as he stared at her. She had shed her sober business clothes and stood before them in a shiny black leather corselet. It hugged her figure, and Richard felt himself growing erect as he stared at her. It was impossible to take his eyes away. Her breasts were pushed up and forward aggressively, her already small waist was almost wasplike now, her sex was both covered and yet somehow emphasised by the tight leather between her legs. She wore dark grey tights and black shoes with stiletto heels to complete the effect.

Hannelore Bern was at the same time immensely charged with sexuality and beyond reach of any contact. The tight leather garment both offered her to view and protected her from any approach. Richard felt his breath grow short as he stared at her. Naked, she would be just a beautiful, desirable and available woman. The world was full of them. But, garbed in this tight leather sheath, she was menacing and impregnable as well. The effect was stunning. And daunting. Hannelore Bern carried a whip in her hand, the end trailing on the floor.

'Gretchen,' she said, 'come with me.' To Richard she added, 'Come back into the front room when you have finished here.'

Richard finished making the sandwiches, found a tray, and arranged the food on it before going back into the front room. Gretchen was nude. Hannelore Bern was in the act of unlocking the padlock that secured her saddle strap. When the strap was loosened, the younger woman relaxed her taut muscles and gave a low groan of relief. She slipped out of the strap and laid it on the sofa beside the holdall she had brought from the barn. Without being told, she opened it and began to take out a different type of harness, more elaborate, more suitable for a horse, it seemed to Richard, than a woman. Yet there was no doubt that it was intended for Gretchen. She was flushed and short of breath as she finished laying the straps out on the sofa.

'Pamela,' Frau Bern said, with another of her ironic smiles, 'you and Gretchen are going to play pony girls. Unfortunately, we don't have a harness prepared for you, but I'll make do with what we have. But first we'll have some tea and something to eat. That's so much more civilised.'

Gretchen looked even more tense at Hannelore's words. Richard guessed that she was already aroused by the presence of her harness, and wanted to get on with it. By forcing her to wait, Hannelore was deliberately toying with her. When Hannelore sat down, she crossed her legs, causing Richard to become aware of his own excitement. He could feel his cock growing erect as she swung her leg idly. Richard and Gretchen drank their tea in a tense silence. Gretchen nibbled at a sandwich, obviously preoccupied. Hannelore was quite relaxed, smiling from time to time as she dawdled over hers.

Finally she was finished. As she stood, she said to Richard, 'First you will help me fit Gretchen into her harness, and then I will deal with you.' She beckoned Richard to her.

Gretchen stood still, silent and expectant, a fine sheen of sweat now breaking out on her face as she waited to be harnessed. Her nipples were taut and crinkly with her excitement. Richard wondered how many women who loved bondage, pain and submission he was going to encounter before this was over. If it ever was going to be over. He didn't want this to end, he admitted to himself. And, if Helena meant what she had said, it needn't. He wondered just how many women and men walked the streets looking for what he had stumbled upon, and never found it. He was one of the lucky ones.

Hannelore handed him a leather belt with several dangling straps.

'Put this around her waist,' she ordered, busying herself with a harness designed to fit Gretchen's head. There was a leather cap which fitted tightly, leaving her long hair hanging down her back. There was a metal bit which went between the young woman's teeth, with rings at either end to which reins could be attached. More straps were designed to secure it in place and prevent her from ejecting it. It was obviously a gag as well.

Richard meanwhile fitted the waist belt, feeling Gretchen tremble at his touch. Or was it merely her excitement at being harnessed? Together he and Hannelore secured the buckles and straps which imprisoned the young woman, leaving her ready to be secured to a cart or wagon. As a final touch, Hannelore added a tail made of horsehair. The wooden handle of the tail went into Gretchen's anus and was secured by a strap, the long tail hanging down her legs as far as her knees. She groaned as the handle was pushed home, trembling as a nervous horse might. She stood still in her harness, waiting to be led away.

Hannelore then turned to Richard. 'Take off your clothes,' she said.

Richard stripped off the skirt, jacket and white silk blouse he had worn for the meeting at the bank. The black nylon slip followed. He laid everything neatly on a chair, as Margaret and Ingrid had taught him. He knew Hannelore would demand the same neatness. He hesitated, standing before her in the corselet and tights, the chain dangling between his legs. A thin trail of sweat descended from under the wig to run down his face. He too was nervous, uncertain of where this was going to lead. At an impatient nod from Hannelore, he pulled the tight corselet off and removed the black tights. The wig followed. Naked, he stood still while she inspected him. His cock, taped to his belly, was stiff and throbbing.

Hannelore took a long thin strip of leather from the pile Gretchen had brought and handed it to Richard. 'Tie Gretchen's hands behind her back,' she directed. 'She does not enjoy this unless she is bound helplessly.'

Wordlessly, Gretchen turned her back to Richard and brought her hands behind her. As he tied her wrists, he could feel her trembling still with anticipation. The horsehair tail bobbed as her stomach and rectal muscles contracted in excitement. Sexual arousal, he reflected, comes from the strangest sources.

When he had done, Hannelore tested the cords. She shook her head. 'Tighter,' she said. 'Gretchen likes the cords to bite in as she works.'

Obediently, Richard unknotted the cords and retied them, pulling them until Gretchen winced slightly. He knotted them and stood aside, waiting for the next step.

Hannelore went to a sideboard and came back with a pair of handcuffs and a long, thin silvery chain. 'Now you,' she said, motioning him to turn around.

Richard turned, bringing his hands behind his back as Gretchen had done. He felt the steel bands close around his wrists, and he remembered how Margaret had done the same thing to him. He tried to repress the slight shiver of anticipation, but Hannelore had felt it.

'You are eager too? Good. I like people to enjoy these little games. Now hold still while I make a lead for you.'

Hannelore fastened the long chain to the shorter one locked around his balls. Taking a broad leather belt from the treasure-trove Gretchen had brought, she buckled it around his waist. Then she gathered Gretchen's reins and Richard's chain and led the two of them towards the door. Feeling that insistent tug on their respective but quite different tethers, they had no choice except to follow. Hannelore led them across the yard in the bright sunlight. Richard was uneasy about being outdoors, in plain view of anyone passing. What could a naked man in handcuffs and being led by the balls say to a passer-by? But there were none. The size and seclusion of Hannelore Bern's estate ensured that there were no strangers nearby. But what about the staff and servants which such a large establishment would require? Surely they would notice. But of course they would not say anything if they valued their jobs. Hannelore looked as if she might be quite severe towards anyone who spoke of what went on here. Losing their jobs might turn out to be the least of their worries.

Hannelore led them into the barn, using the same side door that Gretchen had used earlier. The building was large, part garage and part storeroom. But what Richard noticed at once was the light racing cart standing against one wall, resting on its thin bicycle-type tyres with its long poles standing upright. This couldn't be anything except Gretchen's cart.

Hannelore Bern, severe and exciting in her black leather corselet, tights and stiletto-heeled shoes, strode over to the cart. She set it down on its wheels, turning it so that she could harness them to it. She beckoned Richard to her.

'You first. I want you behind Gretchen, where you can see her but will not be able to touch her.'

The long chain dragging on the floor, Richard moved to stand between the poles of the cart. Hannelore fastened the straps dangling from his waist belt to the poles. She beckoned Gretchen over, and in the same businesslike fashion she set about securing the young woman to the cart. There was a curved wooden frame that slid on to the poles, closing them inside the narrow space. Hannelore slipped this down until it was just in front of the place where Gretchen was secured. Hannelore clamped the bar in place before making the final adjustments to the harness. She led the reins from Gretchen's bit around Richard on either side and laid them on the seat. She led the chain between his legs and laid it in the same place. He could see how she planned to control her team of 'horses'.

'You're not going to shout for help, are you?' Hannelore asked him. 'I don't really want to gag you. You'll need all your breath for our little exercise.'

Richard shook his head. Hannelore smiled briefly and turned away to open the double doors of the barn. They slid easily in their tracks, and the sunlight streamed over the pair harnessed to the cart as she mounted the seat and picked up the whip. When she was settled, Hannelore shook out the reins and let her whip fall lightly across Richard's bottom, a reminder of who was in control. Richard and Gretchen pulled the cart out into the bright yard.

She guided them mainly by Gretchen's reins, as one does with a horse, and they moved over the open ground towards the distant grove of trees. 'Follow Gretchen,' Hannelore Bern commanded. 'She knows the way.'

Gretchen leant into her harness and pulled, her bottom thrust back towards Richard and her tail brushing his legs. Hannelore's whip caught him again, and he guessed that she wanted him to pull harder. He too leant forward, and the cart moved more quickly towards the cover of the trees. Their cover seemed inviting, a screen from the other eyes which he still imagined were gazing at the bizarre spectacle they all made.

There was a bridle path into the grove. It appeared to be well trodden, but not by horses. There was soft grass underfoot. Hannelore guided her team on to it and touched them both with the whip. 'Faster,' she ordered.

Richard did not know how fast they were supposed to go, so he matched Gretchen's pace. If Hannelore was not satisfied, she would soon let them know. As they entered the shelter of the trees, Richard became less anxious about being seen. He was now more aware of Hannelore Bern sitting just behind him in her tight leather costume, and of Gretchen harnessed just in front of him, her bizarre tail dangling down her legs as she pulled. His cock stiffened against his belly, though just what he could do about either woman was not clear to him. What might be done to him was likewise unknown, but exciting. In the meantime, he and Gretchen pulled the cart along the path, becoming warmer and more sweaty by the minute.

Hannelore flicked them with the whip from time to time, not so much to inflict pain as to remind them that she was controlling them, and that it was in her power to make them suffer as much as she wished. Gretchen seemed to know where they were going, and she pushed forward eagerly in her harness. The path was dappled by sunlight and shadow, the light falling through gaps in the canopy of leaves on to Gretchen's nude body as she strained at her harness. The whip rose and fell, touching Richard now lightly, now more heavily.

The ride went on and on. Richard guessed they must be deep in the forest, but he could not tell how far they were from the house, or from any other houses that might lie nearby. He hoped there would be no one to see them. But at the same time, there was a queer excitement in the knowledge that they might be seen at any moment. How would Hannelore Bern explain herself to a casual walker who might come upon them? Probably she would not feel any need to explain. She would not be embarrassed. It was only he who felt that way.

When they came to a wider clearing in the forest, Hannelore tugged on the chain fastened to Richard's scrotum, an unmistakable signal to stop. Richard didn't know if she had tugged the reins to halt Gretchen at the same time, but the young woman stopped as well. There was a creak and a shifting of weight as Hannelore dismounted from her chariot. She came to stand before them, smiling slightly and looking even more stunning and bizarre in her leather costume in the middle of the forest. She reached out to touch Richard's cock.

'I guess this means you like me,' she said. 'Or do you just like the idea of serving me?'

There was no good answer to the question, so Richard said nothing.

Still rubbing his cock and squeezing it gently, Hannelore turned to Gretchen. 'And you, my little one. Are you eager too?'

Gretchen of course could not reply, and he could not see her expression, but Richard saw her shudder in her harness. Her bound hands were twisting restlessly behind her back. In anticipation? Almost certainly she knew what was coming. He wondered if she had come to the woods with other captives, or if she had always pulled the cart alone. He was excited by her: so fetchingly bound, so near, so nude. Would Hannelore Bern offer her to him? His cock stirred at the thought.

Hannelore felt the spasm in his cock and looked sidelong at him. She slowly lifted a corner of the tape which held his cock against his belly, then abruptly tore it away, allowing his cock to swing free. It stood out stiffly, and she grasped it firmly with her whole hand, letting her fingers stroke the underside and tickle him behind the glans. Being so near to two such desirable women, the one nude and the other clad in tight leather, was almost too much for him. He was on the verge of an orgasm, and he knew that Hannelore Bern would not be pleased.

As if sensing the onset of his orgasm, Hannelore let him go and turned her attention to Gretchen. First she loosened the curved piece linking the two poles and slid it off, laying it on the ground. Next, she deftly unbuckled the straps holding the young woman to the cart and led her out from between the two poles to which Richard was still harnessed. She turned Gretchen to face Richard, and he could see her taut nipples and her ragged breathing.

Mischievously, Hannelore said, 'Do you like him, little one?' Pointing to Richard's stiff cock, she added, 'He seems to like you.'

Gretchen looked wildly from her mistress to Richard, then shook her head determinedly. She uttered a sound from behind her bit which could only mean no. She kept her gaze on Hannelore, as if pleading not to be forced into something she feared.

Richard was disappointed at her reaction, as any man turned down by a desirable woman might be. But at the same time he was relieved. If Gretchen had indicated approval, they might both have incurred the displeasure of Hannelore Bern.

Hannelore looked from one to the other for some sign. When none came, she said, 'Clearly it is up to me to play matchmaker.'

Gretchen once more shook her head, this time more vehemently, causing the metal parts of her bit to clink together, her eyes pleading with her mistress. 'Nngghh!' she said. The bit distorted her words, but clearly she was still opposed to the idea.

'You shouldn't be too downhearted,' Hannelore said to Richard. 'Gretchen has been with me for some time, and she has taken well to my teaching and companionship. One might almost believe she was a raging, thoroughgoing lesbian, if one were to judge solely from her words. But she is not.' Turning to Gretchen, she added, 'Are you, little one?'

Gretchen reddened, but she repeated her denial, this time pleadingly: 'Nnnngggghhhhh! Eeeees!'

'She really doesn't know what to say. If she says she wants you, she will get one of the things she wants badly: a man's cock up inside her. But she is afraid I will be angry, because we have been together for some time. So, she's on the horns of a dilemma. We could resolve things by putting her on to the cock of a horny man, though, could we not?'

As she spoke, Hannelore was looking at Gretchen, who was by now red all over with embarrassment at being the object of such a conversation between her mistress and a comparative stranger.

'She may also be afraid I won't beat her if I allow her to have you,' Hannelore said to Richard. 'It is difficult to choose between two pleasures: she is a bit like the donkey who starved to death between two bales of hay.' She paused as if in thought. Then, having come to some decision, she smiled to herself before picking up the curved frame. She slid it on to the poles, this time moving it down to a point just in front of Richard.

The frame, designed to hold the poles together at the front, now resembled nothing so much as a seat, a seat which almost touched Richard's stiff cock. It didn't require too much imagination to guess who would be occupying the seat. Gretchen arrived at the answer almost as soon as Richard did. Anticipation and denial made a battleground of her face. She made as if to run, but stepped on her reins and fell to the ground. With her hands tied behind her back, she was unable to break her fall. The breath was knocked out of her. She struggled to rise but fell back again. Hannelore turned and helped the young woman to her feet.

'Don't be afraid, little one,' she said soothingly. 'You know you like this part of it as much as what comes later.'

Gretchen was trembling as Hannelore unclipped the reins from the bit and led her back to the cart. The older woman led her between the poles and turned her to face

Richard. Hannelore untied the cords binding Gretchen's wrists. She gestured for the younger woman to mount the curved frame in front of Richard.

Gretchen hesitated, looking from him to her mistress in confusion. Richard could see that she was reluctant to mount, and he felt himself grow more excited, rather than the reverse, at the idea of Gretchen's being compelled against her will. The old rape fantasy, he thought fleetingly, though that wasn't accurate either. It would be impossible for him to penetrate Gretchen while his own wrists were handcuffed behind him and he was harnessed to the cart. Gretchen was in a much better position to flee than he was to pursue.

But Hannelore was there to compel the young woman. With a frown, she gestured again for Gretchen to mount the frame.

Richard took the added weight as her legs left the ground and she seated herself in front of him. His cock was brushing her pubic hair, bumping familiarly against her mons veneris, and he felt a stab of excitement.

Gretchen would not look at him. Her body language was saying, I don't want this, but she dared not disobey her mistress.

Richard could see the corners of her mouth drawn back by the bit between her teeth, and the reddened area where the metal had dug into her skin. Even as he thought of the pain and indignity this gag was causing, he was excited by the way it emphasised her captive status. He remembered experiencing the same feelings as Margaret had lashed Helena, and he remembered too how he had wondered how it would feel to wield the whip and inflict pain on someone else.

Gretchen settled in the frame, still not looking at Richard. She sat unresisting while Hannelore bound her wrists together in front of her and then lifted her arms over Richard's head, encircling his neck, and drew her bound hands down his back before fastening them to the belt around his waist. She raised Gretchen's legs over the poles and let them dangle on either side, spreading her widely. Hannelore used the reins to bind Gretchen's thighs to the poles, holding her immobile just inches from impalement.

She reached between them, grasping Richard's cock. 'Good,' she said. 'I see you are not put off by Gretchen's shy virgin act.' She guided his cock between the young woman's outspread legs and into her cunt, at the same time urging Gretchen closer.

Richard felt himself slide home. Gretchen was parted and ready, her juices flowing and her sex warm and tight around him.

But Hannelore was not finished with them yet. She used the remainder of Gretchen's reins to tie them tightly together, encircling both their waists and pulling the young woman against him. Richard could not withdraw; Gretchen could not pull herself away from the shaft inside her. Her breasts were flattened against his chest, the taut nipples rubbing against him.

Hannelore stepped back and regarded them with a look of satisfaction. 'A pretty couple,' she remarked.

Gretchen still would not look at Richard. She held herself rigid, as if expecting to be attacked. Her eyes said no, but the rest of her was now saying yes. Richard too held himself still, not sure what his next move should be.

Once more it was Hannelore who broke the tableau. She positioned herself behind Gretchen, dappled by sunlight and shadow, the shifting light making sudden highlights and shadows on the tight leather garment and the shiny tights she wore. She looked magnificent, Richard thought, as he looked at her over Gretchen's shoulder. Magnificent, and menacing too. She held the whip in her hand, was even then drawing back her arm to strike. Richard braced himself.

He needn't have. The whip flashed forward, striking Gretchen. From what he could see, the blow had landed on her bottom. She jerked abruptly, letting out a gasp of surprise and pain. Her vaginal muscles clamped down on his cock at the same time. Hannelore drew back her arm and struck again. Each time the lash struck her, Gretchen jerked. And each time she jerked, she moved her hips so that he was plunged in and out of her. He felt the rod in her anus, which held the horse's tail in place, hard against him through the membrane between the two passages.

Gretchen seemed to be oblivious of her double impalement, paying all her attention to the whipping. But gradually her movements became synchronised with the lash, plunging forward as she was struck, pulling back in preparation for the next blow. Her breathing was loud in Richard's ear as she lay her head against his chest, her face turned to one side. And gradually she began to moan softly. At first he thought she was in pain, but it soon became obvious that she was not. Hannelore continued to strike her from bottom to shoulders, timing the blows so that Gretchen could move rhythmically to them.

Richard could feel her arousal in the increasing heat of the flesh that enveloped his cock and in her moans. Gradually she lost control, giving repeated gasps as she moved, a rhythmic 'Uh! Uh! Uh!' They were the sounds of increasing pleasure, and they increased in pitch and volume as she was driven to orgasm. Suddenly Gretchen began to jerk and shudder, her muscles clamping down on him. 'Uhhh! Uhhnnn! Uhnnnnnn!' Her orgasm shook them both, but she hardly paused, beginning another almost at once, as Hannelore continued to lash her.

Richard, embedded in Gretchen, was also looking at Hannelore. Her body, outlined by the leather corselet and tights, moved gracefully, showing off her legs, breasts, waist and stomach, as she wielded the lash that drove Gretchen to newer heights of ecstasy. The double stimulus – two magnificent women, one in full view, himself inside the other – was too much for Richard. He could hold back no longer. Gretchen's arms tightened around his neck as she came, and then he was jerking and shuddering with his own orgasm, spurting inside Gretchen and gasping for air.

Hannelore abruptly stopped lashing her protégée, pausing to watch as Richard and Gretchen gasped in mutual pleasure, their bodies straining against one another and against the straps that bound them. She appeared to derive great satisfaction from her accomplishment. She remained silent for a long time.

Finally she spoke, cutting through the aftermath of their passion. 'Gretchen will tell me that she hated all that, that I forced her to have sex with a man, that I do not have any respect for her. But I know what she likes. And, apparently, what you like too.'

Richard had to admit the accuracy of her judgement. He liked what was happening to him. All of it. He spoke suddenly, almost without thinking what he was saying. 'And what do you like?' he asked Hannelore.

Hannelore gave him an angry look and swung the whip, once, with all her strength. The lash caught him across the back and ribs, and he hissed from the pain of it.

'I do not allow my servants to ask impertinent questions,' Hannelore told him.

Gretchen, shaken by her response, looked up at him quickly, fearfully, then glanced at Hannelore, as if afraid of what she would see. But Hannelore merely smiled briefly and set about releasing them. She once more tied Gretchen's hands behind her back and harnessed her to the cart as before. She led the young woman by the reins and turned the cart back the way they had come. Silently, she mounted the seat and shook the reins. Gretchen and Richard, carthorses once more, pulled her back along the path.

Nothing more was said until they reached the barn, where Hannelore unhitched them both. She did not, however, free their hands, nor did she remove Gretchen's bit and bridle. She led the girl to a loosebox with a barred door and hitched her inside it, with the reins tied above her head and out of reach of her bound hands. Richard was led to a similar enclosure, where he was fastened by the chain around his balls. Then Hannelore left them to their own devices, closing the barn door as she left.

Gretchen looked at him once, briefly, from her stall, then quickly lowered her eyes. Richard shrugged mentally and lay down in the straw. Shortly he saw that Gretchen had done the same. Since conversation was impossible, he allowed himself to drift off to sleep.

The sound of a door opening woke him up. Hannelore Bern was back. She had doffed her leather corselet in favour of a black dress that showed off her legs to good advantage. She was accompanied by a young woman in a maid's outfit remarkably like the ones Richard wore in Margaret's house, who was bearing a tray of food for the two captives. Hannelore gestured for her to serve the food, unlocking Richard's handcuffs so that he could eat. Similarly, she freed Gretchen's hands, and removed her bit and bridle. Richard was hungry and thirsty, and he fell to at once. Hannelore went into one of the small storerooms off the main barn, returning shortly with several pieces of light, chrome-plated chain and an assortment of dildoes. She watched while he ate. Gretchen was still eating when he finished. The maid took away the tray, and Richard submitted to having his handcuffs replaced.

What Hannelore did next surprised him. She unlocked the chain which secured him to the wall by his balls and removed the long piece she had attached to it earlier. The short chain swung free between his legs as before.

'Turn around and bend over,' she ordered him.

When he did so, Hannelore selected one of the dildoes from her assortment. Richard saw that it had a ring in the blunt end, as indeed all of the dildoes did. She lubricated it with petroleum jelly and carefully inserted it into his anus.

Richard felt the shaft slide into him with a curious calm. Was this what a woman felt as she was penetrated: full and sensitive?

Hannelore fitted a length of chain around his waist, tightly enough so that he could not slip it off. Then she threaded the chain hanging from his balls through the ring on the dildo in his arse, drawing it up to the chain around his waist and securing the whole thing with the small padlock she had used earlier. Richard was left with the dildo inside him, unable to withdraw it even if his hands had been free.

When he was secured, Hannelore turned him from side to side, inspecting her work. Apparently satisfied, she pushed him towards the central part of the barn.

'You will both spend the night here in the barn,' she told him. 'You can keep one another warm. I may let you into the house later, provided your behaviour pleases me,' she said.

'How long does it take to please you?' he asked. 'At some point I will have to get back to Soltau.'

'I should have told you earlier, but I wanted to have you here before I told you what Margaret's letter really said. You won't be going back. You will remain here with me. She has given you to me – a gift, if you like – for further training.'

Richard was dumbstruck. Not going back to Soltau? Not to see Helena or Ingrid again? This was too much. He could think of no words adequate to express his dismay.

'I see this is news to you,' Hannelore said. 'Margaret likes surprises, provided they do not affect her.' She produced a key which had been hanging on a chain between her breasts. 'She sent me the key to your lead, but I do not think I will be using it soon. It will not harm you to be locked up for a while, until you get used to your new home – like a cat being kept indoors for a few days after the family moves house. You'll soon learn to like it here.' She turned away without giving him a chance to reply.

Richard knew he would not be able to escape immediately, but he also knew that he would have to get away in the end, and sooner rather than later. He didn't like the idea of Helena believing he had deserted her, quite apart from his own desire to get back to her.

Hannelore waited while Gretchen finished her meal. Then she set about securing the young woman for the night. Gretchen submitted quietly as her hands were once more tied behind her back. Hannelore fitted a chain around Gretchen's slim waist as she had with Richard. This time, however, she inserted two dildoes, plugging Gretchen front and back. A chain between her legs and through the rings in the dildoes secured them inside her. Apparently she was accustomed to this practice, as she made no demur, and even anticipated what was coming next, turning and moving to facilitate her penetration and the securing of the chain.

Richard watched from across the floor, knowing what Gretchen was feeling now. Would Hannelore replace the bit and bridle for the night? That might prove to be uncomfortable for such a long period.

But Hannelore had thought of that. She brought a steel helmet from the storeroom. It was hinged at the top to fit over the wearer's head, tapering to a closely fitted neck ring which locked on either side when the hinged pieces were brought together. There were brow ridges, and the suggestion of eyes, though there were no holes. There was a space to accommodate the nose, and another hinged plate over the mouth, presumably to allow the wearer to eat and drink without having to have the helmet unlocked.

Richard wondered how long Gretchen would wear her iron mask. Gretchen herself seemed to have no qualms. As she had with the chains and dildoes, she moved her head so as to allow the helmet to be fitted on to her.

Hannelore pushed her long hair inside the back of the mask as she brought the collar parts together. She secured the collar on both sides, and Gretchen's head was locked inside the steel cage. When she turned towards Richard, he was struck by the impersonality of the mask. It was as if someone had erased all her features, replacing them with this mockery of a face. The iron mask gave her head a swollen, balloon-like appearance. When Hannelore stepped back to inspect her captive, Richard noticed that there were two tubes running from the nostril area of the helmet back over the top. They would admit air, but no light. Gretchen would be in total darkness even with her eyes open, but she didn't seem to mind.

The final step was the binding of Gretchen's feet and legs. Hannelore pushed her, and she fell heavily in the straw on the floor. She then bound Gretchen's ankles and knees with rope, leaving the young woman blind and helpless. She beckoned to the maid, who gathered the remains of their meal and departed. The two captives were left alone with their captor.

Hannelore beckoned Richard to Gretchen's stall. 'Inside,' she ordered tersely. When he was inside, she locked the door. She turned out the lights and closed the barn's outer door. Richard heard her lock it too, doubly imprisoning them.

'Are you all right, Gretchen?' he asked the young woman who lay bound in the straw at his feet.

'Yes,' came her reply, sounding hollow from within the iron mask. She didn't say anything else, and he concluded that she was being careful not to show too much interest in him.

Since there was nothing else to do, Richard lowered himself to a sitting position, bracing his back against the wall as he sat down. When he was seated, he was immediately aware of the plug in his arsehole. It pressed insistently as he shifted position. He made himself comfortable and thought about Hannelore Bern and his present situation. Yes, he liked what they had done this afternoon; he would even like to repeat the experience, or take part in similar exercises. But not at the price of never seeing Helena and Ingrid. At the same time, Margaret's cavalier gesture in giving him to Hannelore without any hint of her intentions made him very angry.

He now thought she had done it in order to get him away from Helena, to avoid losing her and having to make a decision about him. But that knowledge did nothing to help him escape. He was naked, locked inside a barn, in handcuffs, and with a plug up his backside: escape would not be easy. His minimum requirements were freedom and clothing, even if the latter meant donning women's clothes again, as it probably would. He needed his suitcase. But there was nothing to be done about it tonight. He would have to wait for a chance.

He shifted uncomfortably, the dildo in his arsehole moving as he did. Gretchen lay quietly, enduring her bondage and her double penetration stoically. She shifted from time to time, turning over with difficulty in the straw. Richard admired the play of her muscles as she shifted her position. She tugged against her bonds, as if trying to free herself, but of course she couldn't. She relaxed.

The barn darkened as the sun went down, the shadows deepening until Richard could not make out the shape of the interior any longer. Gretchen was merely a pale shape nearby. He drifted off to sleep.

* * *

He came awake abruptly. Something had startled him. The moon had risen, and its pale light shone in through one of the high windows of the barn. The barn had dimension again. Gretchen was once more a definite woman-shape beside him. His shoulders ached from being held behind his back for so long. He imagined Gretchen would be even more stiff in her tighter bondage.

The sound came again. It was a hollow muffled groan, and it came from Gretchen. She was once more shifting in the straw, but it was soon obvious that she was not merely changing position, or struggling against the ropes that bound her. She drew her knees up against her stomach, curling into a tight ball, before straightening them once again. She moved restlessly, then rolled over in the straw and began to raise and lower her hips, as if she were making love to an invisible person beneath her.

As he watched her, Richard realised that she was doing something very much like that. As her hips rose and fell, she groaned again, twisting her head from side to side. The moonlight glittered on the steel mask locked over her face. Her sexual arousal became more and more obvious as she thrashed about. As he watched her, Richard felt the beginnings of his own arousal: the tightness in his stomach and the stiffening of his cock.

Hannelore Bern must have had something like this in mind when she had left them in the barn, he thought. She must have known how Gretchen would react to the bondage and her dildoes. She must have known too that Richard would be aroused by her autoeroticism. So she had locked him in with her protégée, handcuffed and unable to do anything about his reaction. She would be laughing if she were there to watch.

Gretchen was becoming more frantic, bucking and writhing on the moonlit straw. She moaned loudly, the sound rising as she sought release. But evidently she could not quite make it. Had Hannelore known this too, wishing to torment Gretchen as well as Richard?

'Gretchen, are you all right?' Richard asked. His voice sounded queer and tight in his ears.

She lay still abruptly, aware again of his presence. She struggled to turn herself. After a series of heaves, she managed to roll on to her side so that she was facing him. 'Help me,' she said, the words hollow and muffled behind the mask she wore. Her head, and the featureless face, gave her an air of the inhuman, but from the neck down she was a desperate and desirable woman.

'What can I do?' he asked, feeling his cock stir as he looked at her.

'Move over and touch my breasts. Help me! I cannot make myself come alone. And I need to, so badly. It will drive me mad.'

'But how?' Richard asked her. 'She handcuffed my wrists behind my back.'

'Use your mouth, then – your teeth. Lick me! Bite me! Do something! I am burning up.'

Richard in turn heaved himself over on to his side and moved towards her, the plug in his arsehole stirring inside him. His stiff cock seemed to point the way. When he was within range, he manoeuvered himself until he could reach one of Gretchen's breasts with his mouth. Her nipples were erect with excitement. He took one of the engorged nipples into his mouth, circling it with his tongue, nipping gently at it with his teeth, sucking it.

Gretchen gasped with pleasure. She arched her back and thrust forward and back with her hips, being careful not to move her breast away from him. 'Oh, God,' she moaned. 'Oh! More! More!'

Richard guessed that she had worked herself almost to the edge of orgasm by herself, and that his effort had been the final nudge that pushed her over the edge. Gretchen was clearly out of control, jerking wildly and moaning as she came. He marvelled at her concentration, how she never jerked her breast away from his mouth, even while the rest of her body writhed and bucked in the straw. His cock was so stiff it hurt, and the occasional bumps as it made contact with Gretchen's thighs and belly served to excite him even more than the sight of her naked body and her wild movements. Had she not been plugged, he would have tried to penetrate her himself, difficult as that would have been with neither of them able to use their hands.

Her orgasm went on and on, her nude body writhing in the moonlight. Richard imagined her mouth open and her eyes wide with her pleasure, but he saw only the featureless helmet locked over her head and face. That had the perverse effect of exciting him more than the sight of her face had in the woods earlier. Evidently the steel helmet had a similar effect on her, as if it granted her privacy, anonymity, divorced her in some way from the pleasure that racked her helpless body. She was certainly more abandoned than she had been earlier.

Gretchen appeared to have come to the end of her climax. Her breath whistled slightly as she sucked air in through the breathing tubes of her helmet. Her body was bathed in sweat, and small tremors shook her from time to time. She moaned softly, deep inside her throat, the sound muffled by the mask. But she was not finished. When Richard made to draw back, she whispered harshly, 'No! Kiss me! Bite me!' And she arched her body towards him once more.

Richard bent forward again to take her breast into his mouth, sucking on the nipple and feeling it stiffen against his tongue. Gretchen moaned softly as her excitement built. Her hips moved tentatively, thrusting forward and back as she made the plugs move inside her. On the forward stroke, the fronts of her thighs brushed against Richard's stiff cock. He picked up her rhythm, thrusting himself so that the contact became more pronounced. Even though penetration was impossible, plugged as she was, Richard was excited by the increasing wildness of her thrusts and the evidence of her arousal, so close to him.

Gretchen's body was covered by a thin sheen of perspiration, and her breath was coming in gasps as she writhed in the straw. Once his cock slipped between her thighs, which were clasped tightly together to maximise the friction from the dildoes.

At once Gretchen drew back. 'No!' she gasped. 'Madame will see your semen if you come all over me. She will not be pleased.'

Richard wondered how much Madame's displeasure had to do with the matter. He suspected that much of Gretchen's reluctance was due to her own disinclination. He remembered her attitude that afternoon in the woods. Now that there was no one to beat her and enforce her participation, she was unwilling to let a man get close to her. Except on her own terms, of course, which seemed to be limited to ensuring her own pleasure. Mentally shrugging, he resumed work on her breasts.

Gretchen relaxed again as he nipped the engorged nipple between his teeth. She seemed to like it well enough when his attention was restricted to that area, as if she had set boundaries not all that different to those imposed by the girls he had seen when he first began dating: those who belonged to the no-hands-under-the-clothes school. That stage had long ago ceased to excite him. But he was excited by the proximity of the bound woman who writhed and gasped in the straw beside him. And not a little of the excitement was due to her reluctance to allow any further contact. Not for the first time, he wished he had the use of his hands.

Gretchen seemed all the more excited because she was bound and helpless. The steel mask, glinting in the moonlight through the high window, made her both anonymous and doubly a prisoner. The situation was clearly highly arousing to her. All this made her resistance to Richard much less convincing. It was almost as if she were seeking to emphasise her helplessness and fear. Or as if she were testing his resolve.

Richard continued to nip and nuzzle Gretchen's breasts, watching as she had her second climax – a small one, causing a rippling of her stomach muscles and a slight gasp of indrawn breath that ended in a moan. She writhed in pleasure, moving closer to the wall of the loosebox behind her. Richard followed. Gretchen shivered as she felt his mouth on her, giving herself to the spasms that swept through her.

Finally, as she bucked and arched in the straw, Gretchen came into contact with the wall of the loosebox and could move no further across the straw pile on which they lay. She seemed not to notice, being too wrapped up in her latest climax. She drummed her heels against the wall as she came, gasping and crying out.

But Richard had noticed the barrier. He pressed his body against Gretchen, rubbing his chest against her breasts while she cried out in her pleasure. But he also began to thrust with his hips, and now Gretchen had no further retreat. She clenched her legs tightly together when she felt his stiff cock begin to slide between them, but she was too late. Her body was covered by her sweat, and Richard's cock slid between her thighs, against her crotch. He could feel the heat of her as he thrust.

Once more Gretchen cried out in protest, 'No! Don't do that! Madame will be angry.'

'But will Gretchen be angry?' Richard asked her.

She seemed confused by the question, and didn't reply immediately. And when she did, the reply was indirect. 'You will come all over me, and Madame will see it when she comes for us in the morning. She will beat me – us – if you don't stop.'

But Richard never stopped thrusting between her thighs, even as she spoke. He had been too close to Gretchen as she came repeatedly, and he couldn't restrain his excitement. Nor did he particularly want to. If a beating was to be the end of it all, so be it. A stiff cock has very little imagination, he reflected, as he pinned Gretchen to the wall. He could feel his excitement building as the delightful friction brought him to his own moment of release.

Gretchen seemed to catch his mood. Or it may have been that she realised he wasn't going to stop. She began to thrust in rhythm with him, her breath rasping in the moonlit stillness of the barn. 'Oh!' she cried. 'Oh, oh!' She arched her back as her orgasm took her, moving wildly as he spurted between her thighs, his cock sliding in and out. She seemed to have forgotten Madame's displeasure.

Richard never gave it another thought when he felt himself going over the edge. He pushed himself tightly against her and let himself come.

Gradually she became quiet, exhausted by her own climaxes. Her breathing slowed, and the sweat cooled on her body. She shuddered several times – minor aftershocks after the main seismic disturbance of her prolonged and repeated orgasms.

Finally she spoke. 'That was much better than doing it on my own,' she admitted. 'Madame likes to leave me tied up so that I can stimulate myself. When she comes in the morning, she will sniff me to see if I have managed an orgasm. She seems to be excited by the idea of my autoeroticism. But she never joins me.' Gretchen's last remark was filled with regret.

'A bit like Margaret,' Richard told her. 'She gets excited by beating people and then letting them fuck one another. She doesn't join in.' Except the time she had been overcome by her excitement after beating him, he recalled silently. Would Hannelore Bern react the same way? That would be a real treat. Though maybe Gretchen wouldn't think so. So he said no more.

They lay against one another to stay warm, and gradually Richard drifted off to sleep. His last thought was that he had to escape and get back to Helena. And Ingrid. Maybe even Margaret.

In the morning, as Gretchen had predicted, Madame was displeased. Richard thought that one of the most wearing things about being the alpha female was the necessity of being perpetually displeased. Or of pretending to be. Hannelore Bern strode into the barn and came straight to the loosebox. She unlocked the door and looked over her two captives. Today she wore her business suit: the same severe pinstriped skirt and jacket she had worn at their first meeting. Her long, full legs were sheathed in black tights, and she wore stiletto-heeled shoes, also in black. The only relief to the sombreness of her costume was the cream silk blouse that showed through above the jacket front.

Richard managed to return her look, even though she brandished a riding crop menacingly. He watched as she inspected Gretchen. There were wisps of straw sticking to her thighs where the semen, in drying, had acted as a sort of glue. Not that there was any lack of further evidence to indicate what they had been up to during the night. The smell alone would have been a dead giveaway.

'This place smells like a whorehouse on a Sunday morning,' Hannelore declared loudly.

Gretchen flinched away from the harsh tones. Richard wondered just how much experience Hannelore Bern had had of whorehouses, on any day of the week. Not much, he concluded.

Hannelore pushed Gretchen over on to her stomach with the toe of her high-heeled shoe, stooping to examine the backs of her thighs as she had the front.

There too the straw stuck to her flesh. Hannelore wrinkled her nose in disgust and raised the crop, bringing it down with a swish through the air. It landed on Gretchen's bottom with a startling crack. Hannelore raised the crop again and again, striking her from her knees to her waist.

Gretchen screamed, more loudly than she had done the previous day, and sought to escape the lash by flinging herself about in the straw. Richard guessed that Hannelore was using her full strength to lash the young woman. Certainly she was striking harder than she had done yesterday. Gretchen was crying out wildly, seeking to escape the blows that landed on her helpless body.

Hannelore placed her foot on Gretchen's back, the stiletto heel marking her flesh. Gretchen was thus pinioned and couldn't flinch from the crop. The blows continued to rain down on the helpless captive, and she continued to scream in pain. Her screams sounded genuine. She did not look as if she was enjoying this beating as she had the last one.

Perhaps, Richard thought, Madame really was displeased with her young protégée. And maybe with him, too. Was she punishing Gretchen for enjoying herself during the night? Was Madame jealous of her? It might well be so, Richard thought. And in that case there was a good chance he would be punished in his turn. If so, there was nothing he could do to prevent it.

Hannelore continued to vent her wrath on Gretchen, whose bottom was by now bright red. She was sobbing, the sounds muffled by the steel mask but unmistakable nonetheless. When Hannelore shifted her target, the backs of Gretchen's legs began to redden as well. She kicked futilely with her bound legs, trying to evade the rain of blows that continued to fall on her.

Hannelore paused to remove her jacket. Richard saw that there were damp circles beneath her armpits, and that sweat had soaked the front of her silk blouse so that it clung to her, outlining her full breasts as they rose and fell with her heavy breathing. As the blows landed, Hannelore Bern's breasts bobbed heavily, excitingly. Richard admired them even as he awaited his turn. When her arm was raised for the next blow, they too were raised into prominence, defiantly straining against the sheer material of her blouse. Her face was covered with a thin sheen of perspiration. Richard found himself wondering what the rest of her would look like if she were nude. Would the rest of her be as pink as her face and neck? And would she be slick all over as Gretchen had been when she was in the throes of her climax? He felt his cock stiffen at the thought, and he rolled away slightly to conceal his reaction from her. She might be flattered, but then again she might not be.

When Hannelore finally stopped lashing Gretchen, she stood over her captive, regaining her breath. Her arm hung limply by her side, and Gretchen's bottom and legs were covered in red weals from the crop. Finally she turned to Richard. She noticed his stiff cock, and for a moment her eyes lighted with desire, as if she had been aroused by beating Gretchen. She seemed to be considering what to do with him, whether to have him or not.

Richard waited for her to make up her mind, and was disappointed when he saw her desire lose to – what was it? Pride? Too bad, he thought. It would have been interesting to fuck Hannelore Bern. Or to be fucked by her, which was what would have happened as things stood. But it was not to be. As he watched Hannelore, he saw her sense of her place reassert itself. She became once more the dominatrix.

Hannelore looked at him with anger. 'I will deal with you later,' she hissed, turning away and locking the door once more.

Richard lay back in the straw. Gretchen was sobbing

quietly against the wall. When she grew still, he spoke. 'Are you going to be all right?'

Gretchen raised her head, the mask concealing her features, and nodded slowly.

'I'm sorry you got such a beating.'

'It's not the first time,' Gretchen replied. 'Madame sometimes forgets herself. She will make it up to me. She always does. Sooner or later.'

'How much longer will you have to wear the mask?' Richard asked.

'I am not sure. Madame will probably remove it this evening when she gets back from the bank. Or she will have one of the other servants unlock it. It is no great inconvenience.' Gretchen fell silent.

Not long afterwards, the sound of a car departing came to them. Richard surmised that Hannelore Bern was on her way to work. He wondered how long she planned to leave them locked up in the barn. The door opened again shortly, and another young woman came across the barn to the loosebox. She too wore a maid's outfit, almost identical to those worn by Margaret's servants. She unlocked the door and helped Richard to his feet. She motioned for him to move outside before turning to Gretchen. She untied the ropes that bound her ankles and knees. Richard could see deep red lines where the bindings had cut into her flesh during her struggles. They must have hurt, but neither Gretchen nor the other woman mentioned them.

Without untying Gretchen's hands, the woman helped her to her feet and guided her outside to join Richard. Holding Gretchen's elbow, she led the way to the door. She seemed to be under orders not to speak, and Richard didn't know quite what he should say to a strange woman who was shepherding him across the open ground towards the cottage. So he said nothing. Once more he had the sense of being watched by hundreds of eyes, but there was no one else in sight. He was relieved when they reached the house. The maid led them to the back door and into the kitchen.

She signed for him to wait as she led Gretchen away. He pulled one of the chairs away from the table and sat on it, only to get up again immediately. The plug in his arsehole made sitting an uncomfortable exercise. Richard prowled restlessly around the kitchen, waiting for the next development. Approximately a quarter of an hour later, the maid came back for him.

She watched him pacing, then looked at the chair he had tried earlier. 'Not too comfortable sitting down, is it?' she asked with a sardonic smile. 'Madame often leaves me plugged when she wishes to punish me. It is tiresome not being able to sit all day.'

'What about Gretchen? Does she stay plugged all day too?' Richard asked.

'Yes, that often happens. But for her it is not a punishment. She likes it. I imagine that even now she is working on her next orgasm. She can amuse herself for hours that way.'

'Yes, I noticed that last night,' Richard said with a smile. 'But what about me? I mean, what happens now?'

'Madame has left orders that you should be made ready for her arrival this evening. She told me she will attend to you when she gets back from the city. You may find the attention unpleasant. She was not in a good mood when she left a short while ago.'

'Yes. I noticed that too,' Richard said. 'We'll just have to hope she makes a great deal of money today so that she will be in a better frame of mind.'

'Perhaps,' said the girl. 'But now you should come with me.'

She led the way down a short hall towards the south wing of the house: apparently the servants' quarters, if one judged by the number of rooms opening off it, all nearly identical in size.

Richard followed, wondering what Hannelore might

have in store for him. He was in two minds: he knew he had to think about escaping, and at the same time he was beginning to anticipate the next encounter with Hannelore. Whatever happened, it would be a bizarre experience. Ever since meeting Helena and Margaret, the bizarre had become the everyday.

The girl led him to the last room at the end of the hall, then unlocked the door and stood aside for him to enter. Like his room at Margaret's house, this one had a heavy door with strong locks. Unlike the room at Margaret's house, this one didn't have anyone like Heidi near at hand ready to help him with getting out. Escape would not be so easy, but there had to be some way. Or so he told himself as he looked over the bedsitting room he was to occupy.

There was a bathroom leading off to one side, to which the girl motioned him. Inside, she produced a small bunch of keys from the pocket of her maid's outfit. With one of them she removed his handcuffs. While Richard stretched his cramped arms, she unlocked the chain around his waist and pulled the plug from his arsehole. She left the chain hanging from his balls. Either she didn't have the key to it, or she had been told to leave it alone.

'What is your name?' he asked her. 'We should at least introduce ourselves.'

'Gertrude,' she replied. 'And you are Richard. Gretchen told me. Madame wants you to take a shower. Only,' Gertrude said, a hint of apology in her tone, 'I will have to lock you in while I am away.'

'Yes,' Richard said drily. 'Madame's orders.' He heard the door close as he adjusted the shower.

Ten

When Hannelore came home that evening, she sent for Richard, receiving him in the front sitting room whence they had all set off for the bridle path the day before. He had not been allowed to dress, even in the clothes he had brought with him. That was as effective a way of keeping him from running away as any that could be devised. He wore only the chain and ring on his balls, and was beginning to wonder if he would ever have it off.

Gertrude had come for him. She brought the handcuffs with her, and Richard allowed her to cuff his hands behind his back before she led him to the audience with Hannelore.

Standing naked before Hannelore Bern was a daunting experience, Richard thought. Especially when she was dressed, as now, in her leather corselet, shiny tights and stiletto heels. She must have changed as soon as she arrived home, in order to be as daunting as possible. But he was not going to look daunted. There was such a thing as self-esteem. He wondered if she was planning on another outing in the woods, and another night for him in the barn with Gretchen. And a beating for the culprits afterwards. But he said nothing.

Hannelore Bern looked both beautiful and dangerous, regarding him as a cat studies a canary. She appeared to be deciding what line to take with him. Richard decided to speak first, even knowing her preference for silent obedience.

'How long do you plan to keep me here?' he asked, with, he hoped, just the right mix of curiosity and irritation.

Hannelore looked sharply at him. Her eyes flashed in anger. 'As long as I like. Months. Years. Until I get tired of you.'

'No,' he said, watching the anger redden her face. 'I need to get back to Soltau. I want to leave tomorrow morning.'

'You will not be going back to Soltau. Margaret told me why you want to go back there, and why she did not want you to come back.'

'Why I want to go is none of your business. But I am going.'

'Like that?' Hannelore gestured with amused contempt at his nakedness. 'I don't think you will.'

'Give me my clothes, and I will go,' Richard told her.

'I think not,' Hannelore replied. 'I want you to stay here. I need a manservant, if only to make the women here know what they are missing. Later, after you have been house-broken, I will let you into the chateau. In the meantime, you will help out at the bank. No one there will suspect that I have a male assistant. Gretchen knows better than to tell anyone about you. You will be Pamela Rhodes, whom I have hired to take care of translation for our Anglophone customers. I believe you will grow to like it in time, and forget about Margaret and little Helena. And besides,' Hannelore added, stretching like a cat to display herself in the figure-hugging corselet, 'there may be other benefits in staying.' She smiled at Richard.

Despite himself, Richard felt his cock grow stiff as he stared at this beautiful brunette who was half offering herself to him.

Hannelore noticed his interest. She laughed mockingly. 'See, already you are changing your mind.'

Richard said nothing.

The next morning, Richard was woken by the alarm. He heard the distant sounds of feet moving about the house. The smell of coffee brewing came to him. He got up and shaved carefully before beginning to dress. He taped his cock as Ingrid had shown him, then put on a new pair of black tights, threading the chain on his ring through the hole that had been made in the crotch. The corselet came next. Again he fed the chain through the hole in the gusset. Next came the new latex breast pads, provided by Hannelore the day before. He had to admit that they looked more realistic than the ones he had been using. The moulded nipples showed through the corselet.

The sound of the door opening interrupted his routine. It was Gertrude in her maid's outfit.

'I've come to help you with the make-up and the wig,' she announced. She carried a pair of leg-irons.

Richard wondered if Madame had forbidden anyone to say even a simple 'good morning'. Everything here was business, carried out in as few words as possible. Nevertheless he sat quietly as Gertrude locked the leg-irons around his ankles and began to apply the make-up, lipstick and eye shadow. The face which looked back at him from the mirror was almost unrecognisable, his own but yet not his own. Gertrude fitted the wig, combing and brushing the long hair around and off his face. The result was an even greater transformation. When she was finished, she stepped back to inspect her work.

'That will do for now,' she pronounced. 'Madame will tell you if she wants any change. I've been instructed to leave the leg-irons on you. You can finish dressing now, but don't take too long. Madame doesn't like to be kept waiting.' She left the door open as she departed.

Richard guessed that Hannelore Bern was taking his threat to leave seriously: hence the leg-irons. With a shrug, he put on the slip and the blouse. Next came the skirt and jacket. He stepped into the high-heeled shoes. Except for the chains, he looked like any other female secretary setting out for a day's work.

Gertrude was in the kitchen preparing breakfast. Leg-irons had been added to her costume since Richard had last seen her. He looked curiously at her, but she said nothing. He shifted his gaze to her legs, which were sheathed in shiny black nylon tights. Against them the heavy shackles looked at once incongruous and highly arousing.

Footsteps and a faint clinking of chains announced the arrival of Gretchen, whom he had not seen since they were parted after the night in the barn. Although she no longer wore the steel face-mask, she too had been put into leg-irons. There was no outward sign of the woman who had been so strongly aroused by being left bound and helpless. She was dressed for work, a smaller and blonder version of Richard himself. He could see by her unnaturally erect carriage that she wore the saddle strap again. He wondered if the twin plugs had been left inside her as well. She sat down carefully in the chair, keeping her back straight as she ate her breakfast.

'Good morning,' she said to them both. To Gertrude, she added, 'Madame is ready for her breakfast.'

The maid nodded and began to load a tray with coffee, toast and butter. Gretchen said nothing more until she had gone out.

'We will be working today as Madame's assistants. She told me she plans to keep you here and have you work at the bank.'

Richard said nothing of his resolve to leave as soon as possible. Pointing to Gretchen's leg-irons, he asked instead if they would all be wearing them henceforth.

Gretchen replied that today was out of the ordinary.

Normally, she said, she wore only her saddle strap at work. She said she would never dream of running away from Madame. But Madame had decreed that she be shackled as a reminder not to disobey.

Remembering Hannelore Bern's reaction to what they had done during their confinement together, he didn't need to ask what form the disobedience had taken. He asked, 'What about Gertrude? What has she done to make Madame angry?'

'Oh,' Gretchen said, 'she has done nothing. She wears her leg-irons all day whenever she is to be left alone in the house. The chauffeur will be attending to his duties in the city, and Gertrude will be alone here all day. She will be locked in, but the leg-irons are an added incentive not to run away. I do not think she would run away in any case. She likes her work here with Madame.'

Richard thought he detected irony in the reference to 'work'.

'What does she do here?' he asked. 'I mean, aside from maid's work.'

'She dresses Madame and looks after her wardrobe, she cleans the house, and she performs certain other duties for Madame.' Gretchen reddened at these last words.

'What other duties?' Richard prompted.

Gretchen hesitated, obviously choosing her words carefully. She looked over her shoulder to be sure they were alone before speaking. 'She performs . . . intimate services. For Madame.' She reddened further.

'You mean lesbian lovemaking?' Richard said, thinking of the relation between Helena and Margaret.

'Please, not so loud.' Gretchen looked over her shoulder fearfully before nodding.

Richard continued without heeding her signs of alarm, 'So Gertrude is the lesbian part of the household, while you are the resident masochist?'

Alarmed, Gretchen put her finger to her lips.

'Well, are you?' Richard asked.

She nodded.

'Tell me about it,' he said.

Gretchen bridled. 'You have no right to ask me these things. You are only another servant. Madame makes you wear women's clothes and take her orders, just like the rest of us.'

'You're right about the orders, but the clothes are nothing to do with Madame. This is how I arrived. Of my own free will,' Richard told her. 'But you might as well tell me. You know you're going to anyway. As you said, we're all fellow workers – sufferers, if you like.'

'Workers of the world, unite. You have nothing to lose but your chains,' Gretchen said sneeringly.

'So you don't want to lose your chains?' Richard asked.

'Yes . . . No . . . You are confusing me.'

'So tell me about it,' he said, more gently. He could see that she wanted to talk to someone. And he might learn something from her that would help him to get away.

'Gertrude,' Gretchen said, beginning her revelations by talking about someone else, 'is the more passive part of the partnership, though that hardly describes her adequately. She is only passive in comparison with Madame, and only because Madame herself wants to be the one who gives all the orders. If she had her way, Gertrude would be making the beast with two backs every time she saw Madame.'

He thought he detected malice in the description, but didn't want to interrupt Gretchen now that she was talking.

'So Madame – wisely, I think – makes her keep her distance and exercise moderation. Otherwise she would have no time to do anything else.'

Or anyone else, Richard thought.

'As you said, I am the resident masochist,' Gretchen said with a faint blush. She managed to convey that being a masochist was somehow superior to being a sweaty lesbian nymphomaniac. 'Madame punishes Gertrude with the whip. The whip is my reward.'

'It didn't look that way the last time I saw you beaten,' Richard said.

'Ah, but there are ways of being whipped, and ways of being whipped. When Madame takes the trouble to use the whip erotically, there is no greater pleasure in the world. It is not wholly a matter of severity. Intent has as much to do with it. When Madame wants to tease or arouse me with the whip, I wonder why anyone bothers to aspire to heaven. Especially as the heaven to which they aspire is such a sexless place.'

Richard had to agree with her reasoning. Otherwise he would not be here either. Or at Margaret's, he added silently.

'Last night, for example,' Gretchen began.

But at that point Gertrude came back into the kitchen, and she turned the conversation to the more mundane matter of going to the city.

Hannelore herself came in a few minutes later, and they got up to follow her. Richard and Gretchen got into the car wearing their leg-irons. The chauffeur paid no more attention to them than he did to the car. He probably saw this every day, Richard guessed.

The car deposited them at the private entrance at the rear of the bank. Richard and the two women went inside while the chauffeur parked the car. Richard felt self-conscious, but Gretchen behaved normally. He tried to emulate her sang-froid. And he wondered if anyone in the front office had any idea what was going on in the director's office. If word ever got out, there would be an extremely unpleasant reaction on the part of the conservative Swiss. The idea of mixing sex with finance would be deeply disturbing to them.

And there, suddenly before him, was the way out. The whole game depended on a willingness on the part of every player to abide by the two main rules: secrecy and acquiescence. Break either or both of these rules, and Hannelore Bern's hold over him would cease to exist. She might manage to restrain him physically, as now with the leg-irons, but not at every moment. Sooner or later her vigilance would slacken.

There was no one in Hannelore's office when they arrived. She simply walked into the room, and they followed. Hannelore seated herself at her desk and lifted the telephone. 'Do not disturb me until I ring,' she ordered the front office. She settled down to deal with the paperwork that always accumulates overnight. Richard and Gretchen were left to their own devices. Gretchen took herself off to the file room, beckoning Richard to follow.

'It would be better if you had something to do,' Gretchen said. 'Madame doesn't like to be disturbed while she is catching up on incoming correspondence. And she has a strong aversion to idleness. I will show you the filing system, and later you can help me.'

Richard nodded, glancing around the smaller room that adjoined Hannelore's office. It was lined on three sides with tall filing cabinets. On the fourth side, near the door, was the console with video monitors that obviously served the closed-circuit security cameras. Richard saw the view outside the main entrance. Several cameras presented a constantly shifting picture from the main lobby and the public spaces. Other screens showed the vault and the secure rooms with their rows of locked boxes. Richard guessed that the cash he had delivered was in one of them. There were pictures of the inside of several offices, some occupied and some not.

There were several blank screens. Richard moved to the console and studied the controls. There were switches which controlled the operation of each camera, and small joysticks which were used to pan and zoom individual cameras. It was all very neat, each control labelled and the entire console clean and new.

'Gretchen,' Richard said, 'do you know how to operate this equipment?'

'What?' Gretchen looked up. 'Oh, you mean the video surveillance cameras. Yes. Madame sometimes likes to look at the different operations, and I operate the system as she directs. It is very sophisticated. For instance, we can video any area of the building and store it on tape. In fact, that is the normal practice, since no one can monitor all the cameras. The tapes are stored and later one of the security guards will view them at random in case something was missed.'

'What are these blank screens for?' Richard asked.

'Two of them are spare: if one or more of the operating cameras goes down, we can switch to them. And two are used to scan Madame's office during the hours she is away, in case anyone decides to break into the confidential files she keeps here. Those two cameras are not wired into the security guards' console. The tapes are kept here so that Madame or I can review them. Sometimes she tapes interviews with prospective clients. She does that with all of the couriers who operate the cash delivery system with Margaret Wagner. I would guess that you were videoed when you made your delivery. The tape would be here somewhere.'

Richard remembered the striptease Hannelore had forced them to do, and suddenly he knew how he would break away from Hannelore. And how he would ensure that she would never try to track him down or bother him again. That was an important consideration. People with as much money as Hannelore were never good to have as enemies unless one had some way to keep them from exercising their power. Richard knew that Hannelore would not appreciate him leaving, and would be inclined to cause trouble for him or Helena or Ingrid – or all three.

But he said nothing of all this to Gretchen. They filed the documents for the most part in silence, Richard doing the ones in the lower drawers that Gretchen would have found uncomfortable in her saddle strap. They worked undisturbed until lunch time.

Hannelore summoned them both into her office. She had disposed of most of the correspondence from the previous day and was looking carnivorous when Gretchen and Richard emerged from the file storage room. Richard noticed the riding crop lying on her desk at the same time as Gretchen did. He heard her low gasp as she saw the lash. At the same time Richard felt a sharp thrill in his belly and cock as he imagined what was going to happen.

'Take off your clothes, Gretchen,' she ordered.

Richard was taken by surprise. He had not expected the moment to come so soon. It looked as if the afternoon's activity would be just what he needed. Gretchen began at once to strip. Richard had to act quickly. He cast about for an excuse to get back to the file room and activate the cameras in Hannelore's office. The only thing he could think of on the spur of the moment was the old schoolboy trick. Suddenly he had to go to the toilet. Hannelore impatiently waved him away. Her attention was mainly on Gretchen, watching as the young woman undid the buttons of her blouse.

Once inside the file room, Richard quickly switched on the cameras in Hannelore's office. As they warmed up, he sought fresh tape cartridges for them, and fed them into the slots with hands that shook from his need to hurry. The blank screens turned from black to grey, flickered, and steadied down into two views of the outer office. One camera was aimed too high. Richard corrected that with the joystick, then set both to automatic scan. As he watched Gretchen unhooking her brassiere, he noticed that the cameras were set so that one scanned the desk area while the other panned around the room. That might miss some of the action, but it would have to do. He hurried back to Hannelore's office.

Gretchen was standing before Hannelore, naked except for her tights and saddle strap. Hannelore bent down to unlock Gretchen's leg-irons. The young woman then peeled her tights down her legs. She blushed pinkly when she heard Richard's step behind her, but Hannelore held her gaze and silently commanded her to continue.

The leather strap between Gretchen's legs was slightly damp. Richard guessed that she was already wet and excited. The strap would of course have parted her long since. Gretchen's hand strayed to her mons veneris, where she rubbed the strap against her body, rotating her hips slightly.

'It seems our little Gretchen is already excited, does it not?' Hannelore smiled mockingly as Gretchen's blush deepened. Gretchen snatched her hand away as if the strap had burnt her, and then didn't know where to put it.

'Gretchen,' Hannelore said, 'put these handcuffs on Richard. It wouldn't do if he interfered, would it?'

As before, Richard stood quietly while his hands were cuffed behind his back.

Hannelore picked up the riding crop. Gretchen's eyes followed her hand as she raised it and beckoned Gretchen close to the desk. 'Bend over,' she commanded the young woman. 'You know what we are going to do.'

Gretchen bent over the desk, placing her hands flat on the top. She never took her eyes from the whip. Hannelore moved beside her and tapped her knees with the shaft of the whip. Gretchen moved her feet further from the desk until her bottom was fully exposed.

Richard admired the taut muscles in her long legs as she presented herself for punishment. But Hannelore was not yet satisfied. She tapped Gretchen's legs again, between the thighs, indicating she was to spread them apart. When Richard looked this time, he fancied he could see the pink rosebud of her arsehole. Gretchen's cunt lips were fully exposed at the apex of her thighs as she held her bottom up in the air. The strap was dark with her juices where it passed between her labia. She was breathing heavily, and Richard could see that her nipples were taut and crinkly. Gretchen moved her hips, rubbing against the strap so that it pressed deeply between her lips. The strap must have been tight against her clitoris, for she caught her breath on a gasp as she moved.

Hannelore touched Gretchen with her hand, rubbing her labia and passing inside her cunt. She took her time, observing Gretchen's reaction to the intimate touch. 'She's wet,' Hannelore said, as she withdrew her fingers and wiped them on Gretchen's thigh.

The young woman moaned softly. 'Please, go on. I am ready.'

'Should I go on?' Hannelore asked Richard. 'It is such fun to make her wait. When she is really desperate, she will beg me to strike her, punish her, do anything to her. Would you like to see that?'

The question was purely rhetorical. Hannelore could clearly see the lump Richard's cock made as it strained against the tape and the constricting corselet. She moved closer to him and touched him with the whip. Richard gave a surprised grunt and jerked his hips at the touch.

Hannelore smiled mockingly at him. 'It looks as if you are excited too. It will be great fun having the two of you straining at the lead.' She turned back to Gretchen, leaving Richard to his own devices.

Two of those devices, he could see, were working well enough. The red lights on the two security cameras were lit, and they were steadily recording everything in the room. He hoped that Hannelore Bern would be too busy to notice them. If his own excitement was any indication, things should be all right.

Hannelore stroked Gretchen's quivering thighs with the crop, pausing every now and then to give her a light smack, teasing her with a foretaste of what was to come. Gretchen's head hung down between her outstretched arms. She was breathing heavily now, great shuddery breaths. Her eyes were tightly closed, and she was apparently concentrating all her attention on the whip drawing lazy patterns on her body. The saddle strap was pulled tightly into her crotch by her posture, and she was thrusting slowly and steadily with her hips against it. Richard knew she was rubbing her clitoris against the strap, and he wondered what that must feel like. Obviously Gretchen found it exciting. She was moaning softly as she moved.

Abruptly, Hannelore raised the crop and brought it down on her bottom with a sharp crack. Gretchen cried out, more from surprise than pain. She jumped forward, then resumed her pose as Hannelore let the whip trail lazily down the backs of her thighs and over the red weal across her bottom. Another sharp crack, another surprised yip from Gretchen. This time the crop landed across her thighs, just below her arse cheeks. Hannelore resumed the teasing. Gretchen's face was now red as she tried to contain her excitement. She lowered herself towards the desk top, raising her bottom more invitingly to the whip.

'You can see how our little Gretchen loves the whip. She would do this every day if I allowed her. I have to ration her strictly so that she continues to enjoy it. Neither of us would like it if she became too accustomed to pleasure.' Hannelore spoke without breaking the rhythm of teasing and lashing Gretchen.

To Richard, this sounded very close to what Gretchen had said about Gertrude. Hannelore Bern's sadism consisted partly in denying the two women what they wanted. But now Gretchen was getting what she craved.

Her bottom and the backs of her thighs were

crisscrossed with bright red stripes. Hannelore was teasing her now only by letting the crop trail over her cunt and arsehole before resuming the lashing of the rest of her exposed rear. She was squirming and thrusting with her bottom and hips, as if seeking the lash. Her moans of pleasure were almost continuous now, broken mainly when the crop struck her, and then resumed when she had regained the breath that had been driven from her by the blow. Her head now rested on her forearms on the desk top, and her bottom was thrust high to offer the best target. Her legs were braced apart and her muscles taut under the satin of her flesh.

Hannelore broke off the whipping long enough to unlock the saddle strap. She unbuckled it and helped Gretchen to shrug out of it. It fell to the floor at her feet, and her cunt and arsehole were now fully exposed. Hannelore used the handle of the crop to tease her arsehole open. Then she pushed it inside, so that the whip stood up like the tail of a cartoon dog. Gretchen rolled her hips as it went in, and then her eyes opened in surprise as her orgasm took her. She gasped and moaned, shuddering as the waves of pleasure swept through her.

Richard remembered how Helena had responded to pain, and thought he knew how Gretchen must now be feeling as she bucked and heaved.

Hannelore grasped the whip protruding from Gretchen's arsehole and began to move it in and out. The pink hole stretched outward and inward as it was pulled out and then thrust back in. Richard, and the cameras, watched as Gretchen cried out and came, heaving herself backward and forward in time with the movement of the plug inside her. Bent over as she was, her cunt lips were fully exposed. Her pubic hair was damp with her sweat and with her juices. The smell of her musk was strong in the room. She looked as if she would never stop coming. Hannelore reached between her outspread thighs and rubbed Gretchen's clitoris with her free hand. The young woman cried out again as another orgasm swept through her. She thrust wildly with her hips and rubbed herself hard against Hannelore's finger.

Suddenly Hannelore plucked the whip out.

Gretchen shrieked, 'No, please, leave it in!'

Hannelore instead brought the whip up between her legs, striking her squarely on her exposed clitoris. Gretchen screamed, in ecstasy as far as Richard could tell, and presented her cunt again to the whip. It struck her again and again, on the insides of the thighs, on her arsehole, on her cunt, until Gretchen was once more screaming with pleasure and gasping for breath. She was covered with her own sweat and her body was shaking, but she was oblivious to everything except the eruptions in her belly and between her straining thighs. The whip rose and fell and the young woman cried out for what seemed an eternity.

Richard watched, his cock stiff with excitement. He would have gladly buried it in Gretchen's abused cunt – or her arsehole – if they had been alone, and if his hands had been free. As it was, he knew that Hannelore would object. At least. And he wanted to stay out of camera range while she had the stage all to herself. It would be easier for him if he were not on tape.

When it was all over, Gretchen was quivering from her climaxes. Hannelore was glowing pleasantly, a thin sheen of sweat covering her face and neck. She was panting gently, her breasts rising and falling in time. Even though she was still wearing her jacket, Richard could see that her nipples were taut. He suspected that, if he could put his hand on her cunt, it would be wet. For a moment he regretted that he couldn't. It would be interesting to see how Hannelore Bern would react when faced with a stiff cock.

Hannelore laid the crop on the desk and told

Gretchen to go to the bathroom and clean herself up. Turning to Richard, she asked, 'Did you enjoy that?'

'Not as much as Gretchen did,' he replied.

'Yes, she really enjoys the whip. Do you?'

'Not particularly,' Richard replied. 'It's all right when used as an occasional variation.'

'Well, maybe you will change your mind while you are with me.'

Richard said nothing. He hoped again that no one would notice the cameras in operation. Gretchen came back looking more composed and began putting her clothes on. While she did so, Hannelore removed Richard's handcuffs. When Gretchen was dressed again, she ordered them back to work. Gretchen was sent out to collect some letters that needed signing.

To his relief, Richard was ordered back to the file room. He quickly shut down the cameras and removed the tape cassettes from them. These he hid in his handbag, inserting fresh blank tapes and removing all traces of the recording which, he hoped, would be the means of getting free of Hannelore Bern. Nothing else interrupted the afternoon routine, and they were driven back to Hannelore's estate at the end of the day.

Gertrude, still wearing her leg-irons, met them at the door. She wanted to know what time Madame would like her dinner. Hannelore gave her the key and told her to remove her leg-irons and Richard's. After he was locked in his room, Hannelore said, she would be required at the main house. She smiled languorously at Gertrude, so that it was clear what she would be required for.

Gretchen had had her pleasure at the bank that afternoon. Gertrude was looking forward to hers this evening. Only Richard would be left out, it seemed. But he had to view the tapes and make plans for their use. That would be best done undisturbed. Therefore he went to his room without protest. He undressed and took a shower before sitting down with the video tapes.

The cameras had caught most of the action. Gretchen was in almost all of the footage, but was not identifiable because her face was hidden by her posture. Hannelore's face was readily identifiable, and there was no mistaking her excitement as she plied the whip. Richard imagined she would lose a great deal of credibility and face if these images were to be seen by any of the men of high finance in the city's banks. The trick now would be to devise a way of letting her know what leverage he had.

Clearly it would do no good to use the tapes while he was at the country estate. He had no allies there. Hannelore would simply order the security guards to confiscate them. And what she did thereafter would be most unpleasant. Richard imagined that anyone who seriously tried to cross her will or who threatened to make real trouble would be in for a very bad time. Such a person might even be in line for something permanent in the way of silencing. He did not really know Hannelore well, but she had to have a certain ruthlessness to have achieved her present status. So, safety first.

Richard rewound the tapes and stowed them in his handbag. There was no place at the estate where he could safely leave them. They would have to accompany him everywhere.

Eleven

Sometime during the night, as it were subconsciously, a course of action suggested itself to Richard. The day of action would be partly decided by circumstances, but he had to be alert for the right occasion, ready to flee when the chance came. To that end, he packed his bag and left it in the wardrobe. He would live out of his suitcase for the time being. Then he got dressed for the day, taping his cock as usual and leading the chain on his balls carefully through the holes in the corselet and tights. He was dressed once more in the uniform of a female junior assistant, and was ready to leave when Gertrude unlocked the door and summoned him to breakfast. Today there were no leg-irons. Presumably Hannelore was satisfied that lessons had been learnt.

At the bank, Gretchen was employed as usual, fetching documents from the front office and filing them. Richard was given the task of filing and tidying in Hannelore's office. He made the coffee when needed, and retired to the file room behind closed doors whenever a client came to call. Hannelore was no more willing for him to see her callers than Margaret had been. Richard began to think that there might be a shady side to the business. The amounts of cash involved were too great to be solely the proceeds of legitimate business. That sort of transaction was usually handled by cheques or electronic transfer. Illicit cash could not be handled that way. But there was nothing he could do about the situation, even if he had had any desire to interfere.

Richard took the opportunity to duplicate the video tapes while he was sequestered in the file room. He hid the duplicates as well as he could among the rest of the cassettes. At the same time, he used the cameras to watch the meetings in Hannelore Bern's office. It might be useful to know something of what went on in case further persuasion were needed.

Nothing like a good chance presented itself that day. Nor for the next three days, during which Richard worried about letting Helena or Ingrid know what was happening. He knew of no way except by letter, and he did manage to send a short note, of the don't-worry variety, mixed in with the bank's correspondence. That was on the Thursday, and on the same day he was overtaken by events and had to make his move, so that the note scarcely had time to carry its message of reassurance to Soltau.

On Thursday morning, Gretchen was ordered to stay at the estate to do the domestic accounts. 'You will come to the bank after lunch. Call me when you are finished, and I'll send the car to pick you up,' Hannelore told her.

So Richard and Hannelore were driven to the city alone. Richard's plan called for having someone bring his suitcase to the bank. He would need the clothes for travelling. Gretchen would do as she was told. All he had to do was tell Hannelore that he was leaving. And then get away as quickly as possible. He touched the tape cassettes in his handbag as if to reassure himself that they were safe, and began to think of how to break the news to Hannelore Bern.

This time it was Richard who was delegated to gather the morning's correspondence from the front office and convey it to Hannelore as she sat in her private domain. So, for most of the morning, Richard fetched and carried. Near eleven-thirty, Hannelore left a do-not-disturb order with the secretary and ordered Richard to make fresh coffee. He was then sent to the file room and told to close the door. He guessed that she would soon be meeting an important client.

Herr Jurgen Schmidt arrived at eleven forty-five and was shown into the private office. Richard, in the file room, quietly activated the security cameras and settled down to listen to the conference. Herr Schmidt got right down to business. There was to be a large transfer of cash that very day to Margaret Wagner in Stuttgart. Could she, Madame Bern, have a courier ready within an hour?

Yes, Madame Bern said, she could manage that.

'Good,' said Herr Schmidt. 'I admire the promptness with which you manage the delicate business we are engaged in.' He placed the attaché case he had brought with him on Hannelore Bern's desk. 'Ten million Swiss francs and another five million Deutschmarks,' he told her.

Hannelore nodded and accepted the keys to the case. Only then did Herr Schmidt accept her offer of coffee, over which they settled the details and exchanged commonplaces about the weather and their families. Herr Schmidt left only thirty minutes after his arrival.

Richard, watching from the file room, knew the moment had come. He opened the door almost as soon as Schmidt had gone, catching Hannelore by surprise. She was in the act of lifting the telephone receiver, probably to cancel her do-not-disturb order. Richard had to catch her before she did that. Even though he knew that the forthcoming interview would not be pleasant, still the old forms came to mind. 'One moment, if you please, Madame,' he said as he crossed to her desk.

Hannelore looked up in surprised annoyance. 'Yes, what is it?' she snapped.

'I want to be the courier who takes the money to Stuttgart.'

Hannelore looked at him in amazement. 'How did you know about that?' Her look of puzzlement turned to rage when Richard indicated the security cameras, now motionless. 'You . . . you . . .' She was speechless with anger for a moment. When she continued, her voice was low and hard. 'You have been spying on me.'

'Well, yes,' Richard admitted, 'but it was in a good cause.' His smile only enraged Hannelore more.

'Good cause?' she said. 'What might that be?' It was clear from her voice that there could be no cause good enough to allow anyone to take such liberties.

'My freedom,' Richard replied. 'I told you I wanted to go back to Soltau, and this is the perfect occasion. I can carry your money at the same time. That will save transport costs, won't it?'

Hannelore opened her mouth to wither him with a blast of rage, but Richard forestalled her.

'You don't really believe that I only used the cameras to spy on your business dealings, do you?'

'What . . .,' she faltered, 'what else have you filmed?'

'The session with Gretchen a few days ago,' he told her. 'She can't be identified, but your face is plainly visible. Not to mention your excitement as you beat her. I don't imagine Herr Schmidt would be too impressed if he knew how easily you could be compromised. Do you?'

Hannelore's face went pale. She slumped in her chair, all the hauteur gone now, but she still managed to look desirable in her sudden vulnerability. Richard imagined it was not a pleasant situation for someone like her, but now that he had her on the run he must press on. When she recovered her poise, as she no doubt would, it would be much harder to take her by surprise again.

'So I will be taking the trip to Stuttgart?' he prompted her.

'How – how do I know you are telling the truth about the video tapes? You are lying!' she spat at him, her face reddening as her anger rekindled. But there was still doubt there.

Richard could see that Hannelore was already struggling to regain the upper hand. There was no time to lose. 'Come into the file room and I'll show you,' he retorted. 'No,' he said, as Hannelore made a swift movement towards the telephone. He sprang to the desk and moved the instrument out of her reach. As he bent to unplug the phone from the wall, Hannelore sprang at him. Her sudden attack bore him to the floor, winded. His skirt rode up his legs, and a button popped from his suit jacket.

Had Hannelore pressed her advantage, she might have ended the fight there and then. All she needed to do was hit him over the head with something hard and heavy. Failing that, there was always the knee in the groin, which would have put him out of action just as effectively. But she made a lunge for the phone instead, allowing Richard to recover somewhat.

He grabbed her ankle as she reached across the desk, bringing her crashing down with her stomach across the edge. This time it was she who was winded. He hauled on her leg and pulled her down to the floor. Hannelore was an angry tigress. She landed fighting. She tried to claw his face, while Richard struggled to imprison her arms. He didn't want to hurt her, while she had no such compunction. A quick punch to the face would have put her out, but he had to content himself with one to the stomach. When she slumped, gasping for breath, he got astride her and held her arms down with his own.

It was an impasse. Hannelore struggled, trying to dislodge him and managing to look both angry and desirable, while Richard strove to hold her down. His priority was to get away, with or without her cooperation. She was intent on regaining both her dignity and her control of him and the situation. The battle was carried on silently for the most part: grunts of effort from Hannelore and thumps as he pinned her down once more. Her own skirt was around her hips and her blouse gaping open, but Richard had no time to admire the view.

With a heave, Richard managed to turn Hannelore on to her side. He twisted one of her arms behind her back, levering her wrist up between her shoulders until she cried out with pain. He turned her face down and held her arm up until she stopped kicking and struggling. Carefully, he manoeuvered her until they could stand up, then he marched her across to the file room, where packing materials were stored. He would have to tie her before making his escape, and he had to keep her quiet long enough to let her see the tape so that she would know what he could do to her.

In the file room, Richard held Hannelore's face against the wall with one hand, while he pulled down a roll of packaging twine with the other. With difficulty, he wrestled her arms behind her back and tied her wrists together. When she knew she was helpless, all the fight went out of her, though she was still very angry. Richard thought she made a fine sight with her breasts peeping through her unbuttoned blouse and her skirt high up her thighs.

'Now be quiet and watch the screen,' Richard told her. He inserted one of the tape cassettes from his handbag and started the player.

Hannelore's anger faded as she watched the replay of the last session with Gretchen. It was replaced first by worry, no doubt the worry about what would happen if her business clients and partners saw the gusto with which she lashed Gretchen's bottom and thighs. The worry gave way in turn to interest. The next stage was arousal, becoming plain as she watched herself inserting the handle of the riding crop in Gretchen's backside. By the time she began lashing Gretchen between her legs, Hannelore was clearly on the edge of orgasm. And even now, merely watching it on the monitor, she was becoming excited all over again.

Richard, watching her, saw her breathing quicken and her nipples begin to show through her blouse as they erected. He could understand that readily enough. He was excited by the tape himself. But there was the matter of what to do next. When the tape ended, he stood before Hannelore.

'So. What about the trip to Stuttgart? Still don't want me to go?'

Hannelore came back to the present abruptly. Richard could see the excitement replaced by business.

'Of course, I do not want you to go, but I have no choice.' Hannelore managed to include both the matter of the tape and her own helplessness in the 'no choice'.

'Since that's settled, we need to make some immediate plans. When that's done, we can discuss the future.' Richard stepped smoothly into the power vacuum he had engineered. 'You will call Gretchen and have her send my suitcase to the bank with the chauffeur. Tell her that she is to return with the chauffeur to collect you in the evening. You can either tell her you need her to work late, or you can imply that she is in for another session like the one on the tape. Either way, she will do whatever you say.'

'Unlike others,' Hannelore said, with a return of the old manner. She glared at him.

'I didn't mind obeying you. I enjoyed the games too,' Richard told her. 'It's just that I have some things I must do back in Germany. Under other circumstances, I could have liked it here.'

Hannelore was only partly mollified by his words. She shrugged. 'Get on with the next step,' she said.

Richard shrugged in his turn. He had not expected the olive branch to mean much to someone like Hannelore Bern. 'After I have changed clothes, I will simply take the case to the railway station and get on a train to Stuttgart. There I will deliver the case and go back to Margaret Wagner's estate, as I planned.' He didn't tell her what he had planned after that. 'You needn't worry about the money. It will be delivered to whomever you designate.'

'I wasn't worried about that,' Hannelore replied. She did not mean that she relied solely on his honesty. The reliance was based more fundamentally on the courier's desire to remain healthy. 'I meant, what about me? I could have you stopped before you left the bank, and those tapes taken from you. After that you would be returned to me, and things would not be very pleasant for you. My guards will do whatever I tell them and ask no questions.'

'I have sent copies of the tapes back to Soltau for safekeeping,' Richard told her. Of course he was bluffing, and he hoped his voice did not betray him. He also had to make an effort not to look at the copies he had hidden among the other cassettes. 'If I do not arrive shortly after they do, the package will be opened. You can imagine the results. Margaret Wagner might be very interested in the tapes.'

Hannelore obviously thought that having the tapes fall into Margaret's hands would be as bad as having them delivered to her other associates. There couldn't be much loyalty or fellow feeling among the financial sharks who ran the big money operations. The blood from one of their wounded members might well spark off a feeding frenzy.

'In any case,' Richard continued, 'I plan to leave you here tied and gagged. I will need the time to get away in case you change your mind, or decide to take your chances anyway. Gretchen will arrive after I'm gone, and she can untie you – or do whatever else takes her fancy. Who knows,' Richard said tauntingly, 'she might take the chance to repay you for the beating you gave her in the barn.'

'She would not dare,' Hannelore said.

Richard, watching her closely, saw that she was nevertheless excited by the idea. Maybe Gretchen would not beat her mistress. But he could. He said nothing to Hannelore about it, however. Surprise would best carry the day. As he helped Hannelore to her feet, he allowed himself to stare at her nearly naked breasts and the length of thigh above her rucked-up skirt. She reddened with anger but said nothing. Together they went back into her office. He sat her in her chair and tied her ankles with more of the parcel twine from the file room.

While she glared at him in silent anger, he picked up the telephone and began to issue the orders to Gretchen and the chauffeur in Hannelore's name. As he had expected, the orders were accepted without demur. He replaced the receiver and turned to Hannelore.

This time Richard allowed himself to stare openly at her state of deshabille. 'We have a few hours to wait,' Richard told her. 'How do you think we should pass the time?' Hannelore reddened again but said nothing. Was there just the merest hint of interest there? Richard asked himself.

Instead of taking Hannelore's clothes off immediately, he looked around the office. The riding crop she had used on Gretchen was lying on the conference table across the room. He went to fetch it, studying the bound woman who sat in the chair as he came back. Her eyes were wide with disbelief and, yes, just the merest hint of interest and excitement.

'No,' said Hannelore. 'Don't even think of that.'

'You mean you've never wondered what it was like to be on the receiving end? I've been watching you, and I think you want to find out. And I want to find out what it's like on the giving end. A little role reversal never hurt anyone. And your tits are just begging for the lash.'

Hannelore's eyes widened in – what? Fear? Anticipation? Richard never knew. He slashed at her breasts, which were jutting through the front of her blouse, protected by nothing more substantial than her sheer, transparent bra. The blow landed, and Hannelore flinched, almost falling backward with the chair. She cried out at the shock. Richard waited. When she recovered, she hunched forward protectively before he could strike her again. The next blow landed on the tops of her thighs, leaving a red mark beneath the shiny stockings. Hannelore cried out again, jerking away from the lash, and this time she did fall over, landing on the thick carpet with a thump.

She rolled clear of the chair, struggling against the ropes that bound her wrists and ankles. When she saw him raise the crop for another blow, she screamed, 'Help me!' as loudly as she could.

The noise level gave Richard pause. The office was probably soundproof, but there was no way to be sure, and he didn't want the security guards making trouble. He laid the crop aside and bent to untie Hannelore's ankles. She interpreted this as a gesture of capitulation and didn't scream again. Indeed, her face began to resume some of its earlier hauteur.

It was interesting to watch the look turn to incredulous surprise as he took her pants off with one jerk, ripping the flimsy material. Hannelore opened her mouth and drew a deep breath, preparatory to uttering another scream. Richard stuffed the torn pants into her mouth and used the twine from her ankles to tie them in place. Hannelore's face was bright red over the gag. Her fury could only express itself in a series of loud grunts as she fought to free herself and to eject the gag.

Richard stood up and moved across to the file room. The cameras covering Hannelore's office were all ready to run, fresh tape cassettes in place. He switched them on and went back to Hannelore, who was still trying to free her hands. He gestured to the camera near her desk. 'I'll leave the tape with you so you can enjoy this in retrospect.'

Hannelore gave him a furious look and continued to struggle. Richard waited until she rolled over on to her back. Then he brought the crop down on her breasts again. They bobbed under the blow. He could see the faint red mark through her bra. Hannelore let out a loud grunt of pain, even though he had used far less than his full strength. She rolled and bucked as he continued to lash her: stomach, thighs, back, breasts, shoulders, bottom. And as he lashed her, Richard felt himself becoming aroused. Earlier he had wondered what it would be like to wield the whip himself. Now he knew. The familiar stirring in the belly, the stiffening of the cock inside the tight corselet, the shortness of breath, all the signs were there. And he knew what he was going to do.

Richard laid the crop on Hannelore's desk and took off his suit jacket. Next the skirt and blouse. Hannelore watched him with incredulity and growing alarm. When she caught his eye, she shook her head, no. If she could have spoken, she might even have added 'please', though maybe not. Richard caught her mood. He guessed that it was not the shy virgin act. Hannelore knew far too much about sex and sexual arousal for that. It was more likely the loss of face and authority she wanted to avoid: if the dominatrix were reduced to sweaty sexual partner, she would have a hard time resuming her former role.

That might not be so bad, Richard thought, particularly if Hannelore learnt that he could treat her so. She might be more hesitant to cause future trouble for him and Helena. He took off the corselet and tights, laying them on Hannelore's desk, and stood before her naked. When he removed the tape from his cock, it stood out stiffly from his belly. Hannelore, no longer struggling now to get free, stared fixedly at it, as a bird might at a snake.

Richard paused, looking at her and letting her look at him, before he stooped to roll Hannelore on to her stomach. He unbuttoned her skirt and pulled it down and off her long legs, leaving her bare from the waist down except for her stockings and suspenders. Hannelore began to struggle at once, tugging off the ropes that bound her wrists and making strangled noises from behind her gag. Richard waited until her legs were open and then landed a blow from the crop squarely on her exposed cunt, as she had with Gretchen. Hannelore's scream was still loud despite the gag, but even as it died away she seemed to change gear. Her hips began to rise and fall, and she made small, muffled, mewing sounds as she came. The blow had been a release for her. She continued to grind her pelvis against the carpet for a long time.

Richard, watching Hannelore being racked by her pleasure, felt his own excitement peak suddenly. He laid the whip aside and rolled her over on to her back. Without pausing, he spread her legs and entered her, sliding all the way in at once. She was wet and parted, and seemed to have forgotten all about regaining her dominance. She was only a woman in need of a good screwing, opening her legs and welcoming his cock inside her as she bucked beneath him. Her head was thrown back and her eyes were closed as she came again and again, clenching herself tightly around the spear of his cock.

Richard rode Hannelore, staying with her as she came, and holding himself back as her excitement built and peaked and built again. He felt as if he were riding a whirlwind, and when he finally came it was like a sudden storm breaking on a sea coast. He was aware of

Hannelore's moans and writhings as a background to his own orgasm.

Afterwards, he rolled aside and allowed them both to recover. In the aftermath of their lovemaking, the ringing of the telephone was like a dash of cold water. Hannelore looked wildly around as if rescue had arrived. Richard sat up abruptly and lifted the receiver.

It was the secretary, letting Madame know that her chauffeur had arrived with a suitcase for Fraulein Rhodes. 'Tell him to leave it outside the office door and go and collect Gretchen as Madame ordered.' He hung up and rested one hand on Hannelore's stomach, a subtle warning to her to keep quiet. The sound of footsteps grew louder, stopping outside the door. There was a gentle bump, followed by the sound of receding footsteps. Only then did Richard move away from Hannelore. He went to the door, listened for a moment, then opened it and brought his case inside the office.

Hannelore struggled to a sitting position as he came back to the desk. 'Ummmmngg,' she said.

'You need to say something?' Richard asked her.

She nodded vigorously.

'Will you agree not to shout for help if I take the gag off?'

Hannelore nodded again, and he stooped to untie her gag.

'Are you going to leave me like this?' Hannelore asked. She was beginning to think again in terms of position and authority.

Richard was tempted to say yes, but didn't. It is never wise to humiliate someone unnecessarily, especially if he was to count on any goodwill in the future. 'I will have to leave you tied up. And gagged,' he added. 'But I'll dress you again before I leave. There are some things we still need to discuss. We can do that while I am getting dressed.'

Richard opened the suitcase and took out a fresh suit

and blouse. He decided clean underwear would be a good idea as well. The facilities in the toilet would have to suffice for a quick wash. Hannelore watched his preparations. When he went to the toilet, he took Hannelore with him, helping her to her feet and leading her by the elbow.

In the toilet, he tethered her by the ankle to the drainpipe. 'Go ahead and use the toilet if you want to,' he told her, busying himself with cleaning himself up and applying fresh make-up, while Hannelore squatted on the toilet and peed noisily. When she was finished, he wiped her dry.

'I don't intend to let anyone see the tapes I made,' Richard told her. 'Nor do I intend to use them to extort anything from you but your promise to leave me alone in the future. But I will keep the tapes in case you have a change of heart and decide to come after me. I will also leave copies in a safe place with instructions to open them in case I should disappear. Just leave me alone, and I will not trouble you. Fair enough?'

Hannelore clearly did not like being at the mercy of anyone, but she had no real choice. She nodded slowly. 'All right,' she agreed. 'What about the tape of just now?' she asked, with just a faint flush.

'You keep that if you want to. Or wipe it. Take that as a sign of my good faith,' Richard said. He began to dress for the journey. When he was done, Pamela Rhodes looked back at him from the mirror.

He cleaned Hannelore up as best he could, enjoying her little flinch as he cleaned her crotch and applied powder to her sex. 'You'll have to do without pants,' he told her, as he buttoned her blouse and brushed her hair. Then he took her back to her office and helped her get back into her skirt. When she was dressed, Hannelore looked more like the dominant mistress than she had when they were fucking. Except for her bound hands, Richard thought. Once again he sat her in her chair, this time bringing her arms down behind the back and tying her hands to the chair back. He crossed her ankles and tied them together. Finally, he used more of the twine to secure her to the chair by her elbows and waist. 'Any last words?' he asked, as he showed her the gag.

'Just good luck for the future.' It sounded sincere, strangely enough.

'Thanks,' Richard said. 'You too. Gretchen will come along in a few hours and let you loose.' He gagged her with her panties as before. He glanced back at the beautiful woman bound and gagged in her chair as he went out of the door.

Twelve

It was growing dark when Richard let himself quietly into the back of Ingrid's shop. He glanced briefly into the darkened sales area before closing the door. The lock clicked into place, and the light from the street was cut off. He made his way up the stairs by feel. After the encounter with Hannelore Bern and the prolonged masquerade as he travelled, this felt like coming home. He could relax, forget for a while the tension and worry of being discovered as a result of some small lapse. And he was looking forward to seeing Ingrid once more. He had thought of her often on the journey back from Basle. He wondered now if she were at home. There had been several opportunities to call ahead, but he hadn't done so, judging it better to surprise her.

The stairs creaked as he ascended, and he was aware of a narrow slit of light escaping under the door to the living quarters over the shop. He paused on the landing, listening, but there was no sound. He knocked on the door, but there was no response. Nor was there any response to his second, louder knock. The door was not locked, and opened easily into an empty room. All the doors leading off it were closed. After a moment's hesitation, he stepped inside and closed the door. The light he had seen from outside was coming from under the bedroom door. Laying his handbag on the coffee table, Richard went across to it. The knob turned under his hand. He called Ingrid's name softly. She might be sleeping.

There was a muffled noise from across the room. The sound came again: 'Nnmmmmmmgg.' He saw Ingrid as soon as he stepped into the room, and understood why she had not come to greet him. She was lying on the bed, spread like a starfish, her wrists and ankles bound to the bedposts. She was gagged: Richard recognised the inflatable gag that Margaret was so fond of. She was also nude.

He called, 'Ingrid. It's me, Richard. Are you all right?' Even as he crossed to the bedside, he realised how inane the question was. Ingrid could not possibly answer. He knelt to remove her gag, but Ingrid shook her head as soon as she felt his touch. 'Nnnnnnn,' she said, her head moving from side to side. At the same time she arched her back, lifting her hips off the bed and rocking them back and forth. The intent was unmistakable. When Richard looked more closely at Ingrid, he saw that she was highly aroused. Her nipples were hard and crinkly, and her breathing was rapid. The smell of her musk was strong, telling him that she was wet and ready for sex. Seemingly she had been aroused merely by lying there bound, and by the anticipation of what was to come.

Had she been lying there waiting for him to find her and fuck her? The idea excited Richard, even though he knew it was fantastic. She would have had no way of knowing when he might be coming to the shop. So she must have been prepared for someone else. Richard remembered her lover, whom she had said liked to come upon her bound and gagged and ready for him. The gag suggested that Margaret might have been the one who prepared her sister in this way.

Tentatively, Richard touched a nipple. It was taut with her desire, and she moaned softly. Encouraged by her response, Richard bent to kiss her breasts, circling her nipples with his tongue, nipping them gently between his teeth. Ingrid moaned more loudly, writhing on the bed and pulling frantically against the ropes that bound her. Seeing her like this, Richard had trouble remembering the woman to whom he had made love while she was teaching him how to dress and act like a woman. She had been eager and receptive once he had removed her doubts about the difference in their ages. She had responded readily to his foreplay. But this was different. Ingrid seemed ready to explode merely from being touched and gently fondled.

Richard noticed a chain around Ingrid's waist. It ran down between her legs, drawn tightly against her crotch, as Gretchen's had been. It was similar to the chain Hannelore had put on him. He guessed that Ingrid's chain held one or more dildoes inside her, as Gretchen's had done. He had been excited by his chain and the plug, reminding him at every move of his captivity. So, seemingly, was Ingrid.

He reached between her outspread thighs, following the chain down to her cunt. His fingers encountered the small ring he had expected, holding the dildo inside Ingrid. He pushed against the hard metal, drawing a long groan from Ingrid as the plug moved inside her. Richard continued his exploration, touching the plug inside her anus as well. Ingrid's chain was secured by a padlock between her legs, so that her lover could unlock and unplug her more easily.

Lacking the key, Richard had to give up the idea of taking off his clothes and penetrating Ingrid there and then. There was nothing for it but to continue to arouse her with the means available. Ingrid needed little in the way of encouragement. As he pushed alternately on the two plugs, Ingrid began to whimper low in her throat, the sound muffled by her gag but indicating clearly that she was being driven towards her orgasm by his manipulations. Keeping one hand busy between her legs, Richard leant over to kiss her eyes, cheeks and earlobes. He kissed her over her gag, and Ingrid moaned again, softly, the sound muffled. With his free hand, Richard fondled her breast and nipple. He shifted once more to bring his mouth to her other breast, teasing the nipple with his teeth.

Ingrid writhed wildly under his touch, her breath rasping in her throat as she gasped and heaved. The moans were almost continuous, rising and falling as she lost control. Richard could feel her vaginal and abdominal muscles clenching and relaxing under his hand, and he knew that she was having her first orgasm. It went on for a long time. Her gag caused Ingrid's cheeks to bulge, and they were flushed with her excitement. She pulled against her bonds, her arm and leg muscles straining. Her hips rose and fell in unconscious and involuntary rhythm with her excitement. Abruptly she arched her back, thrusting herself against his hands as she came. Gradually she grew quiet, with just the occasional shudder still passing through her body. She was covered with a light sheen of perspiration, and her breathing was still ragged.

Richard was aroused by the sight of this attractive woman being driven to orgasm. His cock was stiff inside the tight corselet, making him conscious of the tape that held it against his belly and exciting him still more. But as long as she wore her plugs, there wasn't anything he could do about his own arousal.

Ingrid opened her eyes and looked up at him. Unable to speak because of her gag, she still managed to show her gratitude and affection. Then she closed her eyes again and lay quietly on the bed.

Richard still knelt beside her, watching as she relaxed and seemed to drift off to sleep. He allowed her a few minutes, then he began to arouse her once more.

Ingrid opened her eyes in surprise as she felt his hands once again on her body. Her breath caught on a gasp as he resumed the massage of her cunt, driving the two dildoes into her once more. His hand on her breast and his lips and teeth on her nipple caused her to tighten her muscles once again. For a moment it seemed that she would try to make him stop. 'Nnnnn,' she said, shaking her head. But he didn't stop, and Ingrid couldn't stop him or protest against his renewed attention. Gradually she became less intent on stopping him, and more interested in the increasingly pleasurable sensations flooding through her belly and outspread thighs. Her nipples became taut once more, and her cunt was wet and ready almost at once. She surrendered herself to his touch, arching herself and spreading her thighs still more widely to present her body to him. When he extended one finger to her arsehole and pressed against the plug there, she couldn't stop herself from beginning another long, shuddering series of orgasms that left her sweaty, limp and exhausted.

Once more he allowed her only a brief rest before continuing her arousal. Ingrid writhed and moaned, flinging her head from side to side as if begging him to stop. But he didn't. Richard continued to caress and kiss her, allowing her no respite. Her breathing became louder, and once more a flush spread over her face and down her neck to her breasts. Her head now began to twist slowly from side to side in exquisite torment. A soft continuous moan came through the gag, becoming sharper and louder whenever she was shaken by another wave of pleasure.

Richard continued the slow, steady arousal.

Suddenly Ingrid's eyes flew open, widening in surprise. If she had not been gagged, she would have screamed in ecstasy. Her whole body stiffened, and then she began to shudder as wave after wave swept over and through her. Her back was arched like a bow, her hips straining upward and her belly taut. The muscles in her arms and legs stood out as she strained against the ropes that bound her to her bed. Ingrid held herself like that for an eternity before slumping back against the pillows, breathing raggedly and moaning softly.

This time Richard let her rest. He rose and sat on the bed beside her, one hand on her stomach, while he brushed the damp tendrils of hair from her face and caressed her eyes, neck and mouth with the other.

Ingrid seemed to be sleeping, her breathing becoming slower and steadier. Her taut muscles relaxed, though now and again a small shudder passed through her.

Outside the night passed slowly by. The village was quiet as only small towns can be. Even the traffic seemed to have gone elsewhere. Richard looked at Ingrid's face and body as she lay sleeping. He could easily see why he was so attracted to her. Why any man would be. It would not be easy to leave her when the time came to go back to England with Helena. If that time ever came, he reminded himself. There was still the matter of avoiding Margaret, who would try to keep him captive. And the matter of stealing the evidence from the safe in Margaret's house. And he knew that he would miss Margaret too: her dominating presence, giving him pleasure even while she forced him to do her bidding with the whip. He realised, too, that his own inclinations would conspire to keep him here where he had discovered the other side to his sexuality. But he couldn't stay here.

Finally it was time to make the next move. Gently, he lifted Ingrid's head and unstrapped her gag. She woke at his touch, and waited while he extracted the rubber balloon from her mouth. He made no attempt to untie her, for he knew he would have to leave her as he had found her. But in the meantime they had to talk.

'What is the time, Richard?' Ingrid asked, as soon as she could speak. 'Margaret told me that Hans would be here shortly after dawn. She told me to sleep if I could, and that my awakening would be a wonderful surprise. She always tells me that when she leaves me here for him. But she could not know that I would have a wonderful surprise before he arrived.'

'It's nearly three in the morning, Ingrid,' Richard told her.

'Then there is no hurry. But where have you been this last week? I – we – expected you to return after making the delivery. When you did not come back, Helena thought you had decided to leave. She was very unhappy. So was I,' she added.

'Margaret didn't tell you, then?' Richard asked.

'Tell me what?'

'That she had given me to her friend Frau Bern in Basle,' he said.

Ingrid looked shocked. 'She did what?'

'Margaret sent a letter to Hannelore Bern along with the money. It was in the case I carried, but of course I didn't know about it because I never opened it. In the letter she gave instructions for the disposal of the cash, and of me. I was to stay in Basle. I imagine Margaret didn't like my involvement with Helena. She must have guessed how things were between us. We made no secret of it. It may have been jealousy: not so much that I had chosen Helena, but rather that she was left out.'

'If that is the case,' Ingrid said, 'it is her own fault. She has always been afraid to let go – to give anything of herself to another. She sees a loss of power, of status, in such a gesture. Perhaps also a weakness she is determined to resist.'

Richard nodded. 'Perhaps you're right. She's a very attractive woman, but distant. It won't get any easier for her as she gets older. Not like you,' he said.

Ingrid smiled softly. 'I am glad you came to me tonight. Glad you came to me at any time. You have taught me not to fear growing older, and to trust people more. It is a great gift you have given me.'

Ingrid did not speak of love or ties: she was clearly allowing Richard to remain free.

'I am glad I found you, Ingrid. You will never grow old.' He too avoided the L word, knowing that he could not stay here, and that she was unlikely to leave.

'The keys you need have been made,' she told him, changing the subject and steering away from the embarrassing moment. 'They are in the top drawer of the bureau over there.' Ingrid nodded her head at the bureau across the room. 'Go and get them.'

Richard crossed the room and opened the top drawer, searching among her lacy underwear and smooth pairs of tights until he encountered something hard among all the softness. It was a small jewellery box. It rattled as he picked it up. He carried it to the bed and sat down beside Ingrid once more.

'Take them with you when you go. I believe they will do the job. You are lucky: Margaret is away for a day or so, and Helena is at the house. You will be able to take the evidence and get away. Then Helena – both of you, really – will be free to begin a new life.'

Ingrid seemed wistful as she said these last words, but then she smiled. 'And I can come to visit you from time to time.' Seeing his expression, half happy and half doubtful, she continued, 'I have spoken to Helena. She would like that very much. She is not possessive, or jealous of her old foster mother. She will make you a good companion, and I will be happy for you both. And one day you will come home and find me tied to your bed, just like this. And I will not be plugged as I am now. You will be able to take me in any way you choose. Helena knows what I like. Indeed, I suspect she got her own inclinations from me, though how I cannot tell. It cannot be genetic, because she is not related to me. So it must have been something in the atmosphere in which she was raised: something between Margaret and me. From Margaret she has learnt domination, and from me, submission. She can be both for you. A happy combination.'

Richard leant down and kissed Ingrid's lips. It was a long kiss, combining gratitude, respect and relief. And love.

When he drew back, Ingrid lay for a long time with her eyes closed. Richard thought she might be going back to sleep. But suddenly she looked at him, smiling, and he too felt glad. Glad he had found her, and relieved that he would not have to leave her for ever. Visits. Yes, they would have visits. They could continue to give themselves that pleasure.

'Now it is time for you to go, Richard. Use my telephone to call Helena. She will come to pick you up, and you can get the papers from Margaret's safe. Go to Helena and get her away from here. And be happy. Kiss me once more, and then replace the gag. I will lie here for a few more hours and then have another surprise awakening.'

Richard bent down once more to kiss her lips. She thrust herself up as far as her bonds would allow, holding herself against him. At length they both drew back. Richard replaced the gag and buckled the straps tightly behind Ingrid's head, leaving her bound and helpless as he had found her. He felt a moment's envy of Hans, whom he had never met, because this was how he too would find her in a few hours. And they would share their own lovemaking, she bound and gagged, but insatiable. He hoped they would enjoy one another.

He closed the door quietly and moved across the sitting room to the telephone. He dialled the number of Margaret's country house. There was no way of knowing who would answer it, particularly at this hour of the morning. It rang and rang. Finally it was answered. He thought he recognised Heidi's sleepy voice. At least it was not Margaret.

'Heidi? It's Richard. Sorry to wake you. Is Helena there?'

Heidi gave a gasp of surprise. 'I thought you were staying in Basle. Madame said you wouldn't be back.'

'I escaped. I'll tell you about it when I see you, but I need to talk to Helena now, if she's there.'

Richard waited for what seemed like an eternity before Helena came on the line. She too expressed surprise. And pleasure, he was glad to hear.

'I did not think you would stay in Basle. Margaret said you had gone for good, but I knew you would come back for me. I am so glad to hear your voice.'

It sounded as if she was crying, but he couldn't ask. He said instead, 'I'm at your mother's house in the village. Can you come and pick me up?'

'Yes,' Helena said, happily. 'Ten minutes. Wait for me!' She put the phone down.

Richard hung up too and crossed to the bedroom once more. He opened the door quietly. Ingrid lay with her eyes closed, the light from the bedside lamp falling softly on her naked body, making highlights and dark shadows. He closed the door again and went silently down the stairs. He locked the door behind him. It wouldn't do to leave it open with Ingrid lying bound and gagged in the bedroom. He stood in the shadows waiting for Helena. The night was clear and cold, the air moving around his legs. He wondered if women were always as aware of their exposed legs as he was. The tights did not provide much warmth. He would have to get used to that.